Covert Ops: Danger in Paradise

Steve Barker

GREEN CAT BOOKS

Published in 2020 by

GREEN CAT BOOKS

19 St Christopher's Way

Pride Park

Derby

DE24 8JY

www.green-cat.co

ACKNOWLEDGEMENTS

Thank you to
Pauline Carter-Rapson
George James
Simon Munnery
for their help with this book

CONTENTS

Meet Up

Sit back and relax and let me tell you a story of danger in paradise, whether this is a real-life story or that of pure fiction, I will let you decide.

Another night ended the same as they had for the last thirty years; go to sleep for a few hours before waking up due to the reoccurring nightmares which involve me dying in some sort of strange fashion. From my brains being blown out, to being eaten by creatures that wouldn't look lost in Jurassic Park.

Cannot lay here all day, besides it's light outside, time to remove my lazy butt out of my pit and hose myself down. Some person once told me when you rise in the morning if you stretch and put a big cheesy grin on your face helps the day go well, what a load of crap. What is there to lose? So here goes. Note to self, don't try that again in the shower, nearly broke my bloody neck!

One of the many vital lessons they taught in the military was breakfast is the most important meal of the day. So, let's go and stare at the food cupboard for five minutes, deciding what to eat before choosing what I always have, Weetabix. Followed by several cups of strong coffee. More than what the silly personages on the TV would say was bad for you one day and acceptable the next. So who cares, I like the taste.

Breakfast out of the way, time to turn on the computer and read my emails, wonder who wants a piece of me this morning. Fantastic news, only two people wanting me to squeeze a stone to discover how much blood I might be able to extract.

Demand from the not-so-friendly people at the council saying I have twenty-one days to come up with several thousand pounds or the bailiffs would be around to seize my home and its contents. Another from the landlord stating my direct debit failed, and my rent is now overdue. Better not open any of the letters piling up over on the dining table, almost certainly more bad news, I will read them tomorrow.

It is the middle of summer, and for once it's stopped raining and the sun's come out to play, so stuff work, can't be bothered anyway. My therapist Tony once said, 'try to start the day on a positive note', simple for him to say, he's not got the arseholes from the local authorities on his back.

In the spirit of giving it a go, I need to go into town anyhow so might as well walk as the sun's out. Plus, I hate getting on a bus because of the numerous amount of annoying people who insist, even though it is empty, sitting behind with their non-stop talking.

Not always easy to find the Chimp, so one of two things happen; I become incredibly stressed out, or I turn around and tell them to shut the fuck up. Best to walk me thinks, anyway, walking is supposed to be perfect for relieving stress.

An uneventful hour-stroll later I arrived at the edge of town, let's hope it is not too packed. One thing I find unbearable is too many people in a confined space, or any place for that matter. Partly the oversight of the Army training me to be hypervigilant. Plus, my time serving in what's known as the Forgotten War, Northern Ireland. Come to think about it, this is all the Army's fault for preparing everyone to a high level, but not un-training you when you leave.

Does not help with arrogant politicians in Westminster on their relentless pursuit of Veterans who served in the Forgotten War, they were the bastards who sent us in there in the first place.

Shame there is no witch-hunt for terrorists making all the killings, oh yes, they can't, thanks to the get out of jail card they gave them on Good Friday.

Positive it won't be long before they come knocking at my door. Saw some stupid Labour politician the other day on the TV saying she would not draw a line under the conflict for veterans, the cow did for the terrorist.

Reminds me of a post I saw on social media, 'If you can't stand behind our military, then stand in their boots for a few days'. Wonder how many of the spineless arseholes mouthing off would do this, especially in a war zone?

Don't really have a lot to do in town today apart from picking up some dobby dust, the washing is starting to pile up and stink a bit, thank fuck for Febreze. Shit, the city is busy and need to make my way to the other end, this is going to take some planning.

Not a problem for the majority of the population but suffering from Chronic PTSD, due to a terrorist putting a pistol to my head and trying to blow me away; fortunate for me, it misfired. Shame the scumbag legged it before the gesture was repaid.

Thanks to my hypervigilance, I am continuously on the lookout for threats, which might come from any direction, even the woman pushing the pram. More feasible from the woman with the pushchair, terrorist organisations use to hide their weapons under the baby before pulling out the gun and taking a shot, then running away like the cowards they were.

One of the many skills I learnt while undergoing surveillance training was the ability to perceive what was going on 180 degrees from the direction you are looking. The refection in windows is a great way to monitor who or what is behind you, would be surprised how many times that comes in handy.

A quick check to where Mickey's hands were pointing, it is 12:00, so it must be beer o'clock. Wonder if the two nutters I encountered on my last visit to nuthouse are in town and fancy a few cold ones?

Met both of them on a two-week stay at Combat Stress, an organisation that provided support for veterans with mental health issues from every service and every conflict since 1919. Like me, they were there for problems affecting their mental health, conditions sustained in conflicts around the world. Probably why we all got on from the start on day one, spent most of the time taking the piss out of each other.

Simon was a slim build, six-foot Cavalryman who served fifteen years as a commander in the Queens Royal Irish Hussars serving all over the world, including Iraq and Afghanistan. Claim to fame, he was the first tank into Baghdad, well that's what he is telling us. Loved taking photos, it goes without saying we would call him a tanky and shout Hussar!

On the other hand, George was a stocky, and a tadge overweight, proud Grenadier Guardsman. Like the rest of us, spend the best part of fifteen years serving in war zones such as Northern Ireland, Iraq, and Afghanistan. For a reason, only he knew the answer, he became angry if someone called him on his mobile. Of course, us being the caring types, Simon and I made him a clay telephone to keep by his door to remind him he was a prat. Goes without saying this was relating to his dislike of phone conversations.

The phone rang several times and was about to hang up when he answered.

"Hi, George, how's life with the Cold Stream Guards?" For some reason he did not like this regiment.

"Do one, you fucking Green Howard!" came the reply; close, as I had spent ten years in the Royal Green Jackets.

"I'm in the city, fancy a couple of cold ones? About to ring our Tanky friend as well. Excellent, meet you in an hour, time to call Simon."

Took several calls for him to pick up the phone, was more than likely changing from his night dressing gown to his day one. Finally, he answered the bloody phone.

"Was about to give up, you old git. George and I are meeting in the pub for a few bevvies, fancy joining us? Fantastic, meet you in about an hour and leave the Polo Donkey in the field."

Took up position in a public house I had used many times, primarily because it had the best prices. There was no way this place be classed as a trendy place, more of a traditional type, didn't even play music. In fact, the only noise besides the chattering of people was the sound of the multiple fruit machines.

Like most pubs, this day and age made more money out of food than beverage sales which, like the drinks, were at a reasonable price.

The bar was along the left wall as you entered and was now occupied by a dozen or more people trying to attract the servers' attention by holding bank notes up or waving like a demented bird with a broken wing trying to be the next to place an order.

Seated myself at one of the tables situated in a small cubical type arrangement, consisting of two bench seats separated by a table, with my back leaning on the wall looking towards the door, so I would see Simon and George arrive.

Now just need to go to the bar and buy the beers, but far too lazy for that; anyway, the place has an app where it possible to purchase beverages from your smartphone.

Had several drinking sessions together since we first met, so didn't need to ask them what they wanted to drink, so requested drinks from the app.

Another fantastic feature of ordering from the phone is no sneaky old bugger is going to steal your table while you are away getting a beverage or two.

Must give the old buggers some credit as they can make one pint last about two hours and leave just enough to keep their table safe on their many trips to the bog.

Was acting like the rest of the morons in the pub, looking at my phone, when abuse from the direction of the door came my way. No reason to raise my head, George and Simon had arrived.

"Been waiting long?"

"Always follow the Royal Green Jackets motto, 'First in, Last Out'. So, what have you two nutters been up to lately?"

"Been doing some security work with the Ministry of Defence and training up attack dogs, before anyone says it, no there wasn't any battle-hardened Chihuahuas. What about you, been up to? anything exciting?"

"Not much, same old rubbish, but had a conversation with a friend of mine from the Cavalry who may have some work lined up."

"Forget all that for a moment, we have a more pressing matter to deal with. Whose round is it, space just opened up near the bar?"

"What are you talking about?"

"A man over there just collapsed, and is now lying on the floor, so more room."

"Talk about insensitive, he might be hurt."

"Yes, Simon, but am I right, is there or is there not now more room for one of you two to fetch the drinks?"

"Leave it to me, lads, got to make a call to wifey to ensure she fed my battle-hardened Chihuahua."

"Cheers, George, a flagon of the bar's best ale."

"What about you, Simon?"

"The same, please. So what about you, Simon? Got to phone home to make sure your other half feeds the Polo Donkey?"

"Piss off".

Once George was back with the beer, the conversation turned to me. "So what you been up to?" That is an easy one.

"Nothing much, little short on the old cash, but did take the kayak out for a couple of days. So I either need to find some work or becoming a trained assassin might be an option, need some money to keep the bastards at the council off my back."

"How about we put all our troubles aside for now, enjoy a laugh and get shit-faced."

"I'll drink to that, cheers nutters."

Not sure if it was in no small part related to the amount of ale consumed or the PTSD kicking in, but the bar seemed to be getting busier and louder as people piled in on their lunch break. I started looking for threats within the room. Glad the other two were here, that is what I love about veterans, they will always have your back no matter how long you have known them.

Soon brought back to the here and now with a gentle slap around the head and the words,

"Got the munchies, fancy any crisps or nuts, what about you, George?"

"No thanks, trying to keep the figure in check."

"Who are you kidding, fat boy?" came the instant reply.

"Make mine a bag of dry roasted peanuts, please, I'm watching the figures of the women sat by the window."

Time was now getting on, far too much alcohol was partaken, so time to head for home.

"Give us a ring at the weekend, gents. Simon let us know how you get on with that work your tanky mate might have lined up. Don't walk home at the speed of a Guardsman, George, you'll never reach home."

Better see what the damage is on the old dosh. As I thought, not enough of the money stuff for a bus home, so what's now become routine in this situation due to lack of funds, I'm walking again. This might even be a positive move; with any luck could have sobered up a bit by the time I arrive.

Appears I slept through the device detonating in the front room during the night, well that is what it looked like to me. The small table, which usually sits close to the couch, was leaning against the wall along with an empty glass with piles of what could only be described as dried food.

Made myself several mugs of steaming coffee before slumping on the sofa trying to work out what may have happened. The caffeine must be doing its job, as now I remembered. Returned home last night and for some stupid reason decided a few more beers would be an excellent idea. Not satisfied with that, complemented this with what was left of the curry I consumed a couple of nights ago. Want not, waste not, is my motto.

Somehow, I had banged my shin on the coffee table while getting up for a piss. Thank God I remembered to do that! Well, the Chimp must have taken another day off as I had launched the table complete with the beer across the room for intentionally hurting my leg.

Must get this anger issue under control. That's the problem with PTSD, you can go from calm to the Incredible Hulk in an instant. I blame the Army.

That is enough of playing Sherlock Holmes for today, better clean up the mess. Now that's what I call a stroke of luck, had thrown the table on top of a £2 coin. That should help with the cost of some strong glue, as I'd taken a massive chunk out of one of the wooden legs.

The plan for the weekend: do bugger all, well at least it is some sort of plan. Turned on the television and sat back on the sofa with control in hand ready for some severe channel-hopping.

Not long before my doing bugger all, I was interrupted by the phone singing its head off over in the kitchen. Don't care who that is, they can sod off; I'm busy, plus I don't have any spare cash to give to charity. Persistent buggers, whoever was on the other line, they rang four times before deciding I needed to answer the bloody thing, if nothing else to tell them to fuck off.

OK, remember the breathing exercise, in for six, out for seven before the mobile becomes the next casualty in the anger games. The display screen said, 'Private Message', well, they can do one. Was about to put the phone down when for some reason unknown to nobody, I answered the damn thing.

Not allowing time for the Escaped Librarian, or as some others might call it the voice in my head to get even the slightest chance of getting a word out, the voice on the other end said, "Steve, it's Simon."

"What the fuck are you doing on a different phone number, was about to give you the verbal equivalent of the middle finger."

"Sorry, but I'm with that Cavalry friend I was talking about down the local tavern yesterday. Has some work we might like, interested?"

This was one of the easiest decisions to make in a while, as the £2 I found earlier was now holding up my financial undertakings.

"Of course, you want to meet to talk about it, or do you need an answer now?"

"Later is fine, shall we say 13:00 at your place?"

"No problem, that will give me time to clean up my mess."

"Ok, see you then, with George."

Pre-Planning

The time now 11:00, which gave me enough time to clean up this place and nip down to Lidl's for a few beverages for when the boys come over, sure there is still money left on the credit card.

That didn't take as long as I had imagined. Throw some laundry in the washing machine, and I'm done. Right, down to the supermarket for the all-important drinks and a few snacks, shouldn't take long, the store is only a short 10-minute gentle walk from here.

Hoped the shop wasn't too busy as I might throw a wobbly and come back with nothing and the boys would not be happy Teddy Bears. Fantastic, not too many people in the place apart from the older generation looking for a bargain. So optimistic this would be a case of straight in and straight out. Not very good at this shopping lark. Looked down into the basket to discover I filled the bloody thing with biscuits, crisps, nuts and cakes, would do, for now, just the beer to procure.

Wish these shops would fucking stop moving things around. Once you're used to where things are some numpty goes and rearranges everything. Only one thing to do now, and that was something I hated doing, I'd need to walk up and down the aisle like a moron until I found the fucking beer.

Beer found; now where were the ones I want? About to pick them up when some stupid personage decides to stand within inches of me. What's wrong with these people, not like the place has limited room. Well, having none of this crap.

"Got a problem, or just trying to give me one, fucking move away."

The man turns around with a dirty stare before he even opened his mouth; followed up with, "Don't even think about it, mate unless you fancy a trip to the local hospital."

Back at the caravan, drinks chilling, an assortment of food all carefully laid out; they're going to take the piss out of me for that. Mickey is now telling me the time is 12:50, so George and Simon will be arriving soon. They are both aware how much that winds me up if anyone is late, so they better not be delayed.

Bang on 13:00 Simon and George arrived at the door carrying more beers, this was going to be an exciting afternoon.

"Throw them in the fridge."

"Who made the puffy decorations with the food?"

Well, what did I expect? "Come over here, Simon and look at what the nancy boy's done."

"I'll sort that out," Simon grabbed the plate and tossed the contents on to the table.

"Better, don't you agree?"

"Pair of twats, took me at least 10 minutes to prepare."

"Plenty of cold ones in the fridge, grab us all one and park your arse over here, let's listen to what employment Simon's mate's got lined up for us."

"OK, Simon, what's your Donkey Walloper friend got for us and what's he willing to pay."

"The job is straightforward in principle. He owns a huge amount of land on a small island in the Caribbean, some thugs moved into his house and took up residence on his property while he's been over here on business. The job is simple; wants us to fly over and evict them."

Finishing his beer, George placed the can down and asked, "So, what's wrong with the coppers, why can't they remove them."

"From what Henry had to say, the police are only a three-man band and might have ties with the group now occupying his place, plus he would rather the mission was completed under the radar."

"Fair enough, Simon."

"So, any more details, like how many idiots need taking out, plans to the property and most crucially who is picking up the tab for us to arrive at this little island?"

"What do you think, George?"

"Sounds intriguing, I'm in."

Come to think of it with my financial situation, I would've taken any job to bail myself out of the shit."

"Need more information, like how much are we getting paid," replied George.

"Once we're all agreed to the work, I will arrange for us all to meet Henry, who can give us more info."

"So that's decided, we are all in, depending on what is said at a meeting with Henry."

"When can this be set this up for?"

"Do my best for Monday. By the way, drying up over here, who's getting the drinks from the fridge?"

Monday morning, with the usual crap out of the way, grabbed my third cup of freshly ground coffee and slumped behind the computer. A new week so better do some work, the vultures should have been off for the weekend, so no bloody emails from people wanting their pound of flesh.

Got that wrong, don't these people ever take a rest and leave people like me alone. First two were from the usual crowd, rent and the arseholes from the council both demanding money by the end of the week.

Not all bad news, one email was from a potential customer looking to book a family holiday, should cheer me up a little if they go ahead.

Hoped Simon comes through and calls today, God knows I need the work, and it sounds like an easy job. Go over to an island and kick some arse, which shouldn't take too long, may find some time for a little R & R in the sun.

Must have been around lunchtime when the phone rang, Simon was on the other end, "All set up for tomorrow in London around 14:00, is that OK?"

"Perfect, got a launch shindig at the Royal Opera House, so couldn't be better. What about George?"

"Just spoken to him, he will meet us at the meeting point."

Just finish this email and the cruise quote then I'm off to the clubhouse for a meal to treat myself. Let's face facts, if this all comes off, and why wouldn't it, there will be more money than I've had for a long time flowing into my bank account.

Thinking logically, better take a notebook and pen to make notes as this job may seem easy but will need some planning for everything to go right and not go off half-cocked.

A significant feature of the complex, there is an excellent stand-off position where a person can recce straight inside without being seen and for any potential threats.

Been here several times so utterly aware of all the exit points. Today the place was empty except for a family sat opposite the TV on the wall. Plus, a man dressed in shorts and a T-shirt with the words 'I drink because I can,' printed across the front. Think he may have consumed one or two too many as he had difficulty walking from his seat to the bar.

Right then, what's on the menu for today, any specials? Something tells me the kitchen manager requested too many chickens. Either that or the country's economic situation brought on by the remoaners trying to keep the country in Europe. Everyone is now doing what we in the trade call a staycation for their holidays. Today's special, fried chicken and chips now half price, will do me.

Ordered with the friendly bar person, can't say barman now in case it upsets some idiot, headed to the table tucked away in the far corner with a pint of the local brew, sat down and took out my notebook.

What do we know about this job so far, well taking everything into consideration all the information we have to date, not much, just that it is on a Caribbean island? Right, let's break this task down into four parts.

First, and the most important, how much are we being paid? I'm not doing this for little money, so who's paying for us to arrive on the island? Or is going to be part of the payment?

Second, how are we getting there, does the place have an airport on the island or do we need to land somewhere else and charter a boat across? Brings the question to mind, do the people running both have links to people occupying the property like the local police?

Third, how are we going to complete the task, as we don't know much about the group? Can't do much planning until we find out more tomorrow.

One topic will need to ask Henry about, are they armed, if so, we are going to need weapons and where we can obtain them from? This always raises the moral dilemma: is it alright to kill someone? As for me, I don't do empathy and if they are aiming a weapon at me, I'm going to shoot first, ask questions second.

Plus, we are going to need detailed maps of the whole island, not a good idea to run from a firefight and not know where you're running to. Then we have the question of transport for us to move around, recces, and making our way out of any tricky situation.

Fourth, this is going to be more challenging than it may first appear if we'd left a trail of destruction and dead bodies lying around the island, someone might be pissed off with us and try their best to block us going. Better think of a second or even a third backup plan for the route home.

Didn't spot them putting my meal in front of me, and I'm the type of person who detects everything going on around me, we must have a stealth barperson. Time to stop this thinking lark, for now, another drink is in order, to wash the chicken down, you understand.

Bloody hell, is that the time, better get back and finish off work from this morning, with any luck that person will book the cruise. Suppose one more beer won't kill me. A comedy show was now going on near the bar. The individual with the 'I drink because I can' T-shirt was now staggering towards the door, hitting tables on the way out.

Stayed for about another hour before deciding I better make the move home, need a clear head, some travel plans to prepare for tomorrow, then there is the task of finding somewhere to stay after the shindig at the Royal Opera House. Knowing me, I will most likely end up spending a cold night at Waterloo train station.

About to call it a night when I realised that Simon had given me the time of our meeting but had missed out one crucial fact, like where in London? Better ring him. Must already be in his night dressing gown as he answered the phone straight away.

"Bloody idiot, you've left out one small detail for tomorrow, like where is it."

"That would be handy, Steve, I'll text you and George the address."

"Thanks, Simon, "now go and tuck in the Polo Donkey. I'm off to the world of nod."

The Meeting

Must have been formulating plans all night, which may well all change once we obtained more information from Henry, so woke up this morning feeling like crap; had less sleep than usual and trust me, that is never enough.

Not only did Simon come through last night. Not only sent us the address of the meeting in London, but also the location of Henry's place on St Halb. Well played that man. Now with the aid of Google Maps, we can work out what type of terrain we may be dealing with. Plus I can now start making plans of getting us three there and back.

Saw from my search of the internet the island did not have an international airport, it was in fact serviced from the neighbouring island of St Bethanie by a daily floatplane service to the south. From what I could work out, this was the most populated part with a small town going by the name of Jal.

On a closer examination of the map, A street called Joshua Boulevard ran up the middle before disappearing into what appeared to be a rainforest, only to re-appear at a crossing. The island is, in fact, two islands joined by, what I could work out, a hundred-metre concrete bridge big enough for commercial vehicles to pass over spanned the gap between them. This will be a problem if we need to make our escape down to the south. The thugs might make it to the crossing before us, blocking our route; will plan for this later.

For the north island, it appeared from the map most of the island was covered with rainforest with small clearings scattered among the woods, in each several buildings. Henry's property is in a clearing to the northeast, various outbuildings and one principal residence, these would need to be cleared.

Behind the house, between it and the sea were rows of planted vegetation, but from the map, I couldn't perceive what, sure Henry will explain what they are later today. Out from the shore in the direction of St Bethanie is what appeared to be a jetty protruding out towards the ocean, which might come in handy if things go wrong on our exit.

Google Maps and the internet are useful to a point, but not knowing how old the charts are, they might have had their drone flown over years ago, now everything might be different.

With the way our luck goes, a town would have sprung up on the north island with hundreds of people; with any luck, Henry will process newer and a more detailed chart of the area, plus a comprehensive plan of his property.

Can't do much more by looking at computer maps, so quick coffee before looking on how to get to St Halb, as the time was getting on and still needed to book my train ticket. Packed my bags for the cruise shindig at the Royal Opera House last night so a little wiggle room on time.

From what I found out, there were flights three times a week from London Heathrow. The issue will be once we land, as the floatplane only operated first thing in the morning around about 10:00 the international flight lands at 11:00.

Due to the problem with connecting flights, we would be spending a few nights on the sunny island of St Bethanie. Will check on boat rentals when I come back tomorrow.

Train ticket booked on my phone, the beauty of this, I can reserve a seat at the back of the carriage. Significant for two reasons; hate people sitting behind me, plus I can keep under observation my fellow travellers and monitor everything that goes on. Call me paranoid, but I like knowing what is happening around me. The train leaves in around two hours so better move my arse, as the station is about an hour's walk.

The train arrived on time, which meant not too long standing with the other passengers who are all in some sort of hurry, pushing and shoving to try to stand where they believe the doors would line up with their part of the platform.

Took up my seat at the rear of the carriage with the small table located in front of me folded down, which now sat my opened notebook. Towards the centre, a group dressed in striped football shirts. All of them seemed to be having a fantastic time with several beers and singing some sort of football song, to the annoyance of a couple of businessmen seated in the seats behind. Doesn't bother me, as long as they don't come annoying me. Reminds me of times in the Army when groups of my fellow Riflemen headed home at the weekends.

Near the other end, a young woman who looked like she wanted the world to swallow her up as her daughter was having a hissy fit and screaming the place down. Other non-descriptive people were scattered throughout the carriage. Either listening to music, reading newspapers, or staring blankly out of the window trying hard not to glance at other passengers sat opposite them.

At this point from the far end appeared the train managers on the lookout for people who were not playing by the rules, and not purchasing tickets before boarding.

From where I was seated I was able to watch people desperately checking bags and coats for tickets. As I used the app on my mobile, my ticket is safely stored. Saying that, I would be fucked if I ever lost the phone.

Still, over an hour until we arrived in London, so time to run through the plans I had so far. Not sure what, but something was bothering me, chiefly if the job is so simple why didn't Henry and a few of his Cavalry mates do the work themselves, not that I'm complaining, I need the money. Read through my notebook several times before deciding to call George.

Tried multiple times before I obtained a signal, eventually got through, and George answered.

"George, it's Steve, are you on your way to London?"

"Just about to leave, any problem?"

Nothing much, but something is niggling me, instead of going straight to the meeting point, let's meet me in the coffee shop opposite, at, shall we say 12:30?"

"OK, I will see you there at 12:30."

Arrived at around 12:00, ordered an Americano with milk then took up a position at a small table situated in the corner next to a window overlooking the road and across the street. This was ideal, not only to view George coming but also gave an excellent vantage point to monitor the comings and goings from the pub opposite where our meeting with Henry would take place.

Received a text from George saying he would be about five minutes, so I went to the counter to be served by a young person who I hardly understood, English not being her first language. Ordered two more Americanos and sat back down. George entered looking around before catching my eye and coming over.

"Took the liberty of getting us both a coffee, if you don't like coffee, tough shit, you can buy your tea over at the counter."

"Coffee is fine, where is Simon?"

"Something is bothering me, George, like, why is Henry and his mates not doing the job themselves, and you know me, only trust people I got acquainted with."

Sipping his drink, George sat back in the chair, "OK, what's the plan."

Showed the notebook to George, who proceeded to spend the next five minutes going through it before saying "Not too bad so far, but why is Simon not here with us?"

"Think about it, George, we've never met Henry, so the only person he could recognise is Simon, so you might say I'm using him to double-check nobody is following him or waiting for him or us in the public house across the road. Glance over in the direction of the pub, you can monitor much of the inside through the front window.

"I Did take a quick peek of the interior earlier to check the layout and exit points in case any issues arise." From what I discovered on closer inspection of the boozer, only one place where a person could be seated without the option of any nosey bastard sitting behind them listening in on their conversation; along with a self-contained private area where we would be able to talk, with the advantage of looking straight out of the window. Knowing Simon as we do, this is where he will sit.

In the worst-case scenario, if anyone were following him into the pub, we would see that from here, plus if he got into trouble, we could also view that from here and be over within seconds.

As he is ex-military, we can guarantee he will be at least ten minutes early, giving us around fifteen or thereabouts to wait.

"Don't know about you, George, but I'm peckish, fancy a sandwich or something?"

"Thanks, a cheese and ham panini would be good."

"No problem, just keep an eye out of the window for Simon while I go and try and order from our non-English-speaking friend at the counter." This should be fun.

Dead on 14:50 Simon appeared, walking down the road to the right of the public house, stopped outside and checked his phone before entering, purchased a drink from the bar and sat where we had predicted. A few minutes later, a man dressed in boots, black jeans and a blue jacket also entered taking up residency near the bar looking in the direction of Simon.

Looking uneasy, Simon could be seen typing something on his mobile, not long afterwards both George and I received a ping on our mobiles, doesn't take brains of a rocket scientist to work out who it was from. The message read 'I'm at the meeting point, where are you two nutters?'

"Better go over and rescue him, best we pretend we don't suspect the person leaning on the bar and avoid eye contact, he might be innocent."

"That's using the old noggin, George."

Walked over to where Simon was sitting, greeted with the words, "Where the fuck you two been, started to feel you bailed on me."

"Sorry, mate." I explained what we had been up to along with my concerns. Plus, that we had been watching him from the coffee shop across the road.

"Well, thanks for using me as bait! That will cost you a pint and a bag of nuts."

"No problem, what do you want, George?"

"Same for me."

Just arrived back at the table when a well-dressed man with short brown hair in black trousers, a pink shirt and a dark blue blazer embossed with a golden logo walked towards us.

"Gents, this is Henry."

After introductions, we all sat down while Henry ordered from the bar. What a relief, at least he is here, and the job is still on, not that any of us had doubted it wouldn't be, but there is always that little thing in the back of your mind.

He returned shortly after with a gin & tonic.

"Right, gents, down to business as I've another engagement in the city at 15:00."

"How about explaining what the job is you would like us to do, starting from the beginning."

"I've been working in London for the last three months so not been back for some time, so friends of mine, Sam and Abbie, have been looking in on the property for me. Both live off the estate near the coast," Henry pointed to the map which he had pulled from his jacket pocket.

"Sam's a good man, ex British military who moved to St Halb a few years back, he'll be the main contact on the island."

"The problem started around six weeks ago when a group of men arrived at the island and occupied my property, forcing the staff to move out. They allowed him back to maintain the generators and other mechanical equipment, he's a trained mechanic. He's been keeping me informed as much as he can via mobile phone, here is his number. The men have been planting under the grapevines which are here on the map."

"So that's what they are, couldn't make them out on Google Maps."

"Yes, my family has been producing wine on the island for over a hundred years, some wines stored in the warehouse are priceless," pointing to a building to the right of the principal residence.

"From what Sam & Abbie's been telling me, the group have armed guards on the front gate along with huge guard dogs, they are kept here behind the gatehouse when not with the guards. Sam thinks may be at least six of them."

Simon and I both looked at George, "This is your domain, mate."

"No problem, I'm on it."

"From what we can obtain, there may be about twenty men and women staying on my property, most of the time they stay on the grounds, only visiting the town of Jal every Thursday to get fresh supplies. I am holding a function there in three weeks to celebrate 120 years of the company, so as you can imagine would like these people gone by then by any means necessary. There has been some dispute by the man who runs the local police, goes by the name of Paul. Believes that some part of the property belongs to one of his relatives, Hadley. Sam thinks he is the person running the outfit. Recognises him from a function we held a year ago.

Now you can understand why I'd rather the police were not involved. Like I said, some wines on the property are priceless; therefore, I am willing to pay decent money for them to be removed, shall we say £500,000, with half being paid upfront?"

I turned towards the other two, "what do you think, gents, is this something we would be able to do?" Both Simon and George nodded in agreement.

"OK, Henry, we are in, just a few questions for now. First, got any detailed maps of St Halb and your home?"

"Thought that might come up, here are the most recent ones of the north and south islands, afraid they are a few years old. When it comes to the layout of the property, Abbie will provide them, she worked for me for a couple of years and knows the place inside out."

"Next question, you said armed guards operated the gate, we will take it as read that there are more people, so we are going to need weapons of our own. Any contacts who can help us in this matter?"

"Have a connection in Jal, Steve who can assist with this matter, her name is Katie, she runs the local coffee shop with her husband Cody on Joshua Boulevard, among others, shall we say not so legal business on the island.

"Give me a moment to note down her details."

Henry went to the bar, grabbed a notebook and pen and was about to start writing before we had to stop him.

"What's the issue?"

"Your acquaintance, Simon, would you like to tell him?"

"Sure, no problem. Writing anything on the notepad will leave an indent on the pages underneath when the top page is torn off. People who know what they are doing will be able to read, therefore, Katie's details. Plus, they will know we have them as well, might put her and us in danger."

"Apart from us, who would have any idea what we've been talking about? I chose this place because we would have no issue speaking in secrecy."

"OK, the man stood over by the bar wearing a blue jacket who followed Simon in and hasn't taken his eyes off us since George and I arrived, one of yours?"

"So, you spotted him, yes he works for me, out of the three you Simon is the only person I know, so had to make sure I was not walking into a trap."

"Next question for now, Henry, we are going to need transport once on the island, is there any vehicles we can use?"

"I'll ask Sam to collect my old Land Rover on the pretence he needs to do some work in his garage. A little old with no roof but should be OK for getting around."

"That will do us."

"Have to go, gents, as I said earlier, I need to go to another engagement in the city. If you think of any more questions, Simon has my contact details."

He turned around to shake Simon's hand while slipping him a large brown envelope with a blue line down the middle. Both Henry and his hired thug were about to leave the pub via the back door when he turned back to face us.

"Sorry, gentlemen, almost forgot. If possible, would you bring back the brown envelope with a blue stripe down the middle that is in my safe, there is only one so easily recognisable. The safe is in the office, I'll text the combination later today, thanks."

"What do you make of all that, gents, you still in knowing our arse-kicking now turned in to an arse-kicking with guns."

"Fantastic, we are all still in."

"You're the one with all the money, Simon, so guess who's getting the food and drinks, anyone else hungry?"

Due to the fact you never know who is listening and a lot at stake, we agreed not to talk any more about the job today and arranged to meet at Simon's place tomorrow morning. Perfect for me, as I still had to go to this cruise shindig at the Opera House.

Planning

As nights go, this had to go down as one of the worst nights for many years, might be something from the meeting yesterday that triggered some bad memories. Must have woken up around six or seven times sweating and having flashbacks from when the terrorist scumbag in Ireland tried blowing me away. The nightmares even managed to throw something new in, just to add to the mix. While driving undercover, the car I was travelling in arrived at an ambush and was blown up; while crawling from the wreckage, some bastard shot me.

Now, while these three events had occurred within two weeks, they have never had them appear in the same nightmare, sounds like a plot for a book. The time was now 06:00, so time to drag my sorry arse out of my pit and grab some strong coffee, God I needed it this morning.

Did not intend turning the computer on first thing, but with so much to organise an early start was required. Another brew was in order while it fired up; really need to purchase a new one, this one is getting too slow.

The first task was to check out the flight times for reaching both St Bethanie and to the island of St Halb. A quick search on the internet also brought up a small ferry that runs on-demand to St Halb. Will dig into this a little more as it might come in handy if the floatplane is grounded for some strange reason. They say better to be over-prepared than under, as the old saying 'failure to plan is a plan to fail'.

The advantage of being a travel agent: I knew where to look for the best flights and the ones to St Bethanie were not a bad price. Shame I can't reserve them there and then as need the gelt first. Looking at this logicality, may be necessary to separate our party with me going on Wednesday and Simon and George flying out two days later.

Will run this past the boys when we get together today. That is the flights sorted now to book a hotel.

From what I could find only three hotels were in the vicinity of the airport and close to town; going to spend a few nights here so why not take time to relax for a while. Let's face it, at this point nobody will be aware of why we're there.

Still, we need to blend in as tourists, so no benefit of picking the two-star accommodation. From the photos, this could well be a pleasant hotel, but furthest from town. Located in the direction of the north of the island away from the coast.

Hotel Osprey looked ideal, a three-star property in the centre of a town called Phoebe, near to local shops and not far from the beach and a small port. Best of all they had rooms free for next week, again need money to complete the booking, now I wish I had grabbed some dosh from Simon yesterday.

Spent the next hour looking over the maps that Henry provided, need to be as familiar as possible with the layout of both north and south island, hate surprises.

From the charts, I can now deduce the south part of the northern island there was a creek, an excellent place to hide a powerboat if we need it. Located on the left of the bridge and out of view might be plan B for our escape, maybe the long way around but better the long way than not at all.

Still, a few hours until the meeting at Simon's place and it is only an hour away on the other side of town. Plenty of time to nip into town to purchase some stuff we will need for the job on the way. Located at the end of the high street was a hardware store where I could buy everything we needed in one place. Better be safe rather than sorry; don't want people connecting events, so will acquire them from different shops.

Another sunny day, so I walked to town, gave me time to mull over possible plans and scenarios in my mind, without listening to everyone else's problems on the bus. Like poor Jenny who got stuck in a lift, now claiming she is suffering from PTSD, unbelievable!

I arrived at the store in no time. From here I was going to require some clothes pegs, about 10 should do it along with a reel of small low voltage wire, next to the stationery shop which is at the other end of the street where I was going to need a box of drawing pins and a pack of cheap BIC type pens.

Only two more shops and I should have what I needed, for now. Don't want to create a paper trail so better break this shopping up and take a rest. Waited for around for about thirty minutes before continuing with a purchase of tiny ball bearings and some high breaking strain fishing line. Not wanting to leave behind a card trail ensured I used a mixture of different debit/credit cards and cash in all the shops.

To the untrained eye what I've purchased won't turn anyone's heads, especially when I carry them through airport customs on the way to St Bethanie. Would be right of course, I could be a tourist who may be doing a spot of fishing while on holiday, it is what I can do with them when used together that counts.

Shopping over, I'd better make my way to Simon's place to meet him and George, to start making plans of how we are going to remove this gang of people from Henry's property on the island of St Halb.

Arrived about half an hour later, George was already sitting outside with Simon around a cast metal patio set situated on a paved part of the garden to the right of the cottage.

"No change then, with you two starting on the beers without me again, anyone going to fetch me one?"

"So, what did your last slave die of?" came the instant response from Simon.

"Not doing as they were told," I replied.

"In the fridge, if you want one help yourself,"

"Thanks, I will, anyone else want top-ups?"

No need to ask where this was located as I had been here several times since we first met at Combat Stress a while back. The kitchen was on the left on entering the cottage. To the immediate right was a small living room decorated in the same colour paint Simon had painted the walls some years back. Grabbed a handful of cold beers from the fridge before joining the other two in the garden.

"Anything else from Henry?"

"Not yet. Will contact him once we finalised our plans and on the way."

Simon's cottage was located at the edge of town, away from any other signs of life or houses as he was one for the tranquillity and peace of living, so it was safe for us to discuss our strategies, nobody around to eavesdrop.

"Wasn't long before the conversation turned to business. I checked the flights to St Bethanie along with a hotel which will suit our needs until we arrive on the island of St Halb. Think it would be best to stop any suspicion of three men travelling to St Bethanie together, we should split up. What do you think?"

"Why would anyone suspect three buddies going on holiday would be anything else but that, what's your thoughts on this, George?"

"Think Steve's right, remember the person who followed us to our meeting with Henry."

"OK, separate flights it is."

"My flight leaves on Wednesday, you two follow on Friday, as the flights only go Monday, Wednesday and Friday.

"Will make all the transport arrangements when I arrive home, can you give me some of that dosh, Simon. Once I'm in St Bethanie and settled into the accommodation, I will check out the local surroundings in case we need to hide out here for a while after the job.

"Did some research on the internet and discovered a small boat company were running on-demand trips over to St Halb, the floatplane only once daily with a departure time of 10:00. Will wait for your arrival before checking out the underbelly of the island for possible purchase of any weapons, in case,

Katie and Cody can't deliver.

"Got the maps handy, Simon, we need to do some planning?" Simon brought over the map and laid it on the dining table.

"Skip the part getting from St Bethanie to St Halb until we arrive and process more information. Let's start with our arrival in Jal on the south island, we're going to need somewhere to base ourselves until we can establish comms with Sam."

"Why don't we call him from Phoebe, he can meet us when we land."

"Excellent idea, George. We all agreed, yep?"

"The less time we spend hanging around, the better. To start with, once we've met Sam, he can take us to his place, and he and Abbie can give us more information on the Island.

"From what I discovered so far, Henry's place is at the end of this road that runs through the rainforest, surrounded by a high fence complete with a large gate, guarded with arm guards and pooches. Over to you, George, you're our dog man, any ideas yet on how we are going to take out the dogs?"

"Been thinking it over since we met Henry, got a few plans almost sorted in my head, going to need to witness the routine of the handlers etc."

"Thanks, we will leave this part to you."

"To the left of the property, there could be a hill covered by rainforest which should give us a fantastic observation point overlooking the residency and the grounds. From the map, we can see a dirt track leading around the back, terminating near the beach. This will need confirming once on the ground, we're going to need transport.

"This leads us properly on to Simon, you're our motor guy, you drove a tank which has an engine; therefore, it makes sense you manage all our transportation requirements.

"Once we've met up with Sam, you need to sort out the Land Rover Henry mentioned and ensure it is not going to let us down when we need it.

"Part of your role will be to check any routes that will enable us access in and out of the property and back to the south island. Take a look here on the map, what appears to be several tracks. May need to complete a recce and find a way across this inlet. It might be possible to hide a small boat here in case we need it for our escape.

"So, we are all in agreement; once on St Halb we are going to do three separate observation posts for at least two days each. One here which I will take on top of the hill, George, will conceal himself at a location where he can monitor the comings and goings at the gate. Paying particular attention to the pooches and their handlers.

"Of course, locations will be confirmed once we have a better understanding of the lay of the island.

"Your role, Simon, will be dropping George and me off then, as discussed, finding the best route in and out, before concealing yourself and the Land Rover somewhere over here where this side of the property can be kept under surveillance.

"Let's break this down into more details once we are on St Halb and speak to Sam and Abbie.

"Any ideas on the escape plan, gents? I personally think we should consider at least three plans for our withdrawal.

"First, make our way at high speed back to Jal where we would have a boat waiting, which could be hidden here at this location where Simon is going to find a way across the creek."

George pointed at the map, "Is that a boathouse? Bet you anything Henry will have a vessel of some sort stored here; we can ask Abbie when we meet."

"Good idea."

"Don't think there is anything else we can plan until we arrive on the island, apart for what to wear on our little trip. Would recommend plain clothes, no logos, or other silly messages, such as the man I witnessed earlier who was proudly displaying a T-shirt with 'I Drink Because I Can' across the front.

"This may seem funny and witty, but it will make anyone stick out like a sore thumb, when describing you the first thing they usually say is something like, 'the man was wearing a green t-shirt with the words 'I Drink Because I Can'.

"Plus, we are all going to need some warm and waterproof clothing for the OPs. Take that stupid grin off your face, Simon, the Land Rover doesn't come with a roof, you're going to be soaked as well if it rains."

"Damn it, I'll go and get some more beers then, might as well be wet on the inside as well."

"Fantastic idea, starting to become a bit dry."

"Let us park the planning for now while Simon goes and makes us something to eat."

"No problem, does sausage, chips and beans sound good?"

"Excellent choice, Simon, do you have brown sauce?"

"What do you think this is, a fucking café?"

"Yes, and with that attitude, you're not getting a tip either."

"Now the Donkey Wallopper is busy making breakfast, any ideas on how we do the observation posts, George?"

"Yes, think we should be dropped off at least two kilometres away from the actual location, this gives us time and space to move in, ensuring we are not seen."

"Makes sense, mate, will find out more about the target area before confirming anything."

"I purchased some equipment that could be used as IED's, these can be used to alert us if we are spotted, and if they try to creep up on us, now all I need to do was acquire some sort of alarm and earpieces."

"Let's take a gander at what's in the bag then, Steve." I emptied the contents of the bag onto the table.

"That's no good, just clothes peg and wire."

"More here than meets the eye, George," as I explained how to make an IED out of the items.

Simon came back with the food. "That didn't take long, mate, thanks. Grubs up, George."

"Have you seen what this idiot can do with some household items, remind me not to piss him off."

"Think that's cool, want to see me make a tilt switch out of this BIC pen?"

Time was now getting on, "I'll have to go if I'm going to book the flights and hotel. Simon, will need some of that dosh, so I make the bookings with and some spends."

"Can do better than that, here is £10,000 each to start with. Best we take all our costs out for the job before dividing up the rest."

With that, I left the boys and headed back home, it was going to be a busy day tomorrow.

Journey to St Bethanie

Up nice and early this morning to ensure the air travel was booked, managed to deposit the money into the bank last night so would be cleared by now. Even managed to find the same flights and prices as the previous day, which is a miracle as flight costs change by the minute; they also went straight through, lady luck must be on my side today. Now need to book the Osprey Hotel in St Bethanie for three nights for myself and one night for George and Simon, who will be flying out to meet me on Friday.

Would give the other two their travel arrangements later; first I needed to do a little more shopping for equipment we needed for the job, which I would do this morning as today was Wednesday, and my flight was booked for tonight from London Heathrow. Shouldn't take long as all I required was the radio transmitter and earpieces for the observation posts. Let us not forget we are going to need four radios.

For some reason, the day was slipping away fast so had better start thinking about getting my arse in gear. May be a good idea to pack my stuff now and take it with me on my shopping trip. Save coming back later, wasting more time. Right, this was the plan; kit, shop, drop travel plans and documents off to Simon on my way to the airport.

For what we were planning and where it was located, didn't need much, so the bag packed in no time, not forgetting the goodies I purchased yesterday. The problem with PTSD; you're not just hypervigilant, you trust nobody, apart from your mates where this was built up over time, so not a simple job of locking the caravan and leaving.

First, close all the curtains, stopping any nosey bastards looking in, set the alarm. A trick learned a long time ago to monitor if somebody had entered your home while you were away on a trip for any length of time: Located a place on the door which would be invisible to anyone trying to break into the home. Next, pulled one hair from my arm, they're lighter than the ones from your head, with two small amounts of clear tape fastened the hair between the door frame and the door. It is possible to use a matchstick, but these are easier to spot. Now if any bugger were to enter the house while I was away, the hair would be free from one end, and I would know someone's been inside and take the necessary precautions.

Repeated this exercise on the windows where people might be able to gain entry, no point on the small window as it wouldn't be possible to fit through; they would need to open the big windows.

Found an electronic store via my smartphone which should have the equipment I needed. The problem, it was on the other side of town; with the time getting on I had to take the bus. Saves lugging the bag around. Shit, it was practically full, just enough room for me to stand near the bottom of the stairs. Well, at least I could put my Bergen in the rack and keep an eye on it.

Travelled a short distance when we stopped at another bustling stop with lots of people waiting to board. This should be fun, no way they were all getting on. Due to the lack of room, some spotty face man stood with inches of me, tapping on his mobile. Now coping with my anxiety levels slowly creeping up to the point of no return, training from Combat Stress, especially the Chimp, a method they taught us to control our anger came in handy. Until the idiot kept knocking into me because rather than holding on, both hands were on the phone.

The first mistake was not listening to me when I asked him to put it away. Unfortunately for him, the Chimp went on a break as the bus came to the next stop, the doors opened — the first thing to leave: his so-called smartphone, which in this case wasn't too smart, swiftly followed by him, with the aid of my right foot and smack to the side of the head. I warned him. Couldn't handle any more of this crap so disembarked and walked the rest of the way, it was only a couple of miles.

The electronic store wasn't too hard to find and was full of every type of electrical equipment anyone could ever need. Why had I not found this shop before? Not long before the helpful person behind the counter came back from the storeroom with what we required for St Halb. On the grounds of not leaving too much of a paper trail, decided it would be best for Simon and George to purchase the radios from here later. I had purchased all the other stuff, so always good to bring someone else in on the purchasing, to throw people off the track.

Simon's place was maybe an hour away by foot, but no way I was getting back on the bus, plus still plenty of time to before I needed to be there. After a pleasant walk I arrived at the house, knocked on the door and walked straight in. Where is the bugger? In the end, found him in an old battered shed to the rear of the house, sat at his potter's wheel.

"That's decent, Simon, what the fuck is it?"

"Give us a minute to finish this vase, and I'll be with you, grab yourself a brew from the house?"

"What a brilliant idea, you want one."

"Now that is perfect timing, Simon the kettle's boiled, where are you hiding the biscuits?"

"They're in the cupboard next to the microwave. Did you manage to arrange the flights and hotels alright?"

"Yes, mate, that's why I'm here. To go through the travel plans, just finish my coffee first."

Simon took a seat next to me, "OK, let's have them, any significant changes since we spoke last?"

"No, not really, I fly out tonight and arrive in St Bethanie Thursday morning. Will take a taxi to the Grace Hotel, go through the door, exit the rear and walk the mile to the Osprey Hotel; can never be too careful. Here is yours and George's travel documents. Flight leaves at 21:00 on Friday night from London Heathrow arriving Saturday morning. Once landed catch a cab and proceed to the Grace, I'll be waiting there."

"That is straightforward enough. I will ask George to come round tomorrow, and I will take him through the travel plans."

"One more thing, I need you to go to this shop," I handed over the address, "and purchase four radios and bring them to St Bethanie; two in your bag and two in George's."

"Anything else, boss man?"

"I'm not in charge, I'm decent at planning that's all and hate changes to routine, with your own sections to run like transport and pooches, there will be plenty to keep everyone busy."

"Time for another brew, Steve before you set off and this adventure turns into a serious no backing down job?"

"Always time for another brew, mate."

"Want a lift to the airport, save catching the bus, we know how much you love buses?"

"No idea what you're talking about; I've no problem with them, it's the arseholes that frequent them I have the issue with, and yes."

"Leave in about an hour, if that fits in with the master plan."

"Fine by me."

"About to make some scran if you fancy any?"

"Thought you would never ask; my stomach thinks my throat has been slit."

"Take that as a yes."

"Yes please, Simon, that would be very nice of you."

No need to take the piss."

That's filled the hole, Simon, tasted good as well.

"But we better make a move, time's getting on, will we be going by Polo Donkey or car?"

"Walk if you fucking like."

"The car it is then."

In just over an hour, we arrived at Heathrow terminal 5

departures. "Before I leave, Simon, any questions on your travel plans?"

"My phone will be on until 20:30 tonight, and once in St Bethanie, I will purchase a local PAYG SIM card, if you or George have any queries, I will answer them then. Will buy you each a card while I'm getting one for myself, there should be a machine like that at most airports where these can be acquired, no questions asked. Talking of which, before leaving the airport can purchase one for yourself as well and text me the number? Right, I'm off, see you on Saturday morning, any issues let me know Thursday, remember I will be five hours behind UK time."

Still time to check out the British Airways lounge. A perk of flying business class, for once I could afford it. Like all the other times visiting these places, the room was full of families and screaming brats running around the place. Think they gave up calling it a business lounge a long time back when travel agents started giving away free access in a way to do more business.

Still, the best place to relax away from the hustle of the main departure hall before your flight with food and drink at no cost. A bonus when you see the sky-high prices in the other parts of the airport.

Can always spot people who are flying economy, and their travel agent paid for the lounge; they're the ones stuffing their bags with drinks and foodstuff due to most airlines now charging for food & beverages on short-haul flights.

Not sure about the prices at the Osprey Hotel in St Bethanie for a beer, so might as well join the game and stuff my bag with a few. Let's hope I won't be checked when leaving the lounge. Seen people stopped and all the drinks they sneaked into their bags confiscated. Time to go to the boarding gate. Would love to meet the sarcastic bastard who thinks it is funny to put your departure gate the furthest from the terminal bars and restaurants.

The last week or so must have taken it out on me as only made it through the first half of the safety brief before I was in the land of nod. Luckily for me, the air hostess decided to wake me for some more bubbly, thanks very much, I'll take two.

One of the strange things about being on a plane; typically, if someone sits behind me, I quickly become stressed, but on a flight, it appears different and safe. This might be something with the fact in business class you are in your own little capsule. The trip is about eight hours so plenty of time to relax and enjoy the hospitality. About an hour before landing, I will run through in my mind the arrival plan with all its variables, from luggage collection to a hailing a taxi to the hotel.

Asked the air hostess, who after several conversations found out her name was Lorna, to let me know when we were about sixty minutes away from arrival; good job I did, as yet again I had fallen asleep.

Before leaving home, I found a map of St Bethanie airport arrivals. Nothing worse than drawing attention to yourself as you wander haphazardly not knowing what you're doing or where you're going. Took out the map along with my notebook and studied the arrivals hall, until I could confirm everything in my head and was sure I could go through the whole process like a regular traveller to the island.

Not long before the plane landed, and I was on my way to passport control. Must be a busy time as the place was full of people all walking half-asleep up and down the sheep pens until they finally arrived at the customs officer sat behind the counter. Doesn't matter how many times you've travelled; you always turn up here looking as guilty as sin, only to find you're welcomed with a smile and told to have a beautiful day. Being no different than everyone else, soon stood at the desk, feeling guilty, thinking any minute my passport will be rejected, and I will be led away and forgotten about. After a quick check and have a lovely day, on my way to collect my bag.

The baggage collection was only a short walk from passport control, so by the time I arrived, the baggage was still being unloaded from the aircraft. Used this time to find the machine selling the local PAYG SIM cards, purchased three. Took my stand-off position away from the conveyor belt a little behind everyone else. Still in a place, I would be able to see my bag arrive and keep it under surveillance for any unusual activity.

From this point on, everything must be completed with military precision using all the undercover skill I was trained to do. Out of the corner of my eye, I spotted my non-descriptive bag appear from behind the curtain. The plan: let it travel around a couple of times before retrieving it. Wanted to find out if anyone else showed any interest in my baggage for two reasons.

My luggage had the equipment I purchased to make the IED's inside, which if the person knew their job, they would be able to connect the items and their potential use. Second, I still didn't completely trust Henry, even though he had handed over a lot of money upfront.

All good news, nobody had been near my bag, so time to spoil its fun and take it off the free ride. A stupid grin appeared on my face as I know how professional George and Simon are. They would be doing everything I've been doing up to now. A quick look around and I had located the area the taxis were parked, on the upper level near departures.

Made the decision instead of going straight to the taxi rank I would head for a coffee shop, fancy a brew. Located one towards the back of the arrivals hall which had seating outside facing the doors.

This is the Caribbean and works like America with everything being served and them expecting a tip for everything. Not wanting to look conspicuous, took up a seat and waited for the young lady who looked dead on her feet, probably from working two jobs, to come over.

Ordered my usual Americano with milk and sat looking in the direction of the doors of the terminal, in front and to the left a shop selling overpriced items nobody really wanted. For me, the perfect place to survey what was going on around me in the refection.

The young lady returned with my Americano, so time to sit back and relax for the next hour. Was waiting for the upcoming international arrival, so it looks like to the untrained eye I have come from somewhere I've never been. Soon the hall became full of people from the flight, so time to make my way to the taxi rank.

To catch a cab, you had to walk to the end, up the escalators through open doors, down the road for about two hundred metres until you reached the taxi rank.

Merged with the crowd up the escalator, instead of heading for the door. Turned left then left again, followed by another left back down the elevators to where I started from. The reasoning behind this madness was not too many people in the world would imminently do three lefts in a row unless they were following you. After waiting another ten minutes, I made my way once more to the taxi rank, this time through the doors until I reached the next available taxi.

Doesn't matter where you go in the world, taxi drivers are the best for local knowledge. Isn't much they don't know about the place and often country. Wasn't long before I had my driver singing like a canary, giving me lots of exciting facts about the city.

The town was named after a beautiful young lady called Phoebe who became an engineer, lived in the town and designed most of the modern buildings. Places to go and not to go soon entered the conversation, with the cabbie telling me to stay away from the area north of the marina. This apparently is where, in his words, gangsters, evil men can be found. This could be somewhere the boys and I may need to visit once they arrive on Saturday.

Told the driver I was a tourist here for two weeks holiday in the sun, so of course he had an uncle who owned a bar and would give me reasonable rates if I mentioned his name, plus the best place to find alcohol and girls.

Between conversations, I had time to check out the local surroundings en route, the area around the airport was mostly open fields which disappeared into the distance. The road was, shall we say, tarmacked with the occasional pothole big enough for the whole vehicle to fit inside. The trail after some time wound its way into a light rainforest before opening near the town of Phoebe.

My taxi made several turns before turning down what must be the high street, with shops of all descriptions lining both sides of the road. The route took us past the Osprey Hotel, which was now on my right and easily identifiable from the other building due to the red-painted exterior, at least I won't have to try to find it later.

The taxi pulled up outside of the Grace Hotel, not too dissimilar to the Osprey hotel, but this one was a light blue in colour. My friendly driver insisted I took his business card and I should call him every time I need a cab. Would ordinarily throw this straight in the nearest bin, but this time he may come in handy over the next couple of days. The fare was $40 so gave the man a $10 tip, and we parted ways for now.

Waited for the taxi to depart before entering the Grace Hotel, doors opened to a brightly painted lobby, a bar and restaurant off to the right, while the reception was to the left under a giant clock.

Again, to ensure nobody was following me I took a seat and ordered a bottle of beer, striking up a conversation with the barperson; with the pretence, I was staying at the hotel and wanted more information, such as where the restrooms and emergency exits were. Emergency exits generally exit into car parks or the rear of the hotel, exactly where I wanted to go in about half an hour or so.

Stayed to chat with the barman for several beers before using the excuse I needed the bathroom. He pointed me in the directions of the stairs, to the left of there, "Cheers mate, catch you later in the bar, I'm here until 21:00," he reliably informed me.

Was right, the emergency exit led me straight to the car park at the back of the hotel. I'd picked up a map of the town while I was waiting at the airport which I now took out of my coat pocket.

If the plan is correct, a side street that runs parallel to the road, should be behind that fence. Lucky for me the back was not kept to the same standard as rest of the hotel, and the fence contained a small hole which I could just about squeeze through.

Quick check nobody was looking, and I squeezed myself through and found myself on the side street. From what I could see, not many people use this road or care about it as the verges were piled up with rubbish and burnt-out vehicles. A few houses with balconies lined the street, which had seen far better days, overlooked the road; several had items of clothing out to dry, so they must be occupied.

Halfway down was a turning to the right that should take me back on the high street. This place was even dirtier than the road I turned off, with dustbins lining each side. On one side was a collection of old boxes piled up where some unlucky sod was calling home. From what I had seen so far, this was a poor town complete with the false facade of the high street and hotels for tourists.

A poor town was good news for me as they will be willing to sell their grandmothers for the right price. Not wanting a new grandmother, but they might be able to provide weapons if Katie over in Jal doesn't come through, may need to nip back over.

Soon back in front of the Osprey Hotel with its bright red exterior, outside were several tables with locals drinking bottles of beer, opposite across the street was a glass-fronted shop. Been a long day and night so went straight inside after a quick look around.

The layout of the lobby was similar the Grace, with a reception on the left and the bar and restaurant on the right, the only difference was the colour scheme. Behind the desk was a tidily-dressed man wearing a jacket and tie buttoned up over a white shirt, he had short black curly hair. Was greeted with a warm welcome and questions on whether I had a good day.

"Hello, sir, I have a reservation for three nights under the name of Barker," might as well use my real name; besides, they're going to want a copy of my passport anyway.

"Yes, sir, room 52 on the second floor, and as requested on your booking, the room overlooks the high street, would you like me to take your bag to the room?"

"That's OK, I can manage, the second floor you said?"

"Yes, the lift is over there, here is the key, have a pleasant stay."

The room wasn't too bad with an en suite bathroom, plenty of storage places and a desk situated under the window. A double bed looking enticing was occupying the middle of the room. Planned on checking out the rest of the hotel, but this could wait until tomorrow. Was now a little on the knackered side and fighting off the urge to fall asleep so went to crash out instead.

Needed to place a tripwire near the bottom of the door in case some arsehole tried sneaking in during the night.

St Bethanie

The alarm went off as planned at 04:00, no better time to check out a new hotel than the early hours of the morning. Generally, only one person will be handling the front desk, which is more likely than not sat in the back office searching the internet. Then there is the security guard who you can guarantee is hidden away in some secluded spot catching a few zzzs.

Put on a t-shirt, and some old tracksuit bottoms, splashed the face with water and went to open the door. Bollocks! Almost tripped over my own tripwire. My own fault as I hadn't turned on the room light. Didn't want to attract attention from outside as it appeared in one of the rooms at daft o'clock in the morning or silhouette myself in the window.

From the sound of the strange noises coming from other guests' accommodation, there wasn't a chance of me waking anyone. Sure, some of them must have been hunting for truffles, talk about loud snoring. The corridor was faintly lit, the hotel probably saving on their electricity bill. Who can blame them as most people, unlike me, are not snooping around the place at this time in the morning.

Crept down the stairs and into the lobby, making my way to the reception, nobody staffing the place as I expected. Will take full advantage of this and check where the person yesterday stored the copy of my passport. Will need this when we leave Sunday morning. Already had an excuse why

I was behind the front desk if someone came out. 'I had locked myself out of my room and didn't want to disturb anyone, looking for a spare'. Found it in an unlocked filing cabinet to the side of the counter, proves security is a little lapsed at the hotel, which is good for us as we plan to bug out early Sunday.

The lights to the bar and restaurant were out, the door was locked. No problem, I would investigate them later today when open. I walked back past the front desk. Spotted the receptionist in the back office sat behind a computer and resting his head on his folded arms. Probably asleep, perfect, made it easier for me to slip into the areas marked 'Staff Only'.

Several doors lead off the corridor behind the staff only door, came to the first one, the door was open with the light on. I had found the laundry room, I need a few sets of bedding for what I have planned, will come back tomorrow night for them.

The other rooms were storerooms of some type or other, apart from the one at the end of the corridor. Through the door, I could see in the far corner of the room, was a sofa facing a TV showing some late-night show. In the darkness the shape of a body tucked under a blanket was easy recognisable, I guess this would be the security guard.

The last door was the staff emergency exit with a push bar to open. Suppose the hotel was not up to code when it came to HSE as they had not installed a breakable locking device, which prevents people from using it as a thoroughfare, but still usable in an emergency. Tried to make as little noise as possible as I forced the door and let myself into the rear yard. Made sure it didn't close the door entirely as I would need to come back this way.

The back of the hotel was illuminated with a single light on the side of the building. Could see that this is where the staff and visitors parked their cars, about twenty in total. Completed a quick calculation in my head, one each for the receptionist and security guard, leaving eighteen vehicles for guests, as this being a twenty-five-room establishment, calculated the place might be three-quarters full.

Like the Grace hotel, a wooden fence ran down the back of the property with the same street I walked down yesterday behind. Good news, an old shed was situated next to it, that would make it easier for us to climb over if we wanted to come this way.

If we did need to come this way, that light would need to be deactivated to prevent us from being highlighted. Might as well sort it now, saves time and noise later when it is not required. Brought down with me my trusty multi-tool enclosed in a rubber sheaf and a small amount of fishing line. The light was powered by an electrical wire which ran down the wall leading into a junction box. Merely a case of unscrewing the front cover, loosening one of the screws which kept one of the wires in place. Tied my line to the cable then carefully replacing the cord back in its socket without tightening the screw.

Then simply put the cover loosely back on with enough hanging out that when required, all we need to do is pull the line. This, in turn, removes the wire and hay presto lights are out. The beauty of fishing line if you're not aware of its presence, it is difficult to find. Of course, I had to do it all without electrocuting myself. Would look rather stupid if someone sees me lying on the floor next to a blown-out light.

Not much more to be seen at the rear, so better head back indoors before our sleeping beauty wakes up. Slipped back past the employee's lounge as our security guard started to stir, through the door back into the lobby as the receptionist fresh from his nap came from the back office and took up position behind the front desk.

Time was getting on with the first meal of the day in about an hour, just time for a quick shower and get ready for the day ahead. Not eaten since the plane yesterday so looking forward to breakfast, bet it's that rabbit food crap with the added twist of pancakes smothered in syrup.

Found myself the first one in the restaurant dead on 06:30 so located a table with my back leaning against the wall, but still close the buffet-style breakfast, of course, I was correct, rabbit food, been to this part of the world far too many times.

Wasn't long before the dining room started to fill up. Two men dressed in pressed black trousers, clean open-necked white shirts appeared first, guessing they are here on business.

Five minutes later they were followed by a young couple who took up a position on one of the tables close to me. Being a nosey bugger, overheard them saying that they were here for a few days before moving on to St Halb for two weeks. They wouldn't go there if they knew what I had planned on that island, they may change their minds.

Finished my second cup of strong coffee and made my way over to the hotplate to discover what delights awaited me. One day I'm coming over here to teach these people how to cook bacon. Just like the Americans, overcooked and hard as a block of concrete. From where I come from this is called pork scratchings. Piled my plate with an assortment of food, including the bacon, will keep these for a snack later. Sat back in my seat and summoned the waiter over to bring me some more coffee.

From my seating position, it was possible to look straight into the lobby through the window. The bloody problem with glass you can see both ways and my friendly taxi driver from yesterday spotted me, came over, sat down and insisted he has breakfast with me. My protest went on deaf ears.

"Not an issue, my friend, my uncle owns the hotel." Now that may come in useful.

"Was there something wrong with the Grace Hotel, did you not like the place, Mr Steve?"

"No, the place was fine. It was me getting my hotels mixed up. When I said take me to the Grace Hotel I meant to say the Osprey Hotel, for some reason I had Grace on my mind, must have been the brochure I read at the airport. So, how's business, Edward?" remembered his name from the card he gave me.

"Not too bad, you need a taxi today, Mr Steve, please phone me."

"Funny you should say that. I was going to get in touch, need a guide for the afternoon to show me the local area."

"Sure, why not, shall we say $200?"

"A bit steep for a few hours, Edward."

"A one-off special deal price for you, at only $100."

"OK, Edward, I will wait outside at 12:00."

"No, Mr Steve, please wait in the lobby. Will come in and collect you." Edward finished his coffee and left, shouting, "See you at 12:00."

Time was getting on so made a move myself, needed to find a general store that has some stuff I still required, plus needed to check the accuracy of this map. Grabbed the mobile from my room complete with the local SIM card purchased from the airport in case Simon or George called.

Exited the hotel and turned right, making my way up the high street for about two hundred metres until I came to a junction in the road, turned right and discovered a small supermarket.

The place was only little, with boxes of produce piled up along one wall. The centre of the shop was lined with shelving, containing an assortment of food from breakfast cereal to canned stuff. Towards the back of the store, chillers providing, among other things cold drinks including the local brew. Could do with a drink so reached inside a grabbed a bottle of soft fizzy pop.

Soon found some items I had been looking for; some children's clay, a box of disposable gloves, three sets of painter's overalls, small square batteries. A quick calculation in my head and worked out I would probably need six of these.

Behind the counter, an elderly gent sat rocking away in his chair. "Good morning, sir, don't suppose you have any small camping stove gas bottles?"

"Not here, my friend, probably best visit the out-of-town store, they should be able to assist you with them. Want me to open that drink?"

Hadn't noticed it wasn't the standard screw-top like the ones back in good old blighty. "Yes, please."

Purchased my goods which the kind gentleman placed in a free plastic bag, makes a change from home where the robbing bastards at the supermarkets now make cough up twenty pence for a flimsy carrier bag.

Took the map out of my pocket and lined it up with the ground to get my bearings. The back street I had walked down yesterday now fifty metres to my right. Good to know if we need to bug out to the rear of the hotel, we will need to turn left to come out here.

From where I stood, the road in front and slightly to my right transverse across open fields for about a hundred metres before disappearing into the forest. The map indicated that the high street ran all the way to the coast. In the opposite direction from where I had walked, the road to my immediate left was the one leading off to the small fishing port I had seen on Google Maps. Still had a few hours before Edward would pick me up from the hotel, so would check this out; needed to find out the distance and layout of the buildings and land.

The first couple of hundred metres of the street were similar to the high street, with shops of different descriptions, from clothes to bakeries lining both sides before the houses came to an abrupt stop. Parked cars occupied each side, some looking a little worse for wear, but who am I to judge.

The road then made its way through open ground, with

little scope for cover apart from a few old burnt-out vehicles. A grassy mound was situated to my right about six-foot-high, and thirty metres long, the open ground lasted for about a hundred metres before entering the forest.

Now stood at the edge of the woods, from the supermarket to here had taken me twenty-five minutes, deliberately strolled to give us a margin of error in the timing if we come this way on Sunday morning. Reckoned at a fast pace, calculated we would easily take off ten minutes from the total time.

Continued along the road, which twisted and turned several times for the next click. From here, the forest thinned out as it came closer to the edge, but still plenty of places for someone to set up an ambush, so not a safe to place to walk. Matching the map to the ground again, I ascertained the road with all its twists and turns, in fact, made a massive curve. Will check if a direct route existed through the forest to the harbour on the way back or even tomorrow as the time was getting on.

Came to the far end of the forest, the port still off into the distance and mickey telling me it was now 11:00, better head back to the hotel, will ask Edward to run me this way later.

Arrive back at the digs in time to dispose of my bag then make my way to lobby and wait for the arrival of Edward. On entering the lobby, the receptionist called me over, shit, maybe he had seen me this morning.

"Received a call from Edward about ten minutes ago. He is deeply sorry, but he is running thirty minutes late." That's a relief.

"No problem, will grab a beer from the bar and wait for him."

Grabbed several beers and found an empty table outside on the pavement, left of the entrance facing the shop on the other side of the street. Even managed to relax for a while; this was perfect, a few drinks in the sun, and someone else was paying, excellent. From where I was sat, could observe up and down the road via the window opposite. Plus, anyone coming from the hotel along with people at tables to my right.

Been seated no more than ten minutes when two youths dressed in jeans and black t-shirts walked up the street, sitting at the table closest to the right side of the entrance. Wasn't long before a taxi drew up in front of me with Edward's familiar face sticking out of the window.

"Ready, Mr Steve?"

"Sure am, mate." Drank the last of the beer and climbed in.

"Can you take me to the out-of-town store? Thinking of going fishing for a few days, need some small gas bottles and a camping stove."

"Sure, no problem, Mr Steve."

"So, Edward, tell me, what's the reason behind your name, doesn't sound much of a Caribbean name."

Looking in his rear-view mirror, "Named after my grandfather who came over here to live many years ago, I think he was born in Portsmouth, wherever that is in England." That explains a lot.

"How far to the store?"

"Not too far, about ten minutes."

This must be the Caribbean for big, the store was about the same size as our standard supermarkets back home.

"Got any idea where in here I can purchase the gas, Edward?"

"Yes, Mr Steve, go through the doors and walk to the end the shop is on the right, owned by a friend of mine. Mention my name, and he will give you a good price." Is there anyone Edward doesn't know?

The store wasn't huge but seemed to be stocked with everything someone would need for a short camping or fishing trip. Found a couple of small stoves with a sign saying, 'please ask for gas at the counter'. On the way to the counter, stumbled across a medium-sized plastic water bottle along with the last two collapsible water containers. Each would probably hold around two litres. Perfect for George and me on our OPs, not an issue for Simon as he had the Land Rover.

Nothing else I wanted from here apart from the gas, found a woman behind the counter displaying a shiny name badge with the words, 'I'm Tracie, happy to help'.

"Hi, Tracie, do you have any gas bottles for this camping stove please?"

"Over by the stoves."

"The sign says they are behind the counter," maybe Tracie is not happy to help.

"How many do you require?"

"Six should be enough." Tracie reluctantly disappeared to the backroom before returning five minutes later, with seven gas bottles, can't be arsed to argue, seven it is.

"Could you put them in a bag for me, please?"

Didn't really want the gas bottles for fishing or camping for that matter, in fact, will probably ditch the stove at the Grace Hotel. The boys and I will be on cold rations in the observation's posts. Last thing we will want is some switched on guard noticing a naked flame in the forest.

The gas bottles come with a concave bottom, making a perfect shaped charge, we will each take one on the OPs to be used as a defence if any of us start to become overrun. This is why I had purchased the clay and nails. Mix both together and stick on the bottom of the gas bottle, instant claymore.

Found Edward where I left him, which surprised me, thought he would be off on another quick job.

"Didn't receive a discount, mate, a woman going by the name of Tracie was behind the counter, not a happy bunny."

"She is always like that, where to next?"

"Need to go to the airport where the floatplane leaves from, and the harbour, you know anyone who takes people to St Halb by boat?" Surprisingly, Edward, of course, had a friend that could help for a price.

"No problem, Mr Steve, they both leave from the port, you want to go straight away?"

The port was in a small built-up area which consisted of the road running parallel with the coast; several fishing boats were tied up against jetties jutting out to sea. A row of shops and cafés ran down one side packed with tourists and locals, one of the reasons we will be leaving early Sunday morning.

"People still go fishing from here, Edward?"

"Yes, Mr Steve, they go out early in the morning, then sell their catch to the cafés or on the Saturday market."

The answers I'd been fishing for. When we leave in a boat Sunday morning, we won't draw attention to ourselves, just like we are going fishing.

"Any good fish restaurants here you can recommend, Edward?"

"Yes, we can stop if you're hungry, it's owned..."

"Don't tell me, a relative?"

"No, a friend, goes by the name of Derek."

"Tell you what, once we have been to the floatplane and spoken to your cousin about the boat to St Halb, we can stop at the restaurant, my treat."

The floatplane dock was to one end of the port, away from the fishing boats. The airport consisted of a small wooden building at the end of a jetty, a single plane was tied up at the pier. With only one daily flight, which left at ten and the time now was 15:00, would surmise this was their single plane? Edward pulled up about fifty metres from the building.

"Sorry, can't get any closer."

"No issue, will only be a few minutes, want to check on the cost of the flight in case we fancy going back to St Halb after the fishing," didn't want Edward to know what we were up to, so left him in the car.

Located inside the building an elegantly dressed woman in a black skirt and white blouse stood behind the counter and welcomed me in with a big smile and 'how can I help you, sir', unlike Tracie this person did want to help. Could see from her name tag her name was Tara.

"Hi, Tara," always used people's title if they could be bothered to wear a badge, only manners.

"Fancy going over to St Halb by boat, with a spot of fishing on the way out and then fly back, could you please give me the cost for three adults?"

"Certainly, Sir, when would you like to come back?"

"Not next Friday, but the following Friday." That should give us two weeks to complete the job.

"That would be $65 each coming back on Friday at 12:00, would you like to book now, sir?"

"Yes, please."

At least now we would now have one booked route off the island after the mission, still planning of having a plan B & C.

"Excellent, that will be $195, cash or card, sir?"

"Cash, please."

Flight tickets sorted, now to find Edward and find out more about his mate with the boat. Found Edward near his taxi talking to a couple of old fishermen sat on the sea wall.

"So where is this friend of yours, somewhere close?"

"Called him while you were inside, he is going to meet us at the fish restaurant in about an hour."

"Does he have a boat moored in the port?"

"Yes, that grey one with the blue cabin, you can see it from here. He normally uses it for taking tourist out on fishing trips, so perfect for your trip as well."

"Might as well go now, could do with a cold beer."

"No problem, Mr Steve, you're the boss."

Derek's restaurant and bar were one of the ones we had passed on the way to the floatplane, so only a short journey.

From the outside, the place was painted in a pale shade of blue with two windows, which hanged an assortment of fishing equipment. Several tables on which stood a small glass light took centre stage outside the restaurant, surrounded by a wooden fence. Inside, more tables all smartly laid out, ready for the next batch of customers. From the walls hung pictures of German cities with many other objects from Germany as well.

Along the right wall was the bar, mounted behind a photo with the words 'Zum-Kuhstall', which I later found out meant 'cow shed' in German; the picture was of Derek's old house before he moved to St Bethanie. Edward parked the car; plonked our arses at the tables outside to wait for his friend with the boat.

Derek soon appeared with two large beers, thought I would try my German,

"Dankeschön."

"You're welcome, mate," came the reply.

Needn't have bothered with the German, the bastard spoke better English than me.

"Can I get you two gents, anything to eat?"

"Yeah, I'll have whatever that is," pointing to the menu, "what you having, Edward, my treat?"

"A sandwich will be fine; the wife is cooking later."

Perfect timing just finished eating when a man in green shorts and a white t-shirt turned up and greeted Edward.

"Mr Steve, this is Joe, a friend of mine who owns the fishing boat."

"Nice to meet you, joining us for a beer?"

"Yeah, I'll take a small one with you."

"That is a beautiful boat you have, Joe. Edward pointed it out to me earlier, is she fast?"

"Fast enough, should get you over St Halb in around one hour. Edward told me on the phone where you wanted to go, am I right?"

"Just looking for the best way, not sure to go by floatplane or sea."

"Will give you a reasonable price, only $200 if you pay upfront."

"Not a bad price, worth considering, can I let you know in the morning?"

"Sure, no problem, give Edward a call, he will let me know."

Finishing his beer, Joe walked off in the direction of the port, Edward also left.

"Mr Steve, would you mind if I leave you here for about an hour? Received a text from my wife, I forgot to go and collect her medication this morning."

"Sure, I've nothing else planned today, see you in a little

while."

Might as well acquire another beer. Made my way inside and took up position on one of the stools facing Derek as he poured several drinks from the pump.

"Derek, another one of those beers please, and have one yourself."

"Cheers, I will, has Edward left you here?"

"Man's got some trouble on the domestic front and had to go back to do something for his wife, he's picking me up in an hour. How long you have known Edward for, he gives the impression of an OK type of guy?"

"Moved here a few years back and known him since then. You're right, he is a nice bloke, but don't trust him too much. Apart from the taxi he also part of the gang that runs, shall we say the black-market activities on the island."

Thank fuck I hadn't told him anything about my real plans.

"So, Derek, what brings you to the sunny island of St Bethanie?"

"Left the British Military while in Germany and decided to stay there for a while, opening up a local pub. Stayed they for twenty years before giving that up and moving to St Bethanie about three years ago with the family."

"So, what regiment in the Army? Personally I spent ten years in 3 RGJ." Talk about a small planet, turns out Derek was in 2 RGJ at the same time.

"So where were you based in Germany?" Something I already knew, testing him to ensure he was genuine.

"Spent five years in Paderborn, Steve."

Seeing as we were 'Brother in Arms' we better drink to that, as they say, beer, beer said the Rifleman.

"Overheard Joe saying something about taking you over to St Halb. Be careful, some people he's attempted to take over never reached their destination. When are you thinking about going over?"

"Sunday morning, two friends from the UK will be joining me here on Saturday, we have some work to do on the island."

"Tell you what, I have a fast boat, slip me a couple of hundred, and I'll take you over and collect you when you've finished your job, no questions asked."

"I'll drink to that."

"I'll pop in on Saturday with Simon and George to discuss more."

"Make it the afternoon, I'm out in the morning."

Decided as I was on a Caribbean island and the sun was out it would be a waste sitting inside. Grabbed another beer and proceeded to sit at the table outside I had occupied earlier. Was not long before Edward pulled up in his taxi alongside the kerb.

"Sorry, it took so long, Mr Steve."

"No need to worry, Edward, had a good time with Derek in the bar, take me back to the hotel please."

The taxi pulled up outside the hotel, the youths from earlier had left. Was getting out of the car when Edward turned around, "Call me in the morning, Mr Steve, if you need a cab and my friend's boat."

"Will do, mate."

Mickey was telling me it was now 19:00, too early to retire so might as well grab a few more beers and sit outside and view the sunset.

Had to remind myself not to drink too much, need to keep a clear mind, plus I still needed to check out the layout of the restaurant. Talking of which, I had the munchies again, an excellent sign of too much alcohol partaken. Time to grab a snack and take it back to my room, still had some things to do before the boys arrived tomorrow.

Replaced the tripwire across the door, same as last night. Unfolded the knife from my multi-tool and slipped it under the pillow, you can never be too careful. Needed some shut-eye before finishing the plans. Must have been a combination of sun, sea and beer, but didn't wake up until well after midnight, oh well the planning could wait until the morning.

Not much to do today until Simon and George arrived from the UK. Might as well call Edward and do a spot of sightseeing; if nothing else, will be able to get acquainted with the full layout of the island. My timepiece was telling me we still had one hour or so to breakfast, so time to kill. A check of the equipment confirmed that the only thing missing apart from weapons was the radios, hope the boys don't forget them.

St Bethanie Day Two

Breakfast was the same crap as yesterday, but hey, it's food; my motor transport officer once told me if a meal is going, never miss it, you never knew when the chance will arise again. Sat at the same table as the day before in the restaurant with the view of the hotel, watching the coming and going of the residents trying to read their body language; a skill I picked up far too many years ago during my undercover & surveillance training.

A quick stop at the front desk on my way to one of the tables outside, "Excuse me, would you mind contacting Edward and ask him to come to the hotel to collect me in about two hours, please?"

"No problem, will phone him straight away, anything else I can do for you, sir?"

"No, that's all thanks."

Found a table to the left of the door and took out my notebook. Still had to ensure everything's been covered, everything we needed to arrive on St Halb. Plus a basic idea of how the mission was going to be completed. Need the other two to plan more. One thing we still need is weapons, not taking a stick to a gunfight. Hope Katie on St Halb comes through. Now I know Edward has some dodgy connections will run it past the boys if we approach him. Saying that, I will check with Derek, he might know some contacts that might help.

Must have been sat at the table for about an hour with the waiter keeping me in coffee, when I observed the same two men from yesterday approached the hotel. One occupied the same table as they had yesterday while his companion went inside only to re-appear ten minutes later with two drinks. Plonked his arse down next to the other, with the occasional glance in my direction.

Could be me connecting to many individual components together, but yesterday these people turned up before Edward arrived to collect me. Plus, it is roughly speaking the time I had arranged to be picked up today. Raises the question, are they checking on Edward knowing his dodgy dealings, or myself. Only one way to confirm my suspicions.

Went back inside and spoke to the person behind the front desk.

"Change of plans. Can you call Edward and ask him to go to Grace Hotel where I will be waiting for him instead of here, meeting someone," a complete lie, but he didn't need to know that.

Exited via one of the rear exits making sure no one was looking and climbed over the fence at the back into the side street. Made my way to the T-Junction, turned left past the supermarket I used yesterday, then left and back down the road and into the Grace.

Grabbed a beer and took up a position where it was possible to monitor the coming and going through the entrance via the window to the right of the door. Now if the men made their way to the hotel, I would know someone from the Osprey informed them of the change of plan. Either that or Edward's been in contact with them regarding the new pickup point.

A yellow taxi pulled up outside, it was Edward. I'll leave him waiting for five minutes, wanted to find out if anyone else approached him, no one did, so finished my drink and left the hotel.

"Good morning, Edward, going to let you decide this morning, show me the sights of your island."

"No problem, Mr Steve."

In the meantime, back at the airport, Simon and George had arrived from the UK. "Any idea where the baggage reclaim is?"

"According to that massive sign, this way, Simon."

"No one likes a smart arse, George."

Walking in the direction of the luggage conveyor, Simon grabbed George by the arm.

"Better stand-off for a while, George."

"Makes sense."

The boys stood back for a while to allow the bags go around several times, similar to what I had done a couple of days ago, but this time someone went to grab Simon's bag but changed their mind at the last second.

"Did you see that, Simon?"

"Yes, mate."

"Better keep one eye on him for a while, to see if he goes for your luggage?"

The moment George's bag appeared from behind the curtain, the same person picked up the bag, placed it on the floor and read the label before leaving it and grabbing a different suitcase.

"Don't like the sight of that, Simon, good job I put a fucking phoney address on it. Quick grab your bags."

"Better follow him, find out what he is up to. You get ahead of him and wait for him the other side of customs, I will tail him through from here; you can pick him up from passport control to find out if he meets up with anyone. Could be innocent, but let's check anyway, George."

There was no problem getting past the customs officer. George took up a position a little away from the checkpoint where he could spot where our stranger came out. Simon followed from a safe distance, takes practice following someone without them being made aware. The intriguing stranger made several stops on the way, once at the currency exchange and another to make a phone call. From where Simon had positioned himself, he could, from a reflection in the glass, verify the man exchanged some British pounds into local money.

As he came through customs, George picked him up from there. Right, let's find out what our friend here is up to. The man came from Border Protection and turned right past a coffee shop. He headed for a paper stall to the right of the terminal and went inside. Stopping short, George pretended to be a tourist; let's face it at this point he was.

Peering through the window, George witnessed our man purchase a newspaper, which is nothing out of the ordinary, apart from that he also slipped the woman behind the counter a brown envelope with a blue line down the middle.

Stood off for a while, George gave our man some distance before following him through the terminal, up the escalators towards the taxi rank. Waited until he climbed into a cab and drove off before George made a mental note of the licence plate number.

No need to worry where Simon would be, standing order on this type of job; Simon would be waiting at the nearest coffee shop to the exit from customs. Purchased two drinks from inside, Simon took a seat outside at one of the tables and waited for George.

"In regard to our friend, what did he get up to and where did he go?"

Taking a seat at the table, George took a sip of his tea.

"Think we were right to follow him, looks like he is up to no good. May be connected or not, but he handed over a brown envelope to a person in the paper shop. Tell you what, Simon, the envelope had a thick blue line running down the middle and I'm sure I've seen this somewhere before."

"Did you catch the licence plate number of the taxi our man drove off in, George?"

"Sure did, do you think we should contact Steve just in case he turns up to at our hotel?"

"Excellent idea, you got your mobile?"

Taking out the PAYG phone he had purchased at the airport before Steve had left, this made more sense than using your own which could be traced, and phone numbers linked.

"Steve, it's Simon. Me and George, we've now arrived in St Bethanie, a few little hiccups with a man checking out our baggage."

"What the fuck was that about!?"

"Not sure, so George and I followed him. Tell you more when we catch up but keep an eye for a taxi potentially heading your way, I'll text you the licence plate number. Are you at the hotel?"

"No, doing a bit of sightseeing."

"Fucking typical, me and George are working our arses off and your off swanning it in the sun."

"Not going to dignify that with an answer. Will be making my way to the Grace and meet you in reception."

"OK, meet you there in a couple of hours."

While Simon was on the phone George had made his way over to a bar/coffee shop situated towards the middle of the concourse.

Once the call was over he walked over to join George. "We still have time on our hands, fancy a cold one while we wait for the next international flight to land?"

"Sure, why not, I'll go inside to get them."

"Cheers, George."

Both waited until the next flight had landed and the passengers started to come out of arrivals, to be met by an assortment of people from families to bored-looking holiday reps, before heading for the taxi rank. Unlike me, they walked straight to the taxi to save setting up any sort of routine.

"Can you take me back to my hotel please, Edward, got some stuff to do."

"Of course, Mr Steve, hope you enjoyed the tour of my little island."

"Fantastic, Edward, will give you a call when back from our fishing trip, so we can discover more of this little island of yours."

Arrived back within the hour, knowing what the other two would be doing; calculated I had about an hour before they would turn up at the Grace Hotel. Plenty of time for a shower, before making my way to wait for them.

It was Saturday afternoon, and the Grace was full of locals watching football and enjoying a few drinks. Perfect if this stays this way, easier for us to slip out the rear of the hotel. During surveillance training, they use to say the best place to hide is not to hide at all but stay concealed in the public domain. No sooner than I walked into the reception when the person behind the bar recognised me.

"Welcome back, my friend," always amazes me that if you give someone a big enough tip, they always welcome with 'My friend'.

Ordered what had become my 'usual' since arriving at the island, a bottle of the local brew, went to find a seat outside. Was out of luck, all the tables were occupied. Was about to turn around and head back inside when a table came free, 'I'll have that one then'.

Almost finished my second beer when a taxi pulled up. The text from Simon confirmed this was the taxi in which the man left the airport. One man climbed out, took his suitcase from the boot. The man matched the description Simon had given me on the phone. Observed as our man picked up his case and went inside, finished what was left of the beer and followed him in.

The mystery man was at the front desk checking in, no rush to follow him any more for now, so purchased another drink from the bar and returned to my table outside.

Simon and George arrived about an hour later, I watched them from the corner of my eye, trying not to make it too evident. As they took their bags from the taxi and made their way inside, made sure we didn't come in eye contact with each other. Left them for another ten minutes to check if they had been followed.

Inside they had booked themselves into the hotel for one night. The man behind the desk had forgotten to take copies of George and Simon's passport. Fantastic news for us, means we don't need to come back to obtain them later. Had no intentions of staying here, just trying to leave a confusing trail as possible. Both of them would also book into the Osprey hotel for tonight as well. Found them where I was expecting to find them, sat talking to the barman.

"Well, you two don't waste much time."

"Sure don't, Steve, you ready for a refill?"

"Thanks, Simon, will have another bottle with you, so how was the trip?"

"No issues apart from the man we told you about, did he turn up at the hotel?"

"Yeah, he turned up in the taxi about an hour before you arrived, he went into the hotel and didn't come back out so guess he's checked-in here."

"Spot anything else out of the ordinary while at the airport?"

"Saw him hand a brown envelope with a blue stripe to a woman at the shop in the airport, George thinks he's seen one like it before it before."

Finishing his drink, George proclaimed, "Got it, I knew I have seen this type of envelope someplace else, Simon, you still got the one Henry gave you with the dosh?"

"Yes, mate, kept a few pounds in it for emergencies, wait a moment, while I grab it from my bag."

From the inside pocket, Simon brought out a brown envelope with a blue stripe down the middle.

"What a coincidence, you don't see many of them around. Maybe our friend is working for Henry, come to check up on us, suggest we have a few words with him later."

"Drink up you two, we need to go the Osprey hotel to book you both in, the exit to the rear yard is over there, no need to push our luck by leaving via the front door."

Similar to before, the emergency door was unlocked, and we soon found our way into the back yard. The plan was to exit from the hotel via hole in the back fence. Made our way down the back street, unlike before carrying on past the side road, which led to the main road. Enter the Osprey over the back wall, glad to find the pile of boxes I had placed earlier were still in place.

After entering the rear yard, we made our way around the hotel to the front and entered via the front door.

"Right, you two check yourselves in, don't forget to make a note of where he puts the copies of your passports, were going to need them back later."

"Done this before, Steve, we know what we are doing."

"Just trying to help. Once you're ready, I'll be sat out the front seated at one of the tables."

Must be my lucky day, found a table to the right of the door. To my left was a table of men dressed in football shirts and in high spirits, their team must have won. To the left of the door sat the man that Simon and George followed at the airport, the one we need the chat with. Between him and me was another table with a couple enjoying the sun.

Both Simon and George emerged from the hotel, looked around, spotted me, came over with a round of beers.

"So, this is what you've been doing since you arrived on the island."

"The second word is off, George, guess the first one."

"Take a glance in the shop window across the road, the man you followed sat at the end table to your left, don't look at him yet, he has been watching me since I sat down."

"Any ideas on how we play this one?"

"How about we play along and pretend we are none the wiser, invite him over to join us for a few drinks."

"Very intriguing, George, tell me more."

"Supply him with too much drink, ask a few questions, if

he gives the wrong answer, we can take him around the back and kick the shit out of him."

"Sounds like someone left the Chimp behind."

"Have any other ideas, Simon, that doesn't involve kicking the shit out of someone?"

"Nope, a kicking sounds good to me."

"Go ask him over, Steve."

"OK, no problem."

"Hi, my name is Steve, and the boys saw you drinking on your own, fancy joining us for a while?"

"That would be nice. My name is Tony, by the way. I'll come over in a minute need to make a call first."

"OK, see you a moment."

"He will be over in a moment; whose round is it?"

"Yours. Mine is a beer, what you having, Simon, the same, mate?"

"Should I do everything then?"

"Stop your whining and fetch the beers."

By the time I returned with the drinks, Tony had come over to join us.

"Got you another drink, Tony, same as what you were drinking," I pointed at the empty bottle he had left on the other table. "Have these to reprobates introduced themselves yet?"

"Yes, and thanks for the beer."

"You're welcome."

"So, what brings you three to St Bethanie, holiday or work?"

"Here for a short holiday, what about yourself?"

"Here on business, arrived several days ago," what a lying bastard, now we know he is up to no good, better play along.

"That's shite, hope it's not all work, and you manage some pleasure time as well. We're only on St Bethanie for a week before flying home."

The beer and conversation flowed for the next two hours, started to build up a picture of our new friend.

"Sorry, Tony, but we are going to have to leave you as we have a meal booked at a restaurant near the port," wanted him to know that if he followed us if he is going to be one unhappy Teddy.

"Go inside and speak with the receptionist to give Edward a call, Simon."

"Sure, no problem, but who the fuck is Edward?"

"The taxi I've been using to get around the island."

About half an hour later, Edward appeared outside the hotel.

"Mr Steve, where do you want to go?"

"Can you take my friends and me here down to Derek's restaurant?"

"Sure, no problem, you still want that boat for the morning, Mr Steve?"

"Let you know later, mate."

My last visit to Derek's place was not as busy as it was today, but still room for us fat boys to sit outside.

"Hi, Steve, spotted you coming through the window, what would you three gents be having?"

"Make that three beers, please, and this is Simon and George."

While Derek was off getting the drinks, I filled George and Simon in on my activities since I arrived a couple of days ago.

"So, you haven't been sat on your fat arse doing nothing."

"Edward knows someone that can take us over to St Halb tomorrow morning. I have been stringing him along, so people think we are leaving in the morning.

In fact, we are not going until Monday morning. Derek is going to take us and bring us back after the job after the job is finished, no questions asked."

"Can we trust him? I think so, besides he is our best option, plus he is Ex-British Military from 2 RGJ, George."

"All we need, another fucking Green Howard."

"Slap him for me, Simon."

Appearing with three huge glasses of beer, Derek placed them in the centre of the table and sat down with us.

"So, what's the plan, boys, you need me to take you to St Halb, tomorrow?"

"Change of plan, Derek, we're going Monday, you still able to take us?"

"Sure, no problem, any idea of timings?"

"At the moment thinking of first light, we could meet you here, or if you give us the location of your boat, we will meet you there."

"No problem meeting at the boat, she is easy enough to find, it's that green one across the street at the end of the pier."

"Perfect, will meet you at first light Monday."

Made sense to meet at the boat as this gives us time to arrive a little earlier and stand-off for a while to ensure we were not followed, or someone waiting for us.

"Hungry anyone? Might as well indulge in something to eat as we are at a restaurant."

"Don't know about you, Simon, but I am starving. You have any recommendations, Derek?"

"House specials it is, I'll bring them over when they're ready."

"Thanks, Derek."

"Look over there, gents, isn't that Tony sat on the wall?"

"You're fucking right, Simon, anyone seen the Chimp lately? No? Good time to talk with our friend Tony."

"Let's finish our meals first. If he hasn't moved when we've finished, we can take him somewhere quiet for a chat."

Must have taken us around twenty or so minutes to finish our meals when George got up and looked out of the window. "Can anyone still see Tony?"

Simon joined him at the window. "Yeah, a little further along the wall than he was before, he's still looking our way."

"OK, time for a little word with our new friend. Derek, we need to borrow your tablecloth."

"Leave that one where it is, Steve, I'll provide you with a couple of blankets from inside, and here is the key to the boat if you need to take your friend somewhere inconspicuous."

"Right, here is the plan, Simon, you walk down the road past Tony. Believe there is a side street that runs parallel to this one behind the restaurant. Take this blanket, George, and come from our left, and behind him. I will approach him from the front. Once you see me start talking to him, move in from both sides at once in case the fucker tries to make a run for it.

Once Simon and I have hold of him cover him with the blanket, I'll bind his hands with this cable tie. Once we have him, we can take him to Derek's boat for a few questions. Don't give a flying fuck if he is innocent, we can't afford to take chances. Better to attack first, ask questions later, shouldn't have been following us."

Once I could confirm Simon and George were in position, I made my way to where Tony was sat. Bollocks! The bastard is making a sprint for it. Didn't manage to run too far before running straight into Simon, who was heading for him at high speed. This part of the operation went effortlessly. Anyone would think we had done this type of thing before, OK, several times.

The blanket was held firmly over his head by George, secured in place by Simon, who now had him a very tight headlock while I concentrated on tying his hands up.

"No need to panic, just need to ask you a few questions," at this point, Tony decided to start protesting and mouthing off; I soon shut him up with a smack to the side of the head with a piece of wood which happened to be lying on the floor.

Derek's boat had an open deck to the rear leading off into a wheelhouse, at the opposite end was a wooden door which led into the sitting area.

"Right, boys, throw the arsehole in here," as George launched him through the door, yep that will do nicely.

Use of one well-placed cable tie to make someone immobile is something we all had learnt. This involved laying the prisoner, in this case Tony, on his belly, crossing one leg over the other and top leg and foot tucked in behind his hands.

"Why have you been following Simon and George and checking out their baggage at the airport. Furthermore, what was in the envelope you gave to the woman in the shop and why? Yes, we were watching you as well."

"Fucking not telling you bastards nothing."

"Give Tony a little persuasion with your right foot, if you would be so kind."

Lifted his leg high off the ground, Simon gave several hard kicks to the chest, which made Tony flinch and gasp in agonising pain.

"Ready to talk now?"

"Fuck off!"

"Now that's not nice," George lifted his hands up a little, Tony gave out another painful cry as his body was arched backwards.

"Tell us who you're working for, and we will leave you in peace."

"I'm working for fucking Mickey Mouse."

I glanced at my wristwatch, "Sorry Mickey says you're lying," as I slammed my fist into his face, which George had kindly lifted off the floor for me.

"Doesn't look like he going to talk, let's throw him over the side."

"OK, Henry sent me here to check on his investment."

"Now that's better, Tony. Grab him, boys, and launch him on to the dock. Must be your lucky day, I'm not going to kill you," as I hit him again, for no reason, but he had pissed me off.

"The building at the end of the pier, George, check if it's open, we can chuck him in there."

"Sure, no problem."

"Need to look in Derek's boat for a few items, make sure he doesn't make a sound."

"Catch that, scumbag, don't make a sound," to check he understood Simon gave him another kick in the stomach.

Appears like Derek always travelled prepared, and soon found what I was looking for; a ballpoint pen, a reel of thin wire, can of petrol, a small battery and a piece of a metal rod. Once I had everything, I needed I laid them out on the table next to Simon.

"So, what are you going to do with them?"

"A little reassurance our friend doesn't leave too quickly."

The plan was to place a small booby trap on the door handle. First, I unscrewed back part of the pen and removed the ink cartridge. Next step was to cut off a small piece of the metal rod and check it slid up and down inside, perfect. Put one end of the short wire into where the nib was located. The second wire was placed into the small hole you find on all this type of pen. Made sure the bare part was inside and ran a short distance within the enclosure.

A check confirmed the rod was still functioning, this would act as the connection between the two-wire and completing the electrical circuit. Would finish the booby-trap off once we had the bastard locked inside.

George came back to where Simon still had Tony pinned to the floor.

"Get it open?"

"Yes, took a little persuasion, but the door is open now."

"Fantastic! You two take our friend and show him his new home, I'll join you in a moment."

Both Simon and George were using their boots to help Tony inside the building when I arrived.

"Listen carefully, Tony. If you're lucky, someone comes here sometime next week to let you out; in case you're thinking of leaving early, there is a tilt switch secured on the outside handle, I think you know what I'm talking about."

Right, close the door while I finished the mechanism, concealing the switch as best I could behind the handle, led the two thin wires down the crack in the door towards the floor; most people only pay attention to what's directly in front of them taking no notice of what's near their feet.

Ran the cables along the bottom of the wall to the rear, one wire led to the battery, another coming from the battery. Emptied some petrol out of the can, ensuring plenty of room for vapours.

This is what was going to ignite and trigger the explosion. The two free ends being twisted together, leaving just a small distance apart that the current would cause a spark. Both were then placed in the can before sealing it tight. Gave it a shake to be safe. Now, when someone pushes down on the door handle the metal rod will slide inside the pen, creating a circuit and send a beautiful little spark to the end of my wires and boom.

"Right, boys, anyone fancy another drink at Derek's place before we head off back to the hotel?"

"Fine by me, you up for a few more, Simon?"

Arrived back at the restaurant and took up a position near the bar.

"Make that three beers please, barman."

"So, your friend left quietly I take it?"

"Like a church mouse on its way to choir practice. Just one thing, that building at the end of the pier, I would stay away from it if I were you, may go bang."

"Understood."

Time was getting on, better head off back to the hotel; needed to rebook another night.

"Can you call a taxi for us, Derek?"

"No need, I'll give you ride back; the wife can watch the bar for a while."

There was no problem with booking the extra nights with reception. "It's getting late, gents, I will catch up with you at breakfast in the morning."

"OK, Steve, see you in the morning, you definitely need your beauty sleep, you ugly bastard,"

"What's that saying, something about who's calling the kettle black."

St Bethanie Day Three

Another shitty night with enough flashbacks to produce a bloody film, plus my head was still mulling over the plans for today. A quick check of Mickey informed me that it was only 04:00, might as well get up, becoming bored with all this tossing and turning. Dragged my sorry arse in the bathroom for the morning 3 S's, Shit, Shave and Shampoo before getting dressed into jogging bottoms and a light sweat top.

Remembered that I still hadn't checked out the route through the forest towards the port where the road takes several turns on itself, If I'm quick, should manage to complete this before breakfast.

Removed multi-tool from under the pillow, placed it in the pocket of joggers. Even at this daft hour, I remembered to remove my tripwire before opening the door and stepping out into the corridor. By the sound of it, few doors down someone was still hunting for truffles as they slept. Decided a deaf person was staying in the last room as a woman was shouting at the top her voice, 'I'm coming'. Wonder where they are going at this time of the morning?

The same situation as the other night with nobody behind the front desk. A check confirmed the man was once again sleeping in the back office, let's hope he is still on tonight as well before we bug out.

Exited the building, turned right heading up the high street until I came to the junction in the road; it was still dark, so the street was illuminated with several lights which gave off a faint glow.

Needed to confirm the timing from here to the spot where I'd walked to before. This time it had to be accurate. A quick check of my wristwatch and set off at a fast pace until I came to the edge of the forest. Took a look at Mickey who verified it had only taken me fifteen minutes.

Was starting to become light, which should make trying to find a way through a lot easier. Located the track I spotted the other day and headed off into the woods. The trail continued for about 100 metres before turning right through some bushes that had overgrown the path. Will probably be moving through here fast, so spent a little time ensuring they would move when required. Didn't want to move them now as it would confirm someone had come this way, plus they would need to fall back into place once we had passed.

Followed the path for another kilometre (Click) before coming to a Y-Junction; this idiot had forgotten to bring the map, so would need to go by my acute sense of direction. Decided the right fork would be the best option so bordering the track leading off to the right.

Found a small sapling and bent it near the bottom making sure the longest part pointed the right way. Grabbed a handful of dirt, rubbing it into the newly exposed clean-cut on the arch, making sure it was not visible to anyone coming this way.

Carried out the same process on every junction I discovered on the route, until I reached the far end of the forest and met up with the road again. For people who know what there're looking for, this is the best way to mark a trail.

Most people don't acknowledge what's staring them in the face. Anything happened to me, Simon and George would find their way without me.

Time was getting on so headed back the way I had come, this time making a mental note of any good ambush points along the route, working on the principle that if I would make one in a particular position, a good chance this is where someone else would make one. Would mark these down on the map once back at the hotel.

Arrived back with about fifteen minutes until breakfast, time for a quick wash and change before meeting the other two. Both were seated in the restaurant when I entered, sat at a table to the rear.

"Morning, sleeping beauty, glad you could join us."

"Second word is off, George. Pass the coffee," Simon poured me a brew and I filled the boys in on my morning activities.

"Any of you sampled the delights of the continental/American breakfast yet?"

"Wouldn't like to start without you."

"Don't know about you, but I'm bloody starving. Anyone coming up to grab some brekkie?"

Same rubbish as yesterday, but hey, food is food. Loaded the plate with one of everything, this was maybe going to be the last proper meal for a while. Sat back down and poured yet another coffee, guess the waiter is getting to know me as he had left the pot instead of keeping coming back.

"Think you left space on your plate, George."

"Know what you can do, Steve?"

As usual, Simon returned with a few offerings of the rabbit food.

"How the hell do you survive on such little food?"

"Practice, mate."

"Who's up for a bit of a stroll after breakfast? Don't worry, Tanky, it will only be a short walk, we need to discuss the plans on how we are getting to and from St Halb."

"OK by me, Steve, could do with stretching the legs, need to wait for Simon to finish his lettuce leaf."

"Know just the place where we can talk without the chance of anyone eavesdropping on our conversation."

Exited the hotel and turned right up to the junction in the road and turned left, was heading for the open ground I had seen the other day on the way to the port.

Usual practise on this type of operation, something we had learned over time; nothing was discussed about the plan on the route. Doesn't matter how good you think you are; it is always possible for someone to overhear your conversation.

"Right, gents, the open ground I'm heading for is about 100 metres from here. Simon, if you take a right here and making your way around from the right and stand-off until you see me and George approach. Spot anything out of the ordinary, give me a missed call, one ring, two rings if the target area then becomes clear, George and I will stay at the end of the building until we are confident there is nobody around."

Didn't expect any issues, but better to be safe than sorry, especially with Edward's connections and still not too sure about the two men that kept appearing at the hotel.

"Clear from my point, George, you see anything?"

"Apart from the group of men over in the doorway, it appears to be fine to me."

"OK let us proceed to the mound and meet Simon."

Was about to move when a miss call came over the phone, one ring, "Fuck, what's the issue."

"Let's stand-off for a while, George, I can't see anything, can you?"

"No, mate."

About five minutes later when I received another missed call, this time two rings.

"OK, let's go."

"What was the problem?"

"Nothing much, two men was hanging around over in that derelict building, but they've gone now."

"Right down to business, here is what's been done to date since arriving Thursday morning. Firstly, I purchased the rest of the stuff we need for the mission such as gas bottles, clay and nails for the home-made claymores, we will not assemble them until we reach Abbie and Sam's place on St Halb.

"Talking of Abbie & Sam, can you give them a call this morning, Simon, to let them know we will be arriving one hour after first light on Monday, we will update them on where later today after we talk with Derek.

"Second, leaving St Halb. Plan 'A', acquired return flights via the seaplane returning, a week Friday at 12:00, so we need to aim to complete the mission by then. Plan 'B', we will arrange Derek to pick us along the coast, more than likely from the creak we talked about before we left."

"Got a plan 'C', Steve?"

"Yes, Simon. Don't fuck up plan A or B."

"Let us talk more about this once we're on St Halb, when we have a better idea of the layout of the island. May need to go to the shopping centre on the outskirts of town if you need anything for our poochie friends, George."

"No problem, give us the number of the taxi you use, will nip off once we've finished here."

"For tonight, gents, our normal safety precautions will come into force. Come to my room later and collect the sheets I acquired the other night plus the disposable overalls, gloves etc. Will go and purchase three more mobiles and SIM cards from several shops around the town. Planning to play it safe and throw the phones over the side of the boat, somewhere after leaving St Bethanie. Can't be too safe in this type of situation. Anybody could have cloned our phones or installed a tracker.

"Around midnight, we'll bug out. Simon, you collect the copies of our passports from behind reception. I will deal with the lights in the rear yard, the one I prepared the other day, George if you ensure the security guard stays asleep and doesn't watch us leave.

Once we are at the back of the hotel we will exit through the hole in the back fence, turn left until we reach the junction at the end, take the road we just came down. The Rendezvous Point (RV) if something goes wrong, will be where this road enters the forest, I will prepare an RV once I have the phones. Any questions, gents? OK, let us RV at Derek's place, shall we say 15:00?"

Once our conversation was over, George and I headed back in the direction of the hotel. Simon stayed behind to make his phone calls to Abbie and Sam, along with making the first contact with Katie over on St Halb regarding the weapons and other stuff we are going to need for the mission.

After making sure nobody was near him, Simon dialled his first contact, Sam. "Is that Mr Peeps, it's Simon," a code word given to Simon by Henry before we left the UK. If the reply was 'Sorry Mr Peeps is out at the moment' this meant Simon was talking to either Abbie or Sam, but this was not a good time to speak due to their location on the island, probably at Henry's place. If the reply was, 'Yes this is Mr & Mrs Peeps,' it was OK to continue with the conversation as this was them. The response Simon was hoping for came back, yes this is Mr & Mrs Peeps, thank fuck for that.

"Hi, Sam, it's Simon. We will be landing in St Halb about an hour and a half after first light on Monday morning, I can give you a better idea of time and location when we depart St Bethanie."

"No problem, Simon, would you like me to pick you up or leave the Land Rover somewhere?"

"Picking us up, Sam, would be perfect as we will need to go to meet Katie in Jal as well to collect up some supplies."

"OK, Simon, no issues. Will be on standby from first light,

let me know when you're close, this isn't a large island so won't take long to get to any location."

"Probably need your assistance for most of the day, plus would be great if we could meet with Abbie at some point to gives a rundown of the property. Any chance you could obtain a detailed plan of Henry's place as well, that would be fantastic?"

"Leave it all with me."

Simon ended the call with Sam before finding the number for Katie in Jal. Henry had also provided a code word for this first contact as well, let's hope the codes had not been compromised.

The code for Katie was, 'Hi is that Katie from Perth?' If she replies 'No, this is Katie from Headland,' we knew we were talking to Katie.

Took several attempts before someone answered the phone,

"Hi, is that Katie from Perth?"

"No, this is Katie from Headland."

"Fantastic! This is Simon, a friend of Henry who owns the property on the north of the island."

"Been waiting for you to get in contact, Henry said you would be calling."

"Did he tell you what we would need from you?"

"Yes, Simon, I'll make sure everything is ready for when you arrive, when will that be?"

Better play it safe and not give away too much info on our

movements. "Sometime on Tuesday."

"Katie, besides the weapons we will also need around twenty electrical detonators, can you help with this?"

"Shouldn't be an issue as I have contacts with a small quarry company, will arrange them to be here ready for our meeting."

"Thanks, Katie, see you Tuesday."

Simon finished all his calls, for now, so head back to the hotel to wait for the other two nutters.

Meantime both George and I had made it back at the hotel.

"Steve, have you the number for your taxi driver chum?"

"You have the memory of a sieve, I gave this to you earlier, so not giving it to you again, ask the person behind the desk to call Edward, they will know who you're talking about, that bugger knows everyone."

George walked over to reception, "Excuse me, sir, could you give Edward the taxi driver a call and ask him to collect me up in about half an hour?"

"What name should I give, sir?"

"George, a friend of Steve."

Edward must have been local as he turned up in around twenty minutes. "George, Edward's outside."

"OK, mate, catch you later."

"Where to, George?" came the voice from the front.

"Having a problem sleeping, Edward, do you know where it is possible to purchase some strong medication?"

"Yes sure, my friend owns a pharmacy in the shopping centre.

"Steve said you knew everyone."

Edward laughed, "You known Steve long? Bet you're looking forward to the fishing trip."

"Yes, for about five years now. As for the fishing, not a great fan but the other two are, and hey the journey comes with beer, so I'll be fine."

The taxi pulled up outside the shopping centre, "George, if you go inside, turn left, proceed to the end and the pharmacy is on the right, tell them Edward brought you here."

"Thanks, Edward. Going to be some time, you might as well go and shall we say come back to collect me in a couple of hours, going to look around the place for a while."

"No problem, George, will be back for you in two hours, I'll be parked here."

"Thanks Edward, see you then."

Once inside, the place opened with a vast array of shop of all descriptions. To the right of the door was a map of all shops from which George took his bearings.

Took a gander around the place before making his way to the pharmacy to find out what sleeping drugs are going to be needed—the more reliable the better, to knock out the dogs. Now just needed a way to deliver the drugs. Infusing meat is not an option if they are trained dogs, they will have been instructed not to pick up any food they find. So, a different way is going to be required.

Spotted a sport/hunting shop, in the window, were several types of spearfishing equipment, now that would be perfect as a last resort, saying that if it came to that might as well shoot the little fuckers.

Out of the corner of his eye, George spotted a sign reading 'Poisons For Getting Rid Of Your Pests, Behind The Counter'. Bingo, that should do the job. A bit of luck, they would not ask too many questions when a stranger tries to buy poison.

Would say Edward recommended the shop, worth a try. Behind the counter was a young man dressed in jeans and a T-shirt, lost in his own world as music blasted from his headphones.

Just the type of person required for this purchase, as the man gave the impression he would not care who the fuck he was selling poison to as long as he received his paycheck at the end of the week.

Took several attempts to attract the man's attention, all it took was reaching over and tapping him lightly on the shoulder, the fucker almost jumped out of his skin as he was suddenly brought back to here and now.

"Sorry to disturb you and the music, but Edward sent me here. I seem to have a pest problem that needs dealing with."

"No problem man, how big is your problem?" as he reached under the counter and produced several tins marked with 'Caution, Poisons, hazardous to health'.

"Huge, a pack of wild dogs taking the piss around my mates' property and killing the chickens."

"Then you will need this one, mate, you can lay your traps with this neat or add water and leave if for them to drink."

"That one it is, I'll take two cans."

"Perfect, $30 per tin if you're paying by card or $20 if you're using cash and don't need a receipt."

"Cash it is then," the bugger was probably going to rip his boss off, but not our problem, "do me a favour, mate, put them in a bag."

Right, pooches sorted, now for our sleepy security guard; the pharmacy would be the best place for this. The pharmacy was a completely different place than the sporting shop, the staff were dressed in white clinical coats complete with shiny name badges.

"Hi Aimee," she had a name tag, might as will be polite and use her name, "the taxi driver, Edward said this would be the perfect place to help me with my problem."

"Sure, what's the issue?"

"Nothing much, having difficulty sleeping, do have some powerful sleeping tablets?"

"Must be your lucky day, these arrived this morning and brand new on the market, they should allow you to sleep for hours."

"Thanks, can I have two packets please."

"Sure, but being drugs, I will need your name plus the details of where you're staying for the records."

"No problem, my name is George James, I'm at the Grace Hotel," well it's almost accurate as don't want someone tracing the drugged-up security guard to us. That's all the purchases completed, for now, might as well grab a coffee and wait for Edward to come back, shouldn't be long. True to his word, Edward was back smack on time.

"Ready, George?"

"Yes, Edward, can you take me back to the hotel, you can take the longer scenic way if you like, would love to see a little of the beautiful island." Of course, this wasn't true, just wanted to vary the journey around the island, keeps people on their toes.

The journey took them along the harbour past the shed we had stored our friend in, wonder if he was still there; not detected any explosion from the trap we had left, so guess he is still sitting tight. Guided tour with running commentary from Edward completed, arrived back at the hotel.

"Thanks, Edward, enjoyed the trip, here is the fare plus a $20 tip."

Entered the hotel and heard the routine verbal abuse coming from Simon, who was sat at a small table not too far away from the bar.

"Stand by your beds, the Cold Stream Guards have arrived."

"Nice to see you too, Simon, now get the beers in, I'm parched."

"How was your shopping, purchase everything you wanted?" Simon and George were old hands at this and knew people were listening on purpose or being nosey bastards and not to discuss anything unless they were in a safe location.

"Yes thanks, Simon, you make contact with our friends?"

"Yep, all sorted, have you seen Steve since this morning, George?"

"Yes, he has gone out to finish his shopping will be back later. We might as well grab some lunch."

"Sounds like we have a plan?"

Purchased the last two of the phones which now meant Simon and George had a spare phone for when we landed in St Halb. Bearing in mind I had purchased them from the local phone shop goes without saying, paid with cash, so no paper trail of bank transactions. Now needed one more phone for myself once on St Halb.

Next stop, the hardware store I used the other day. Needed a short plank of wood, a small trowel and some six-inch nails for use at the RV. That's what I love about small islands, purchased the wood and nails with no questions asked.

Soon arrived at the track as it entered the forest, with all my equipment; now needed to find the right place for tonight, which needs to be off the track with easy access and cover from view.

The marks I placed this morning were still in place at the Y junction, as we would be going right when we bug out, the RV needed to be close to the track. Stopped to study the area for a while, surprising how much more you observe if you take time to stop and survey rather than piling in headfirst.

Spotted what should be the perfect place about fifty metres up the track on the left. The last thing I wanted to do was to leave footprints on the trail in front of the RV, so best to enter from the rear to throw off any nosey bastard who may have spotted any tracks. Turned left, made my way just inside the woods along the left fork in the track for about fifty metres. At this point, I had to cross the trail. Lucky enough I'd learned a trick from some Jamaican soldiers who I did some training with several years back.

Instead of walking across the track and leaving footprints, which any idiot could see you had crossed the path and in which direction you were travelling, the trick was to take a giant leap, fewer marks the better. Land on one leg, then swivel 360 degrees before taking another leap. This only leaves a small circular mark with no indication of the direction of travel.

Once on the other side, stood off for a moment to select the best way forward. Again, the route had to provide cover, but also, not cause too much movement of vegetation which could be easily seen. Would be coming here once the light had faded and was dark enough to mask our activities. To my right was an opening leading off towards where I wanted to go, with the right amount of protection.

Found the perfect RV which stood about twenty metres off the trail, the one we would be travelling down early tomorrow morning; which gave protection in all directions including from above, plus still being able to monitor for people coming our way.

The floor of the RV was covered in dead foliage which would create noise when laid up. Spent time carefully pushing them to all sides being careful not to pile them too high, which would be noticeable if anyone looked this way. Need to deal with the issue of protecting our way in from any intruders. Wouldn't want anyone to creep upon us.

Located two small trees, one either side of the small clearing I came through, planning a little something for any idiot who tried to take us by surprise.

Opened my bag and took out two clothes pegs in which I stuck two drawing pins, one either side of the inside of the open jaws, to that was attached some of my small electrical wire.

One end leading to a battery, the other was a longer piece which led off to one of the transmitters Simon had brought with him, another wire led from the transmitter to the other side of the battery.

Placed the components in a plastic bag to keep them waterproof, ensuring the clothes peg was left protruding, concealed this under the dead leaves on the floor. On the other side, I attached a length of fishing wire to a tree, making sure I had enough to stretch across the opening at about six inches from the ground.

At the other end of the fishing line was attached a small piece of wood, this would sit between the jaws of the clothes peg, acting as an insulator.

Once someone tripped the wire, the wood would be pulled out causing the two drawing pins to come together creating the electrical circuit for the transmitter, which in turn would send a signal to our receiver.

Always good to have a backup, so on the RV side of the tripwire I dug a hole more significant than the piece of wood purchased earlier, and about ten inches deep. Into the plank was placed the nails, making sure they were not too close together and stood up vertically, to cause the most pain as possible; this was put into the hole.

Grabbed some thin twigs, laid them over the hole before covering them with leaves from close by, needed to look the same. Now if some smart fucker saw my tripwire and tried stepping over it, they would be getting a foot full of sharp nails for their efforts, that will teach them.

The RV all set, a quick scan to ensure nothing looked blatantly obvious, hide the dirt from the hole. Wouldn't put the tripwire in place until we were in the RV, accidents do happen. Made my way back the same way as I came until I reached the edge of the forest. A quick check of my person for dirt and foliage. Couldn't go back to the hotel looking like I had literally been dragged through a hedge backwards.

Arrived back to find Simon and George still propping up the bar. "Looks like you two lazy bastards have been busy."

"Keeping the stool warm for your fat arse, mate."

"Take it no issues today then, boys, and everything is set?"

"Yep, nothing to do for the rest of the day," replied George, as he ordered a round of drinks from the bar.

"After this round, anyone fancy a meal and a few more cold ones down at Derek's place?"

"Brilliant idea, what about you, Simon?"

"Yeah, sure you can count me in."

"Derek's place it is."

Couldn't be arsed to wait around for Edward, so we grabbed a taxi from the taxi rank across the road.

"Where would you fine gentlemen like to go?"

"The fish restaurant, Derek's place at the port, please."

"Sorry don't know that one." Shit! Being taken everywhere by Edward, the idea of checking the name of the joint hadn't even crossed my mind.

"Drop us off at the port we can find it from there."

"OK, no problem, you tell me where you like to be dropped when we arrive."

The taxi dropped us off at the far end of the pier, so just a 200 metre walk to Derek's place.

The place was empty, apart for a small group sat at stools situated in front of the bar and seeming to be in good spirits or too many spirits in them more like, fantastic for us as service would be quick. Only been seated at the table for a couple of minutes before Derek appeared with three beers.

"On the house, gents, would you like to order some scran?"

"Yeah, can you bring over the menu."

Being a meatatarian, the 12 oz steak was looking promising.

"You eating from the list, Simon or should I go around the back and steal the rabbit's food?"

"Fuck off, twat, for that, I will have the steak as well."

"Bet he doesn't eat much of it, hey George."

"While Derek is away preparing the scran, do you think we should let him know a little more about the mission, due to the fact he could be picking us up in a gunfight if all goes arse over face?"

"No harm in letting him know a little more, what are your thoughts on this, George?"

"OK by me, plus if we all agree we should pay him a little more than a couple of hundred."

"OK, agreed. I'll call him over when George and I have finished eating."

"What about me, boys?"

"With all respect, mate, we only have two weeks to get this done, and by the time you've finished eating the whole steak the mission could be over, and we'll all be back in the UK."

About ten minutes later, the food arrived.

"Derek, once we've finished eating, could you join us, want to discuss a little more about our trip in the morning."

"Sure, no problem."

Now that's what I call a steak, must have covered half the plate along with chips and rabbit food.

"Has everyone finished, if so, I will call Derek over."

"Yep, all done here, Simon may be struggling."

"OK call him over, can't eat any more."

"Take it you two would like another beer while I'm getting Derek's attention?"

"Might as well collect a few while you're about it, saves you going back again."

The bar being full, Derek was busy serving the gents with a mixture of alcoholic concoctions, as they had now started some sort of drinking game.

"When you have a moment, can you come over, Derek."

"Yeah, give us a few minutes."

"There, you ugly bastards, two beers, drink up. Derek will be over shortly."

"Sorry for the delay, gents, had to finish serving the group at the bar, now how can I be of assistance?"

"Not a problem, once Simon and George have stopped gas bagging, we can talk about why we asked you to come over. I suggest we whisper from this point, don't want the boys over at the bar overhearing our conversation. Right, here's a quick overview of what we are doing on the island of St Halb. Simon, George and I are going to St Halb to remove some people from the Winery. The owner is a friend of Simon's.

"The people we believe to be armed and will put up a fight when we ask them warmheartedly to leave. Now if it all goes fucking wrong, we could be doing a tactical withdraw in a hail of bullets. Going to need you with the boat to make sure we all manage to make it the fuck out of there.

"Now you know that you could be picking us up under heavy fire, you still willing to take us and bring us back, we're prepared to increase the money we're going to give you from $200 to $5,000 to ensure you are where we want you to be."

"Sure, I'm in."

" I have something for you," Derek placed a black bulging bag in front of us. "Was going to give them to you tomorrow on the boat. But from what I've heard, you may have some night activities planned, and this place can be dangerous at night, especially for foreigners due to the organised underworld on the island.

"Already informed Steve, it's run by Edward, the taxi driver."

"WTF, Steve, something you forgot to mention."

"May have slipped my mind."

"So, what time do you want to leave in the morning?"

"Be at your boat at first light tomorrow ready to go, we will be around and meet you at your vessel. One last thing, can you give us a lift back in about an hour? Me and the boys have a busy night planned."

Was around 21:00 by the time we returned back at the hotel.

"Gents, you fully understand what you have to do before we bug out at 02:00? Come with me now, I will give you the sheets, overalls and gloves I procured earlier; to confirm we will meet out in the rear yard at 02:00, check your watches, don't want anyone being late."

The boys collected the sheets and their share of the stuff I had purchased and disappeared off to their respective rooms. Put on a pair of the disposable gloves then spread one of the new sheets on the floor and emptied the contents of several bags into the middle.

Need to place them in my Bergen in such a way there was no movement, and hence noise, when we bugged out and made our way to the RV. Will need to be up in three hours so might as well grab some shut eye.

Back in George's room he had placed the sheet on the floor, and now just needed to crush the sleeping pills and add them to some water. He'd decided the best and quickest way for the mixture to enter into our security guard's bloodstream was to inject them directly. The tricky part would be stopping him from waking up and making a run for it. May have to drug his coffee as well, it appears like George will be joining him for a brew until he feels drowsy then inject him.

This is the advantage of doing your groundwork, as he had spent last night with him at daft o'clock in the pretence that he needed a coffee and everywhere was shut, the security guard fell for it hook line and sinker so tonight shouldn't be an issue.

Need to ensure all the rubbish was taken away in the bedsheet, to be ditching at sea tomorrow.

Finished packing my Bergen, better give it a few shakes and listen for any rattles; that would be the last thing we needed and very unprofessional. The time was now 22:00, set the alarm for 01:00, time for some shut eye.

Managed to grab a little sleep, but now's the time to put the guard to sleep before the boys made an appearance. Time to put on the overalls, dust mask and gloves, the same as the others would be doing when they wake up.

Bed stripped and remade with clean sheets etc. Wiping down all surfaces, including the bottom of my Bergen, as that will soon be sat on the cleaned floor near the door. One last check to ensure nothing connected to us would be left in the room.

Stood in the centre of the sheets, removed my overalls, placed several wipes on floor in the direction of the door before tying up bedsheets into a bundle and putting them next to the exit along with the Bergen.

George's plan was to place his Bergen outside in the rear yard before going to see our friendly guard for coffee. The light was on in the backroom, fantastic looked like the security guard was still awake. Turned into the room and the guard wasn't about. Crap! This was going to be an issue if he appeared when Simon is looking for the passports.

Was about to leave when the little fucker came up behind me.

"Hi, George, you come for more coffee? You're in luck, about to put on a fresh pot."

"Yes please, couldn't sleep so came down to see if you had a brew on."

"Help yourself, just need to go for a piss."

Perfect, couldn't have been planned better. Poured one cup and added the sleeping powder mixture, then waited until the guard came back in the room.

"Here you go, mate, only manners to give your friends the first cup," the truth was, didn't want him suspecting anything with a cup already sitting on the counter for him, handed him the brew and poured one for me.

Not sure how long this was going to take, so given this task one hour. Walking over to the corner of the room to turn down the volume on the TV, emptied the cup into the sink; the last thing I needed was to be lying in an OP bursting for a piss.

"That went down well, fancy another one, mate?"

"Yeah, little on the dry side." Again, made sure he wasn't looking and poured more mixture into his coffee. Repeated this four times before the bugger started to drop off.

"Back in a moment might have drunk too much coffee, need a piss." This was just an excuse to give him time to fall asleep before hitting him with the syringe.

On the way back from the bog, George ran into Simon on his way from behind the reception.

"Got the copies?"

"No, we have a problem, the receptionist is being a hero and is still awake in the back office."

"Got any of that sleeping stuff left, George?"

"A little."

"What's required here is teamwork, you take him in a coffee and keep him busy while I collect the passport copies."

"OK, Simon give it a few more minutes for my security guard to go night night, and I'll grab a cup."

The drugs seemed to be working, our guard didn't make a twitch when the syringe was inserted into his arm. Now that should keep him asleep for about eight hours. Felt sorry for him in a way, as he will be sleeping when his boss comes in the morning. And receive a right bollocking with a bit of luck, not the sack.

"Here you go, Simon, one coffee with milk and drugs," what more could a receptionist need!

"Thanks, you go and give it to the bastard while I grab our stuff."

Once George had engaged the man in loud conversation to drown out any noise from the filing cabinets being opened and closed, Simon looked for the passports behind the reception desk.

Found the buggers, and just in time as it was now 01:50; time for the RV outside, as Simon turned to attract George's attention, George came from the back office.

"The bugger is asleep now, didn't take him long."

"Probably bored to sleep by you."

Like George, Simon had placed his kit outside before collecting the passports. "Heard from Steve this morning?"

"No, but knowing him, he will be out in the yard already."

Trip to St Halb

I was already at the rear of the hotel and dealt with the light by pulling the fishing line I placed in the socket several days ago, and the backyard was now in pitch darkness. Simon and George entered the yard and picked up their Bergens.

"Steve is over near the fence, better join him."

"Morning, gents, you retrieved the passport copies?"

"Yep, all tucked right here," as Simon tapped his jacket pocket.

"Our security guard friend?"

"Placed enough sleeping juice in his coffee to knock out a rhino, he will not be disturbing us any time soon."

"Right let's go! As discussed, I will leave first, followed by Simon then George taking up the rear. The rendezvous point is where the road enters the forest. Once we've all arrived, I will lead us to the night RV I prepared yesterday, any questions? No? Good, let us make a move."

Perfect, the back street was in complete darkness, apart from a light coming from one of the windows at the far end. This should not be an issue as it was high up, and unless they were looking down, they wouldn't spot us passing by. Once I reached the junction, took time to stop and listen to what was going on.

All quiet, so bent down before looking around the corner of the building. Seen too many people being killed because they put their head around the corner at head height, where someone had a rifle aimed. Once I confirmed the situation was safe to move, turned left and headed towards the road leading to the forest.

Always great working with professionals like Simon and George, without any words being spoken, they had spaced themselves out with a fifty metre gap between us. All went without a hitch until we came to the open ground where we had our meeting yesterday; again, I took time to stop and listen to my surroundings. This time a group of young men were sat on the mound drinking and talking noisily to each other.

Signalled for Simon to close up, took out my 9mm and headed across the 100 metre or so while Simon covered me; once across without being seen, George would move up and cover Simon while I observed the road in the direction we had come.

Took about another twenty minutes to reach the edge of the forest, again without a word being spoken. We fanned out, taking up position facing toward the way we had come, in case someone had followed us. Wasn't expecting one too, but better to be safe than sorry.

A short time later, sure no one had tailed us, I whispered to each of the boys, in turn. "Follow me to the rendezvous point and walk where I do due to the Punji trap I laid earlier."

Once we were all passed, placed the tripwire across the track, we continued the last fifty metres to the RV. Nothing fancy, just enough to give us cover and protection for the next three hours.

Once in we took up positions, with each of us facing with different orientations. Positioned myself, pointing the way we had come. George was covering up the track in the direction of the port, which left Simon looking down the path towards the town. To keep noise to a minimum, everyone was in such a position they could be tapped by the foot of each other. We would be taking it in turns to stag on for an hour.

At least the sky was clear with no chance of rain, plus with the warm heat of the tropics meant it would be a comfortable stay. Nothing like the ambush in Northern Ireland laid in a hedgerow for four days, where it pissed it down the majority of the time we were there. Waterproofs of the time were not as good as you can buy them now, they made a noise when you moved so not worn.

What annoyed me as much as the rain, was the fact the patrol commander decided this would be a good time for a kip. Left me to make the decision when to bring down fire. Mind you, there is always a silver lining. Now there are several members of the terrorist organisation won't be bothering anyone anymore.

Took first stag, which was uneventful with the usual sights and sounds of a rainforest at night, surprising how the brain plays tricks on you in these situations, you would be amazed at how many things you see which are not really there—case of training the mind to filter them out.

Gave Simon's right leg a hard kick to wake him up, as he was on stag next. Was no need to pass him the receiver from the tripwire as we all had receivers and earpieces. Ensured Simon was totally awake and checking the ground down the track. Then after a quick glance over to George who was sound asleep, settled down to try to for some shut-eye.

Felt like I had been sleeping for seconds when I received two hard kicks from Simon. Shit, two boots meant someone was approaching. Looked over to where Simon was, he was pointing towards the track leading from town. Gave him the thumbs up to confirm I understood what was going on. Already alert, George was looking in the opposite direction to ensure we were not being circled.

The noise of the alarm from the trip wire was ringing loudly in my ears. Enormous scream of excruciating pain came from the where the tripwire was set. Shit, someone had not only tripped the signal but had found my Punji trap.

George and I immediately launched towards him to shut the fucker up; being the first to reach him I grabbed him in a headlock with one hand over his mouth to cut out the noise. George was close behind and sat on him to enable a better grip of his now flailing arms.

"Right, my friend, when my buddy here moves his hand from your mouth, want you to stay quiet, and we are not going to hurt you unless you scream again, do you understand me," the man shook his head to confirm he understood what we just said.

"Right a few questions, and don't lie to me or a will stick them nails through your other foot," the man nodded again to show he understood.

"Don't really care who you are. Why are you here, and are there any more of you around?" Released my grip over his mouth slightly, giving him the ability to talk.

"Work for Edward. He knows you would be heading for the port at some time, so he had us keep surveillance on the hotel during the day and the road from town once it had become dark, in case you left on foot. One of us saw you pass the open ground on the way, so I was sent ahead to find out which way you went. I'm on my own, please don't kill me."

"Nobody is going to hurt you, in fact, the complete opposite. My friend here is going to give you something to take away the pain from your leg," George looked straight at me, no words were needed.

I placed my free arm around the back of his head, ensuring the arm went entirely around the man's throat. Resting his hand in the other elbow, I squeezed as hard as possible while making a jerking motion, snapping his neck. Kept the lock in place until I was sure he was dead.

"Help me drag his body under that bush, better check his pockets while we're here as well, George."

"Good idea."

"Anything unusual?"

"There wasn't much in his wallet apart from a few dollars and some bank cards; in his back pocket was something fascinating, an envelope with a blue stripe."

"These are appearing far too often, George."

After collecting the transmitter from the tripwire, went back to where Simon was still covering towards the direction of town in case any of the man's friends turned up, and they would.

Let's not hang around waiting, gents, let's bug out and head for the port, we have enough darkness to cover our movements."

Led off first with George bringing up the rear, spacing ourselves out enough so you could see the person in front and behind.

Had about two kilometres to go through the forest before hitting the open ground between it and the port. The journey through the woods was straight forward, due to the fact I had checked the route several days ago and because now, thanks to no artificial lights, we all had our night vision. You would be surprised how much you can see at night once your eyes have come accustomed.

Using a trick picked up while driving armoured vehicles through the forests of Germany in the blackness of the night, with the only light being that of a tiny convoy light of the APC in front to guide you, the skill was to look up and line up between the trees, navigating your way by following the gap down towards the track. Wasn't long before I came to the edge of the forest, stopping around fifty metres short. No way I was going to just walk out from the woods, seen too many of my colleagues killed that way.

Signalled for Simon and George to close up. Once they had reached my location, we entered the trees at right angles to the track. Then moving forward, using the available cover and stopping just inside the edge, watched for any movement in the ground to our front. The area appeared clear with no vehicles or people coming down the road towards us.

Now we had two options, stay off the road and head cross-country or use the tarmac which would be quicker, but risk being spotted. Time was getting on and needed to be near to the location of Derek's boat at least an hour before sunrise, it was agreed we take our chances down the latter.

Been travelling for about thirty minutes when a set of car headlights appeared in the distance. No need to act now, need to keep an eye on the direction it was driving. Seemed to be looking for someone, as every couple of minutes it would stop for a while before moving off. Maybe they were looking for their friend, who was now providing food for the numerous insects that frequent the undergrowth in the woods, or even us?

Had walked for about a kilometre when the car headed straight for us. Automatically took up cover in the ditch to the left of the road, Simon and George followed suit. The vehicle stopped about two hundred metres from our location for about five minutes before speeding off in the direction of town. This had cost us precious time, we now needed to pick up the pace if we were going to arrive at the harbour in time.

Approached the dock just as the first rays of the morning light started to appear over the horizon, estimated we only had around forty minutes until sunrise. The port was still empty of people, apart from a couple of men setting off in an old fishing boat and heading out to sea, in the distance spotted Derek's boat at the end of the pier.

"Here is the plan, boys. Simon, if you proceed to the dock that runs parallel to the one Derek's boat is on and take up a position overlooking this area," I pointed towards the other pier.

"Take up a position at the end of the dock, George, while you're there check our friend Tony is still where he is supposed to be. Will make my way along the dock and wait for Derek to appear."

Not that we don't trust Derek, but someone could have overheard our conversation in the restaurant, plus as we now know Edward's mob know we are heading for the port at some stage, best stand-off for a while.

"Once I start talking to Derek at the boat, give it ten minutes or so and then if all coast is clear join us ready for the off."

Smack on first light, Derek arrived at the boat, watched as he climbed on board and started preparing for the trip. Waited for a couple of minutes to ensure he was alone before joining him on deck.

"Hi, Steve, where are Simon and George?"

"Around. They will join us soon, everything ready for the trip?"

"Yes, all fuelled up, and the weather is good, waiting for you to give the word."

At this point, George appeared walking down the dock; at the same instant Simon climbed onboard from the seaward side.

"What the fuck, Simon, how did you...." I was cut short.

"Walk on water, mate, or I may have borrowed that little dingy down there."

"Smart arse."

"Right, let's get this mission underway, ready when you are, Derek. How long do you think it will take us to reach St Halb?"

"With this weather, we should arrive at the island in about one and a half hours."

"Perfect. Simon, could you call Sam and let him know our ETA and pickup location."

"No problem, give us a few minutes."

Must have only been travelling a couple of minutes when a loud explosion was heard from the direction of the pier.

"From the sound of that, our friend Tony has finally gone to pieces."

"Think you may be right, George, he will not be bothering anyone any time soon."

"Any luck with Sam, Simon?"

"Will be at the RV ready with the Land Rover when we arrive."

"OK there, George, you're starting to look a little green around the gills."

"You three may be wannabe sailors, but there's a reason I joined the Army, not the fucking Navy, I suffer from seasickness."

"No problem, George, me and Simon will only hold this against you for the rest of your life."

"Bastards."

"That's what mates are for, George."

"Fancy a brew anyone, I'm putting the kettle on? So, two NATO standards, how do you like your drink, Derek?"

"White with two sugars please."

"Three NATO standards coming up. Of course, I'm sweet enough so no sugar for me."

"Who are you trying to kid, fat boy?"

"Must be, my mum told me."

"Yeah, and the Pope's a Jew."

"Not far to go, gents, you can see the island appearing over the horizon at our 12 o'clock."

OK, time to ditch the mobile phones we've been using in St Bethanie, and bedsheets. Ensuring he wrote down Sam's number before taking out the SIM card, Simon tossed them over the side. George and I copied suit and confirmed we removed the SIM card before launching it overboard. Ensured we left a 100 metre gap between them before doing the same with the phones. With technology these days you can never be too careful, someone could have cloned the smartphones or SIM card and added a tracker.

Reached into my Bergen, and pulled out the three new mobiles I had purchased on St Bethanie, I hadn't put the SIM cards in yet to switch them on, we would not be doing this until we reach St Halb and made contact with Sam.

Derek called out, "Gents, best you all move inside and stay out of view if possible, a boat is heading towards us at high speed, seems to be the local police, they may have been informed of the explosion at the pier."

They say the ideal place to hide is in view of everyone, but let's not make it easy for them as we have gone out of our way to keep our identities under wraps.

Simon concealed himself in the forward cabin while George and I sat in the wheelhouse but hiding from anyone giving a cautionary glance in our direction. To make the scene more plausible, we both started handling the equipment; Derek kept up the pretence that we were all on a fishing trip.

Once the police launch pulled alongside Derek called out, "Hello officers, can I be of any assistance this fine morning?"

"We're looking for a group of five men who may be heading this way from St Bethanie." Thank fuck someone can't count.

"Any reason, officer? I left around 04:00 and have not seen anyone in my vicinity," a complete lie, but hey they didn't need to know the truth. The boat tilted to the right when one of the officers transferred from the police launch to our vessel.

"Mind if I take a quick look around?"

"Not at all."

The Policeman was about to enter the cabin via the door when a shout came from his colleague, "Bob, leave it, a boat been spotted to the north of the island, we need to go."

"Shit, that was close, Derek, well-played, mate."

While on the phone, Simon had arranged for Sam to meet us at a small sandy beach to the right of the port which had a secluded inlet, ideal for us. When we arrived, Sam was stood on the shore next to a battered-looking Land Rover with no roof. Fantastic news, he was here. Throw the anchor over the side and let's park for a while.

"Just before you leave, Derek, let us go over the plan for your part if everyone could gather around the map. Your primary task, mate is to ensure you and the boat are located in this area at 07:00 on the seventh day, with today being the first day, let's synchronise our timepieces, in three-two-one the time now is 09:30."

"No problem, will see you at 07:00, seven days from now."

Time to introduce ourselves, "Sam, I'm Simon, we spoke on the phone, that over there is George and this fat, ugly bastard is Steve."

"Nice to meet you all, I suggest we climb onboard the Land Rover and head back to my place. Abbie is there once we arrive, once we are there, we can fill you in on what's been happening."

St Halb Day One

The route to Sam's place took us along a dirt track winding its way through some dense forest, with any luck this is what the area around Henry's home will be like and give plenty of cover for the RV's.

"Tell us about the town of Jal, Sam, like how many people live there, how big it is, where is the police station, how many officers, plus anything else you may think is essential."

"Where do I start? Jal has around five-hundred locals all year round, which can stretch to five hundred and fifty during the holiday season, with people coming over from St Bethanie to work in the two hotels.

"For the size of the town, hard to say as it is spread over a fairly massive area. Joshua Boulevard itself is around five-hundred metres long with shops, a café, and one of the two hotels running off from it. The station is located at the end of Joshua Boulevard near the port. The police force is made up of two constables and an inspector.

"The people are on the whole a friendly bunch with everyone knowing each other and what's going on, so be careful of what you say to anyone as it's worse than bloody Chinese whispers here, you say something to one person before you know it, it's all over the island.

"You are perhaps aware, the island is split into two parts, with only the one road between the two. Henry's place on the north island where the road comes to an abrupt end, I believe he had it extended to his home once he took over the family business.

"Takes around forty-minutes to drive from the police station to the plantation, might be handy to know that for what you're planning."

"Thanks, Sam, some fantastic info, will come in useful later. What's the distance from Henry's to yours and Abbie's place?"

"Not too far, around 15 minutes or so."

"The idiots in the back are quiet, any questions?"

"Not from me."

"Not from me either, not yet anyway, but sure we will have a few once we arrive at Sam's place and get a full brief."

"Here we are, gents, welcome to my humble abode, not much I know, but it's home for Abbie and me."

Sam had pulled up into a clearing in the woods, a slight breeze blew through and over the trees, making them sway gently in the morning air. At one side was a wooden structure, the doors were open, a Land Rover was parked inside along with other broken vehicle parts scattered across the floor. Between it and the house was another building in need of some repair work, one side had crumpled and required fixing.

The house, this was a single-storey affair with a tile clad roof, windows and a door slightly off-centre. This being the Caribbean tarmac must be reserved for the roads. So, the whole area was covered in a light dusting of sand. Didn't need to look too hard to see where Abbie had done her best to keep the dust entering the house. Making sure Sam only drove his vehicle and the ones he repaired from the gate to the workshop. Surrounding the house Abbie had placed a white stone circle which prevented parking too close to the house.

"Beautiful place you got here, any problem with the wildlife wandering in? When I said local wildlife, I was referring to the two-legged kind."

"Not anything worrying about, I put an electric fence all around; with just the one gate in or out we manage to keep them away from the property. Shall we go inside? Abbie will be expecting us."

Abbie was a woman around 30 years old with long fair hair and about 5' 6" tall and was waiting for us in the kitchen, which was to the left of the front door when you entered the house.

Not bad, as kitchens go, and where the home was located they had done a fantastic job in equipping it with everything you would need, from the range cooker, storage and a big dining table taking up the majority of the space in the centre of the room.

"Abbie, this gentleman here is Steve, that's Simon, the man over there is George."

"Great to meet you all, would anyone like a coffee, tea, or if you prefer there are cold beers in the fridge?"

"No, that's OK, coffee would be fine for me."

"Same for me."

"Sorry, but I am more of a cup of tea person when it is available," replied George.

"Not an issue, please take a seat, I won't be a moment."

"Might as well come with me while waiting for your brew, gents, let me show you where you'll be getting your heads down." Leading us through a small living room, Sam pointed out the washing facilities en route, out the back door to where an outbuilding stood about two metres from the building.

Inside were three wooden beds, each with a blanket and pillow, a small window let in light. "Not much, but sure it will be fit for purpose for gentlemen like yourselves."

"Perfect, Sam, thanks."

"Once you've dropped your kit, I will meet you back in the kitchen where Abbie and myself can give you an update on what's been going on at Henry's place."

By the time we re-entered the kitchen, several maps and drawings had been placed on the table, along with aerial photos of Henry's home and the north island."

Give us a shout when you're ready to go over this stuff." Sam pointed towards the table.

"Now is as good as time as any, might as well start straight away, let's begin with the layout."

"From the photographs taken about six months ago, you can make out where the property is divided into three areas, the house and a few outbuildings are situated towards the back. Over here are the wine production and bottling warehouses, the vineyards stretch from here all the way to the edge of the coast.

"The men and women are using the vineyard to hide the growth of marijuana plants, our sunny climate with the gentle breeze coming off the sea makes this place ideal for growing the stuff outdoors. The two huge water tanks, one at each end, are topped up frequently from a supply in the bottling plant.

"To gain entry to the property, you need to go via the front gate at the end of the tarmac road. On the majority of the days, at least two people are monitoring the entrance 24 hours a day from the small gatehouse. Nearly always they are armed with rifles and two dogs. The rest of the gang, when they are not working, are housed in either the house or warehouse."

"How many people are staying at the property, Sam?"

"Around twenty altogether. They are led by a man called Hadley, I recognise him from a function that was held here, he is a relative of Paul who runs the island police."

"Any idea of the firepower we'll be dealing with?"

"From what I've seen on visits to repair vehicles and other equipment they are all armed, some with SMGs, AK47s, seen a few M72 LAW, Light Anti-Armour Weapon knocking about."

Crap, don't fancy one of them up the rear end as we drive off, definitely fuck up anyone's day.

"A few questions before Abbie gives us a more detailed look at the inside of the house, sure George will have a few on them dogs as well."

"You have any questions on the transport side of things, Simon?"

"What vehicles do they have, Sam, are they reliable, and do you know a way you can nobble them to prevent the fuckers using them to give chase?"

"There is one lorry which they used to go into Jal on a Thursday to pick up fresh supplies, plus a couple of Land Rovers; which reminds me, Henry's old one is in the garage for you. Then there is a speedboat kept at the boathouse," Sam pointed at the map.

"A quick question from me. Do you know if they're in high spirits or any signs of friction? Always an advantage if a little unrest is taking place, people don't tend to put up a good fight if they're not completely into something."

"Some shouting and gun pointing the other day, apart from that I couldn't say."

"Next time you're at Henry's, Sam, do me a favour, swipe one of their bins."

"What the hell for?"

"Trust me, you can tell a lot from the enemies rubbish they leave behind. For example, if they are well-fed, have a proper diet, empty bottles along with excess bog roll could indicate illness, plus lots more, all handy to find out if our boys are in a good mood and well-organised and ready to put up a good fight or not."

"Got any questions on them pooches, George?"

"A few, Henry said maybe six of them. If so, where are they kept and how well-trained do you think they are?"

"From what I can tell there are at least six, they are housed in kennels at the rear of the gatehouse," again Sam pointed to the map. "Not being a dog handler, couldn't tell you how trained they are, sorry."

"Any questions, Simon?"

"Can see from the map that only one road goes to the property, any more tracks that go around the north island, if so, where are they on this map?"

"Yes, but they are not marked, as they are only old dirt tracks used by a few people, apart from this one that leads up the hill. I could sketch a rough idea of their locations, but it won't be very accurate."

"Could you give us an overview of the house, please?"

Abbie grabbed a piece of paper which she had sketched a plan of the building. "The house consists of two floors. The living room, kitchen, study and dining room are all on the bottom floor. Upstairs are six bedrooms, all en suite, the master bedroom is on this side of the house. Below the house is a small cellar that includes a tunnel leading over to the warehouse, the family used it when the weather outside was terrible.

"The living room is complete with French doors leading out to a patio at the rear of the building, the same goes for the study. The back door leads off the kitchen."

"Thanks for that, all we need to do today is check out the town of Jal, could you show us around, Sam?"

"Would love to, but I have to go and repair a couple of broken-down vehicles for a friend, sure Abbie will show you around."

"Of course, I have to do some shopping. Don't allow cars near the house, blows the bloody dust everywhere, including inside the home, so you will have to walk over to the garage with me."

"OK, you're the boss, Abbie."

Inside the garage was an old Jeep, parked next to a battered old Land Rover. Abbie reached up on to a shelf, grabbed a set of keys and tossed them in Simon's direction.

"May have a few hours work when we arrive back, mate, to get that heap back into working order."

"Cheers, Steve."

"No problem, it's what you cavalry types were born to do."

"Is the centre of town hard to find from here, Abbie?"

"Not particularly, you basically just keep following this road until you reach the edge of town, then a few turns and hey presto you're in Jal!"

"Hear that, Simon, even you couldn't become lost."

"Know what you can do, maybe Jal's got a town square you can go and stand on."

The drive to town did not take long and as Abbie had indicated the route was straight forward with not too many turns, more importantly the roads were not in a bad condition. Which meant to us if we needed to bug out this way, we would be able to do so a speed. Abbie pulled into a small car park and parked the car.

"That's it, gents we are here."

"Have to go to the supermarket and do some other stuff. I'll be about two hours, want me to wait for you or will you be making your own way back?"

"Best we play it safe, the fewer people who know we are here or connected to you the better, so we will wait around the corner from here in two hours from now. Word of warning, Abbie, be careful of how much you buy."

"OK, have fun, boys, Joshua Boulevard is there, where you will find the best public house in town."

"First stop, the bar it is then, gents."

"Suggest before we grab some scran we do a complete recce of the town, find what's located where, just in case we have to come this way off the island."

"Let's start on Joshua Boulevard."

At first glance, Jal seemed a lot bigger than Phoebe on St Bethanie, perhaps due to this being the only town on the island. Joshua Boulevard ran down the middle, one street over from the road which ran parallel with the shoreline.

Reminded me a little of the Grand Bahamas, with colourful wooden houses lining the street and the open-air market running down the centre of the road. Made a change to see the stalls selling fresh food and items people needed rather than full of the tourist junk nobody really wanted.

Along the street, at least two hotels were looking not too similar to the ones in Phoebe. Halfway down on the right was a coffee shop ; with any luck, the one ran by Katie and Cody. Could leave the visit to after we had checked out the rest of Jal. Need to make a plan, not as straightforward as walking in and asking to speak to Katie.

A little further down Joshua boulevard but on the opposite side was a local bar. Now that could be worth a visit, the best place to listen to the local gossip, could even hear something about our friends at Henry's gaff.

At the point where the road comes to an end, you are faced with a T-Junction. The right went to the port and left to another road similar to the street we were on.

"Just check out the port, then who's up for a quick beer?"

"Thought you would never ask, got a mouth like a camel's flip-flop."

"Don't you mean Polo-Donkey, Simon?"

"Fuck off, fat boy, or you're on the soft drinks through a straw."

"Oh no, I'm shaking."

The port, which was now in front of us was a little busy with lots of people—a mixture of locals and holidaymakers milling around, going about with not a care in the world.

At one end was a building which looked like it hadn't seen a lick of paint in a few years. Above the door was a sign, 'Police Station', to the right was an iron gate, beyond that was the jetty. Now that might be an issue later next week. Still keeping our options open on our escape plan. Always have more than one method for an exit has always been part of the plan. Towards the far end, next to the pier was a floatplane moored next to a small wooden building. Will be time to check that tomorrow, now was beer o'clock.

Usually, on a mission, we would take a different route than we just made, but at the moment nobody knows anything about us or why we are here. Hence, we went the same way back and started to head up Joshua Boulevard towards the local bar we had seen on the way to the port. Halfway along was a side street leading off the main drag; was virtually past when I caught something in the corner of my eye, which needed a closer look.

"What the fuck!" A group of men hurling verbal abuse at a woman and small child sat on the pavement, I grabbed Simon and George. "Now that is out of fucking order."

"Leave it, Steve, it's not our problem." At that moment the woman received a smack to the side of the head. Nope not having that.

"Steve, leave it."

"Any of you see a fucking Chimp?"

Yelling at the top of my voice in the direction of the attackers. "Any of you fuckers want to pick on someone who can fight back?" while charging towards them, immediately followed by Simon and George. The attackers initially tried to stand their ground, but after the biggest one hit the floor, as a result of a perfectly placed hard kick just below and upwards on his right knee, they all fled as the other two caught up.

"Calmed down yet?"

"Excellent thanks, now the Chimp's arrived."

"So, what was all that about?" The woman lifted her head while trying to comfort her now crying child.

"Not sure, I only asked them if they could spare some money as we have not eaten for a few days. Then they came abusive, one of them hit me."

"Right stay here for a few minutes with these two, don't worry, you'll be safe."

Was not long before I returned carrying two large bags.

"What you got there, Steve?"

"Some food for these two, can't let these good people go hungry."

"How do you know she isn't pulling your pisser and taking you for a ride?"

"Trust me, I know, Simon."

Placed the bags by the feet of the still sobbing women and reached into my jacket pocket taking out some money. With an outreached hand. "Here take this as well as the food, there is $200. Go home and take care of yourself and your beautiful daughter."

With this, the two disappeared into the distance.

"Never known you to be such a soft arse before, Steve, maybe we are seeing a new side of him, Simon."

"Doubt it. That man is as cold-hearted as they come, probably hasn't even got a heart."

"Why don't you two go forth and multiply, who's getting the beers in?"

The bar was your typical Caribbean local bar with an old-style TV on the wall, complete with a small bar which ran against the back wall. A few bottles of the local brew and spirits were neatly lined up along the top shelf. A few locals were inside drinking and playing cards. So we grabbed a few beers and went outside. Occupied several seats at one of the wooden tables covered with a plastic tablecloth overlooking the street.

Anyway, we still need to make contact with Katie, without people eavesdropping on our conversation. Not that Simon would give away too much on the phone, he's far too much a professional for that.

A quick check on Mickey told us we were running a little late for our pickup time by Abbie. "Better call Katie and arrange a meeting for tomorrow, Simon."

The phone rang a few times before a man answered. Shit, now what, time to think on his feet. This was absolutely the right number.

"Hi, is Katie there?"

"No sorry, she is out. Try calling back in a couple of hours. she should be around then, anything I can help you with?"

"No , I'll call back later."

"Time is getting on and due to no small part to this idiot," George pointed at me, "playing Robin Hood and rescuing the poor. We've no time for another drink, so better leave now if we are going to meet with Abbie." Time we returned to the pickup point, Abbie was waiting for us.

"Had a good time, boys and get everything done you need to?"

"All good, thank you."

"Excellent, thought I would treat you all to a Caribbean barbecue tonight."

Once we arrived at Abbie's place, Sam was already back. "You manage to repair all the vehicles?"

Sam paused for a few seconds before answering. "Repaired

the car in no time, an easy job."

Was going to question him on the fact he said he had two vehicles to fix, but left it at that and grabbed the beer I was being handed.

"Will start the barbecue in about thirty minutes, if you gents would like to get cleaned up, that includes you, Sam."

"On our way, boss lady."

Would be fantastic to wind down for a while, something none of us has really done since we arrived in St Bethanie last week; what could be better than sitting around a barbecue, a few beers and good friends on a warm evening in the Caribbean.

"Don't get too comfortable and start to relax too much, Simon, you still need to make contact with Katie."

"No issue, you two arseholes rest while I carry on working."

"Stop your complaining, you'll be done by the time George finishes his shower."

"True, there is a lot of him to wash, think on George washing it for more than thirty seconds is classed as a wank."

Picking up the phone Simon redialled Katie's number, a woman answered the phone this time when Simon called, "Hi, is that Katie from Perth?"

"No, this is Katie from Headland?"

"This is Simon; spoke the other day."

"Yes, Simon, I remember. Are you on the island now?"

"Yes, can we arrange a meeting for tomorrow, say around 11:30 at the coffee shop?"

"No problem. If for any reason I'm not about, ask for Cody, he's my husband, he is fully aware of what's going on. Great, see you at 11:30."

"Take a seat, the food will not be long, the beers are in the cooler, help yourselves." A small fire was started in a circle of stones by Sam, a little distance from the house, guess Abbie had a rule about smoke going into her home as well as dust.

"Give us a hand with these old sofas, Steve, we can put them around the fire; might as well be comfortable. "

"So, what's your story, Sam, how did you end up on St Halb?"

"Well, left the Army after four years in the Royal, Electrical and Mechanical Engineers before I bought myself out and settled in Farnham where I was employed as a mechanic for about three and a half years, before becoming bored with the job and finding it more of a challenge to living the rat race, plus was getting into debt.

"Moved here about five years ago with Abbie, worked for Henry most of the time here as knew him from a posting in the Army."

"Grubs up, folks. Sam, give us a hand to carry it over to the table, hope you like it. Mind you, if you don't like it, that's all you're getting." Laid out in front of us was a wide selection of meat, fresh salad, fruits, and my favourite, jacket potatoes.

"Thank you, Abbie, what a genuinely fantastic feast, far better than Simon's egg banjos."

"What's an egg banjo?"

"Come on, you said you were in the Army, Sam, and you haven't told Abbie about egg banjos, what sort of squaddie was you?"

"Have you not guessed yet? Abbie is a strong-minded woman, if you tried to say she was making an egg sandwich wrong you're likely to get a slap."

The whole evening was spent sitting around the fire, merely chatting and telling the odd war story and of course, far more than we intended to drink. Must have been the small hours of the morning before we called it a night, but hey, we needed to relax, the next week or so is going to be hard on us all.

St Halb Day Two

The sun was now shining through the small window, as I opened my eyes slowly, as my feet landing securely on the ground. "OK, which one of you arseholes hit me over the head and shit in my mouth, how much did we drink last night for Christ's sake?"

"Did anyone say anything about last night, must have been about 02:00 before we called it a night?"

"Where is George this morning?"

"Fuck knows, knowing him he is probably having breakfast."

"About time you two lazy bastards got your arses out of bed."

"Good morning, George, anybody else around this morning yet?"

"Yes, Sam's gone to Henry's to fix a water pump, but Abbie is around she will be back in a moment, coffee is in the pot, mate."

"Ready for breakfast?" Abbie had entered the room carrying a basket of eggs she had collected from her chickens. What will it be, a 'full English,' or what did you call them yesterday, 'egg banjo'?"

"Egg banjo will be perfect for me."

"Same for us please, Abbie."

"That will be three egg banjos, coming right up."

"So, what's the master plan for today?"

"The Land Rover needs to be checked over by Simon as we will require that later, George and I can go over the kit we will need for the observation posts. Once this is completed, it's a trip to Jal and Katie's place to find out what weapons she may have for us; not going into a firefight with three 9 mms and very little ammo."

"Empty everything on the floor, George, so we can check all the equipment individually, split the items required for observation post into separate piles as each would be different.

"To make things easier once we arrive at the OP, we put as much together now as possible as we will be entering the observation posts just before first light."

The first task was to mix the nails and clay then stick them to the bottom of the gas canisters. Electrical detonator wouldn't be placed in until they were in place, for safety. The home-made claymores would be protecting the front of the OP. We're planning a simple tripwire for the rear; this would be the same type we had used in the RV on St Bethanie.

"I Just need to check the transmitters and earpieces are working, once this is done, the wire itself can be wrapped around the batteries, with the clothes peg secured to it with an elastic band.

All three water bottles were filled in turn to ensure there were no leaks, placed one in each pile. The two smaller collapsible ones were for George and me and the larger one for Simon as he had the Land Rover. When it came to our own personal kit, we all had our own way of packing and wearing, something fine-tuned over many years.

They were observation posts so we would be travelling light with the bare essentials for the two days, food, water, weapons, ammo, equipment and claymores: luxury items such as sleeping bags were definitely out, in case we had to bug quick. From experience, if you get too comfortable and warm, the higher the chance of you nodding off.

While George and I were busy checking the equipment, Simon made his way to the garage to check over the Land Rover. Both electrical and hand tools lay on the benches in the garage, by the side of the workbench stood a 250-litre drum half-filled with used motor oil. Towards the rear was a row of vehicle batteries on charge, 'perfect', 'will take an extra battery, you can never be too careful'.

Better check the old girl over to see how she runs. Now that was a welcome sound as the Land Rover burst into life on the first turn of the key. An inspection underneath confirmed there were no signs of dripping oil or water that might cause any issues. In fact, the car was running perfectly, better turn the old girl off, need to do a service before they take the vehicle out later.

Let's make a few alterations while she cools down. First, I needed to find somewhere to secure the spare battery, along with a few emergency tools. Between the two front seats was a metal plate, perfect locations to store the extra one. It was possible to connect it with the aid of some wire to the charging system, without the leads getting in the way.

The Land Rover was going to be acting not only as transport but as the actual observation post — time to move on to removing or hiding any objects that will give off any type reflection. The windshield is easy as this was a mark 2. The front screen folded down, preventing any reflection off the glass while in an OP.

Came with the benefit of being raised when driving, stopped you getting a face full of annoying bugs. Would take it off entirely but that may attract some nosey bastard when we go to town later. A search of the garage uncovered some old hessian sacks, these can be stitched together to form a complete cover for the front of the vehicle.

Grabbed the welding gear and proceeded to erect a removable machine gun post in the rear of the Land Rover. This would be constructed once the mission got underway, plus of course, Katie came up with any type of machine gun, if not will make an excellent rifle stand.

Time was getting on so better carry out the service, should not take long.

Just finished when a call came from the house, "You ready, Simon, we need to make a move."

"We'll be a couple of hours, Abbie."

"OK, Steve, see you when you get back. If you find my husband in the bar, kick his drunken arse back home."

"Roger, will do."

"Right, Tanky, you remember the way?"

"Any reason I should dignify that with an answer."

Halfway to town, spotted Sam driving like a mad man in the direction of his home, probably about to receive an enormous bollocking from the missus. Guess Abbie called the bar, wouldn't like to be in his shoes when he gets home. Parked the car in the same spot as Abbie had done yesterday for convenience plus, we knew where we could park so no need for driving around looking for a parking place.

This time, instead of walking down Joshua Boulevard and immediately to the coffee shop, we took the street opposite, stopping within a hundred metres of the rear of the place. The mission was getting close, so every precaution now needed to be made, if not more. Spent the next twenty minutes or so sat on a small brick wall observing Katie's place. Taking it in turns to be the one watching while the other two did anything but look at the location.

"Right, gents, my Mickey is telling me it's now 11:00. Wait here until 11:25, Simon, before entering the coffee shop via the rear exit, George and myself will make our way around the front and enter via Joshua Boulevard. Will order coffees and take a seat somewhere in the café where we can be seen by you as you enter from the rear. Once you enter, if you can't see us, assume something has gone wrong and leave by the front door, we will meet back up at the Land Rover, let's go."

Arrived at the front about six to seven minutes later and entered. Looks like Katie had gone out of her way to make the place look nothing like your typical Caribbean coffee shops. Gone were the tables with plastic tablecloths and containers, replaced with stylish linen ones and glass sugar containers.

Opposite the door, a little off to the right and along the back wall stood a glass counter containing an assortment of cakes and pastries. Behind which stood an elegantly dressed woman in her early thirties, a slim figure and long black hair. Not being lunchtime, only a few local people were sat in the café, plus a handful of tourists of European complexion. Perfect, we wouldn't stand out too much in the crowd.

11:25: Entering via the back door, Simon spoke to the woman behind the counter before taking a seat at a table near to George and myself.

On the pretence of striking up a conversation with a stranger, I leant over, "Excuse me, do you know where Headland is?"

"Yes, it is about ten minutes from here." Now we know that was Katie he was talking to, and she will be with us in about ten minutes.

Reappearing after a short time this time, Katie was accompanied by a well-built man about 5' 8" in height, cropped brown hair and well-groomed beard. Walked over to where Simon was sat and signalled for him to follow her as she disappeared again via the back door.

Gave Simon five minutes before we followed them, no need to panic, we knew Simon would have them stalled near the back.

"Katie this is Steve and George; I take it that this man is Cody."

"Correct. If you go with him, he will take you to where we have the items you requested, I need to go back to the shop."

Cody led us down a small road past the port to a small industrial park, I felt inside my pocket to check my 9 mm protection was still where I'd placed it.

After several twists and turns, Cody stopped, turned to face an old metal door and preceded to remove three padlocks, before turning and, facing us saying, "You can't be too careful," and showing us the locks.

The door led to a barely lit room about thirty metres square with many piles of objects, each covered with a grey tarpaulin.

"What's under the cover, Cody?"

"Let us say it's where Katie stores her business stuff!"

Walked across to the centre of the room, Cody uncovered several wooden boxes. Opened the first one box, inside was three L1A1 variants SA80 which was the first on the SA80 to be produced.

"God, I remember these from my Army days when they first came out in the '80s. Now if I remember rightly, there was some issue with the reliability of the mechanism holding the magazine in place."

"Yep, I remember the pile of crap too," said George.

"Hold the damn thing close to your chest, the magazine would fucking fall off, plus they kept miss-firing on you." Had its positive side as well, it was hard to miss with the optical sight, with an effective range of 400 metres. Call me old-fashioned, but I preferred the 7.62 mm SLR, kicked like a mule but a fantastic weapon.

Opening another box inside was the LMG version of the SA80 the L86 Light Support Weapon, Simon had just the place on the Land Rover for that, as long as we have ammunition for it. Whilst Simon was admiring his new toy, Cody uncovered some metal ammunition boxes, enough here to start a war, around a thousand.

"The missus said you might be interested in some electrical detonators as well."

"How many you got?"

"What type do you want, Steve? I have instant electric detonators or shock electric detonators."

"Tell you what, Cody, I'll take some of both, do you know the length of the electrical wire?"

"Would say about 6 metres."

"Have any safety fuse?"

"Sure do, how many reels?"

"Three reels."

"Who do we pay for this little shopping list, Cody?"

"Why not pay me, Steve. Katie said if it's cash no questions asked, you can have the lot for ten thousand dollars."

A deal, had been carrying two envelopes strapped in the small of my back, each containing ten thousand in high-value notes, not sure how much or if they could supply.

"Go and pick up the Land Rover, Simon, while I sort Cody out."

Both Katie and Cody came through with this job, will be keeping their contact details for any future work.

That was all the goodies loaded, time to recce the route from here via Abbie's gaff to Henry's home. The way from town was easy, primarily due to only one road going from Jal to Henry's place, plus we had now completed the journey twice. Once past Abbie's and Sam's home, the road narrowed as it twisted its way through the forest, which seemed thicker here than before.

Wasn't long before we arrived at the bridge. Simon pulled off the road, driving a little way through the trees until we were clear of the road. Must have been all those years in the Army, without anyone saying a word Simon was covering the vehicle tracks we had made coming into the location.

"OK, if we follow the tree line, we should be able to get a clear view of the inlet the other side where Derek will be meeting us, if not we will have to take a chance going crossing over and to take a look."

Kept inside the tree line, not wanting to be exposed to anyone that might be on the other side. Not sure yet if Hadley's men patrolled this far out, unlikely from what we've been informed but can never be too careful. Made our way to a position directly opposite the inlet. From what I could see, the channel was around 50 metres wide and 150 metres long, the trees that lined each bank reached inwards giving plenty of protection from the air.

The tide was out as we turned back towards the bridge. "Gents, we may have a problem here if the tidal flow is in, will Derek's boat be able to pass under the bridge?"

"Could let Derek know about the low bridge concerning the tide, to ensure he checks the tidal charts and arrives when the tide is out."

"But that is not the issue. If we end up running from a gunfight and the flow is in, we're fucked."

"Think I may have a solution to that, Simon as part of your OP can you come back and check the bridge construction."

"Sure, no problem."

Staying clear of the inlet, no point in leaving tracks at this point, Simon can check in more details later. Drove further down the road and closer to the target. Just as we reached the apex of a sharp bend, George shouted out, "someone is coming from the opposite direction, if you look over there you can see them through the gap in the tress."

Times like this you were glad you had people like Simon by your side, with all his experience of being in the Cavalry and all the years of forward recognisance. Automatically looking for exit points as we drove, he soon had us leaving the road and into the undergrowth and concealing us from the vehicle coming in the opposite direction.

"Think it's best we call it a day, gents, and head back to the digs. Simon, home if you please."

"Yes, master!"

"Better park the Land Rover back in the garage unless you want your arse-kicking from Abbie. Safer not to leave the SA80s in the vehicle in case some idiots come snooping around. Take one SA80 and the LMG, Simon; as you built a beautiful little stand for it, George, grab yourself a rifle and the ammo, I'll grab mine and the detonators."

The sound of crack & thump echoed from within the tree line. Did not have much of a choice, we had to risk the noise of the weapons being fired as they need to be zeroed. Both Simon and George had set up a makeshift target range, consisting of targets constructed of wood almost half the size of a person, similar to a figure 12 target which they found in the garage. This had been placed about a hundred metres from where they were laying. All located a little way inside the tree line to muffle the noise as they zeroed their weapons, to ensure bullets landed where they aimed.

"Fancy putting fifty quid on whose rounds land closer to the centre?"

"Now that would be fucking cheating, George, we all know you were a sniper before becoming a dog handler. Then there is the little matter of you taking part in a bit of shooting competition at Bisley, what was it called, oh yes, Army Operational Shooting Competition, so no. Besides, Simon is a crap shot unless it comes from a Chieftain 127 mm gun."

"That is where you two arseholes are wrong, not too bad with the L7 machine gun."

"Take it the bets off then."

"Not terrible grouping, Steve, think you got the target scared."

"Fuck off, you sarcastic bastard, give me time to zero the rifle then I'll show you. All five rounds in the centre of the target, so suck on that."

"Heard you shooting in the woods, kill anything?" asked Sam.

"No, but plenty of deadwood out there."

"The kettle just boiled if anyone fancies a brew."

"Cheers, Sam, could do with a cuppa."

"Been up to anything exciting today Sam? We saw you hurtle past us at the speed of light earlier."

"Yes, Abbie called the bar checking if I was in. The barman

is a friend, so said I wasn't and hadn't been in all day. I'm not brave enough to argue with Abbie, she can be a mean person when she wants to be."

Something about Sam that I couldn't put my finger on, not sure if I completely trusted him or not. "Did you manage to fix the water pumps at the winery?"

"Sorry, no water pumps, that was what I told Abbie as I had other business in Jal."

At that moment, Abbie came into the room, "I'll make dinner in about an hour, if that's OK with your gents?"

Perfect, as we have some planning and equipment checks to do."

Another radio check to ensure they were working, this time Simon relocated himself to the far end of the property,

"TS; this is S3, radio check, over."

"OK, over, you picking this up, George?"

"Over and out."

Responses came from all radios. Once everyone finished packing their own personal equipment into the Bergens, we shared the ammunition; equally, this was also either placed in the Bergen or placed in our combat jackets for ease of use.

Took it in turns to put on all equipment, jumped up and down a few times, running up and down the room and jumping to the floor, while the other two listened for any unwanted rattles or clanging of metal.

The purpose being the last thing you needed when making your way into an observation post trying not to make a sound was the constant clanging of metal. Especially at night, as noise travels further.

"This is the plan for the next 48 hours," laying out the map.

"Sunrise in this part of the world for tomorrow is 05:40, so Zulu time for the start of the OP part of the mission will be 04:00. Leaving here in the Land Rover, Simon first dropping me off at this point; from where I will make my way to this position, here on the map. Here, I will be able to see the vineyard and buildings with part of the main complex.

"Next, drop George off at this point along the track past the road. If you could double back and find your way to a position around here, George, where you can monitor any movement of the guards at the gatehouse and those bloody dogs."

This leaves you, Simon, first find a way to the inlet where we will meet Derek, then finding a way to insert you and the Land Rover somewhere in the tree line at the top of the hill overlooking the whole complex.

All being well, we can all be in position by first light, then at 06:17 a simple radio check to confirm you're in your designated locations. Consciously chosen 17 minutes past the hour as you would be surprised how many people either use on the hour or half past the hour to check-in and could be listening for any radio traffic.

Keep the message and radio time to a minimum, a simple 'S3 OK' for example, will be sufficient if you encounter any issues and need to leave your position call 'S3 bugging out'. After the initial check, we will call every odd hour such as 09:17, 11:17, well you get the picture.

"Will reach an end to the OP's on the second night, to confirm that is not tomorrow night but the following night, one hour after sunset, that will be 19:30. The process will be in reverse of the insertion plan, once you've sent the last radio check this will be the signal to bug out; Simon, you will leave at 19:45, giving us time to arrive at the relevant pickup points.

"Then drive steadily down the track you dropped us off on. Not knowing where George and myself will be, it will be up to us to attract your attention, we will do this with two flashes of a red torch, so better keep your eyes peeled. Once we are all back on board, we will make our way back here.

"The continuity plans are as follows; all stay in position, if you hear over the radio any call sign, say 'bugging out'. We will all leave and make our way to the emergency RV. Now, if 'All call signs bug out', or gunfire coming in the direction of our locations, goes without saying, gents, if there are only a few shots it might be some drunken bastard shooting widely into the trees."

Pointing to the map, "If we come under attack, everyone makes their way to the emergency RV which is located here, near the bridge. Once there, we will head back to Abbie & Sam's place, taking up position near the front gate in case we are followed.

"By any chance one OP is being attacked, the other two will make their way to assist, if the path is blocked, all call signs retreat to the emergency RV.

"Any questions, gents? If not, I'm sure Abbie mentioned something about scran being ready at 16:30, and I'm starving."

"No questions from me."

"What about you, Simon?"

"Nope nothing from me, the only thing to do now is to wait and eat."

"One last thing, gents, better synchronise Mickey, time now 16:21."

Back in the kitchen, Abbie had prepared another fantastic meal. "Good timing, boys, tuck in."

"Will be leaving in the morning for a couple of days," not wanting to give too much away; as they say, careless talk can cost lives. Nearly happened to me once in Northern Ireland as a young driver, told some civilian I was taking a lorry out that night, the bastards had a car bomb waiting for me, learned quickly after that.

"Would you like me to make you some sandwiches to take with you on your little outing?"

"That would be perfect, Abbie, could you wrap them in tissue or anything that wouldn't make a sound when unwrapping?"

"Yes, sure, I've some napkins around here somewhere."

"A few cold ones, anyone?" Sam entered the kitchen clutching a pack of beer in each hand, suppose a few won't hurt, plus may help me sleep later. From experience never got a good night's sleep before a mission, the head will be doing the overthinking thing it does just to piss me off.

"Glad your both here, we've been talking and would like to give you a little thank you for your assistance since we've been here, just in case of any change in plans." slipping a brown envelope containing $5,000 across the table towards Abbie.

"No need for that but thank you."

***

As suspected, hardly slept a wink with the mind playing every possible scenario over in my head.

Looked over to where Simon lay fast asleep, I hate that man, he could sleep anywhere, lucky bastard. Was only a short time left before I had to be up anyway so might as well get the kit on, including the war paint.

Had always carried on a mission my own concoction of camouflage cream mixed with aloe moisturising lotion, made it easier to apply, and reduced the number of blackheads afterwards; along with a 1.5 m x 1.5 m square of camouflage netting and a small foldable shovel.

Time to kick the sleeping beauties out of their pits. Once awake, both Simon and George followed the same routine without a sound. Being the only sniper in the group, George put on his ghillie suit. For the rest of us, we made do with our old dirty combat jackets which undoubtedly stunk a bit as well. Let's face it, if we were upwind of the bad guys the last thing we wanted was the buggers getting a whiff of fabric softener wafting through the air.

"Zulu time, boys, let's get this mission going."

Steve's Observation Post

The vehicle slowed down to about 25 mph when I jumped, landing in the bushes that grew along the edge of the tree line, knocking the wind out of me. Once I'd grabbed my composure, realised I had fucked up and had leapt out on the wrong side of the track, shit. Only one thing for it, going to have to walk back up the trail for about two hundred metres and cross over before making my way back to this point, but on the other side of the road.

No signs of movement, time to get over to the other side. Took a massive jump, and landing on one foot around a third of the way across, steady, a full 360-degree turn on one leg followed by another enormous leap. Had to repeat this three times to reach the other side. Perfect. Looking back, the only trace of anyone crossing was two semi-circular marks in the track. Quick adjustment to the foliage around the edge of the trail to hide the fact someone may have come this way.

Glanced down at Mickey, the little detour had cost me twenty minutes, better get my arse into gear. Learned a long time ago to take a bearing on my compass, pick out an object in the distance. Walk to it before taking another tack. Nothing worse than always looking down at your compass, looking up to find someone pointing a weapon at you.

The undergrowth wasn't too thick so made steady progress, making up valuable time; finally reaching the edge of the woods overlooking the target. A short search uncovered two potential locations for the observation post. The first was behind a small grassy mound between two giant trees located right on the ridge.

The second, a small indent in the ground, a little more to the right and marginally back from the tree line overgrown by a small green bush which grew over the area, but still allowed sufficient room to crawl underneath, and even gave a good view of the property.

The first would be perfect spot, apart from the fact I would be skylined while looking over any object. Plus the camouflage net placed in the front would stick out a mile, so the second location would be home for a while.

Better sort out my priorities. The first task, cut away some bush to allow me to crawl into the indent, ensuring any parts chopped away were concealed inside so they couldn't be spotted. Right, a few adjustments to the front, camouflage net in place and the location was ready. Now to get set up in a position enabling me to scrutinise the target with as little moment by myself as possible.

Dragged in my Bergen and took out my binoculars, radio, receiver and notepad to record any significant movements, times plus anything that would be important to the mission to come.

The time now 06:17, time for the first radio check pressed transmit button, with a CLAP (Clear Loud as An order with Pauses) spoke into the mic, "S3, OK," followed by, "GD, OK."

Wasn't a long wait; seemed to last forever, but in reality was only about twenty seconds before, "TS, OK," came over the airways, all three of us were now in position.

Radio checks out of the way, two more tasks needed to be completed; first, need to set up rear protection and tripwire alarm. Now if I was to sneak up on myself, where would I come from? To my right, I could see the direction I approached the position. Chosen this way because it provided me with cover and ease of access. So if I had used it, it makes sense someone else would most probably come this way.

To the left of that was another likely route from which people may consider. The solution was simple as a thin branch of a bush was sticking out and upwards between the others.

Grabbed the tripwire and transmitter from my Bergen, stopped to listen and watch for a few moments then proceeded to the right of where I came in from, about 50 metres from the location of the OP.

Tied one end of the fishing line to a tree about 25 cm from the floor, around the small branch, confirming it had free movement and could not become snagged. The other end with the receiver and clothes peg was attached to a tree to the far left. Once I had inserted the wire into the clothes peg, I went back along the line, ensuring I had not accidentally left any traces of my presence.

The second task of placing the home-made claymore would have to wait until after nightfall, this had to be positioned forward of my location. Spotted an old stump almost fifty metres away down a slight incline, which would be perfect.

Now back in the OP position, got as comfortable as possible and looked over the target, the observation part of the mission was now entirely underway.

The time now 07:30, the only people seen on target were two men standing by the water tank between the vineyard and the house, noted this down on my pad with additional comment, 'looks like the lazy bastards don't like getting up early'.

Nothing changed for the next hour until two people emerged from the house and stood on the doorstep. From my location I couldn't see what they were doing, ten minutes later they re-entered the house.

The small things could be significant in any mission; for example, if the same people came out and stood in the same place and this was happening every day, this might indicate a pattern; such as the time people were getting up, how many people do you know who's first sign of life in the morning is to light up a cigarette? Noted this down on my pad along with the time of 08:30.

Just finished the 09:17 check with the boys when a Jeep pulled up outside the house, Sam and woman I couldn't recognise, but sure it wasn't Abbie got out of the vehicle, spoke to someone before entering the house. Same as before noted this down with the time.

10:45 - Three men in their mid-thirties dressed in jeans and blue T-shirts enter the warehouse building, resurfacing around thirty minutes later carrying several fully bulging sacks between them and headed towards the vineyard. Passed the two men still stood near the water tank, then continued into the middle of the neat rows of the vines where they disappeared underneath the plants, guess they were replanting more crop.

11:05 - The woman, accompanied by Sam left the house, walking in the direction of the gatehouse. Strange, why is he holding this woman's hand? Could see more clearly now she was around 5' 8" tall with a figure that wouldn't be out-of-place on some glamorous modelling shoot; her long blonde hair reached halfway down her back, dressed in a light blue dress. Lost sight of them crossing the yard; with a bit of luck, George can pick them up from where he was located somewhere near the front gate. Bet that bastard is cheating on Abbie.

The time passed rapidly as I lay there, as plenty was going on and I was still fresh, tonight would be a different completely matter with less going on and the bloody body clock telling you it's past your bedtime.

Must have been in my own little world as the radio burst into life,

"TS, OK," followed by, "GD, OK," shit, almost forgot about the check-in, fumbled for the radio,

"S3, OK," that was close, get your act sorted, idiot.

Been lying in the OP motionless observing for four hours now and the body was telling me I needed to urinate in a public place; came prepared, been into many long ambushes in my lifetime.

There are only two ways to deal with this as I couldn't leave the OP for a piss, of course, depending on where you are. In this type of situation, your two options are pissing yourself or the place you're laying in or bring along a big enough empty container, I chose the latter. Would dispose of its contents tonight when it's dark.

12:00 - Both Sam and the woman climbed back in the Jeep and drove off, after shaking hands with a well-dressed man around 6' who was standing near the front door to the house. Picked up the binoculars for a better look, it was Hadley, I recognised him from the photos Sam had shown me back at his place.

Now, why would Sam be shaking hands with him, knew there was something about this bloke.

12:25 - Another three men and two women joined the two men from earlier in among the rows of vines. One man left the vineyard shortly after, carrying one of the sacks I had seen taken into the field by the others this morning. After a short stop to talk to the two armed men at the water tank, he continued on into the warehouse. Thinking about it, this is the first time I had seen anyone with weapons. Not saying they don't, but some reasons not seen anybody carrying any guns, apart from the two men at the tank.

Besides the hustle and bustle of what's happening down at Henry's place, the whole area was silent except a few birds singing their heads off in the treetops. At this point, the senses started to tingle as the sound of something making its way through the undergrowth. I Grabbed the SA80 and turned my head towards the sound to try and get a better fix. The noise started to grow louder as I took aim ready to take a shot.

While I listened, I detected something approaching.... My finger took up the first pressure on the trigger when two wild pigs emerged from the trees. That was close, they nearly ambled into my tripwire, setting it off.

14:00 - A commotion came from the rear of the house. Picking up my binoculars for a better view of what was going on, a stocky woman and Hadley were stood facing another man knelt down with his head bowed forward. Behind him stood a tall man around six feet dressed in shorts, a white Polo-shirt and resting a 9 mm on the back of the man's head.

From my location, it was not possible to understand what they were saying, but without question, without doubt, Hadley was shouting and waving at the man on his knees. Seconds later the distinctive sound of a pistol shot echoed around the grounds and the man fell face down on the lawn. Ambling over to where the dead body lay, blood oozing from the hole in the back of his head, Hadley took something from his pocket and went back inside the house, closely followed by the other two.

Well, that answers my question on weapons issue and the fact people down there willing to kill for the drugs. Wonder who the man was and what he had done to piss Hadley off so much; thinking about it they are all drug-related so who cares.

14:10 - Three people and Hadley leave in Land Rover.

Reached into my Bergen took out the food parcel Abbie had made us all, as feeling a little on the peckish side. Contained within were several meat sandwiches, a couple of oranges, along with some cookies; well played, Abbie, makes you think why the bastard Sam is cheating on her, suppose it's not my issue.

Nothing much happened for the rest of the afternoon, besides from shift change that occurred around 15:30; saying shift change out of habit. In reality, the people in the vineyard went back indoors, and the two men who had been near the water tank most of the day had changed over.

These were the worst times in an OP, with nothing to keep the brain alert at the quiet times at night, which are a killer. Managed to build up an extensive list of things to keep the mind occupied from going over nursery rhymes, poems to singing songs; all in the head of course.

18:30 - Now that's strange, Hadley's Land Rover had returned. Hadley, Sam, the woman he had left with earlier and two small children around the age of 4 - 9 stepped out.

Hope there are no kids about when this all kicks off, have no issue disposing of any arsehole who deals with drugs but not at all comfortable with unintentionally killing kids, saying that if it comes to them or me.

What was strange, Sam now had his arm around the young lady as they walked into the house. Well, that confirms it to me, the bastard is cheating on Abbie, which raises the question tell Abbie or kill the bastard.

The light was now starting to fade as it approached 18:30. Sunset will be on us soon, but still plenty of light down on the property, in fact, the place was lit up like a football stadium, take it they didn't want anyone sneaking upon them.

Usually, you get your night vision after thirty minutes or so, that is if the whole place remained in darkness, which it wasn't. Solely for this purpose, I came prepared, brought along an eyepatch, made me look like fucking a pirate, but who cares. Wore the patch over my right eye as this is the one that would be looking down the optical sight of the SA80 if it all kicks off tonight.

Will wait until after the 19:17 radio check then go and place my claymore in the old tree stump, George and Simon would be doing the same and setting their own claymores.

"GD, OK."

"TS, OK."

Replied with my own call sign, "S3, OK."

Then reached in my bag, pulling out the claymore before slowly and without making a sound, crawled out of the location. Spent the next few minutes acclimatising to the darkness and listening for any sounds of movement, all good so far.

After making my way to a position about fifty metres to the right and ten metres before the ridgeline, laid down and crawled to a place, observed over the ridge, paused for a few minutes before sliding over the rim as flat as possible. Crawled towards a small clump of bushes, again, stopping for a couple of minutes to survey my surroundings and listen for movement. Once I was sure it was safe to do so, continued to the stump.

Looked even better than I imagine when I arrived. Laying right in front was part of a rotten stump facing out through the trees in the direction of the property. One thing I didn't spot from the OP. This made it perfect for placement of the gas bottle into the tree. Yes, it might blow small shards of wood everywhere when it went off, but not before bombarding anyone who was approaching with a shower of nails.

Strapped the detonator to the side with plenty of duct tape, ensuring the wires were free to be reeled out, and inserted canister into the stump.

Crawled back to the small bushes, attached the end of the wire to a rock then launched it in the direction of the OP, landing just to the left.

Arrived back in the location via the same route I took on the way out, again, making sure I stayed as flat as possible while sliding over the edge and back into the tree line. Took out the square battery from my Bergen and located it to the right of my notepad where I could get to it quickly if required. Attached one wire while ensuring the other was nowhere near the terminal, didn't want that unexpectedly going off.

20:30 - A group of six people emerged from the house one of which was Sam. Splitting into two smaller groups, they started to shine powerful torches into the tree line, one in my direction and the other in the path of where Simon would be.

Now, this can't be a coincidence that they're doing this with Sam, hope he hasn't compromised the whole mission; if he has it will be one of the last things he ever does. This lasted for about ten minutes, before they gave up and went back indoors, apart from Sam, who jumped in his Jeep and drove off.

Must have started to rain about 02:00; at first, it was a gentle trickle before opening up into a full-blown tropical rainstorm. Thank god I had lined the inside of my new home with my poncho or I would be getting soaked.

There didn't seem a lot going on, so spent the next hour or so listening to the gentle pitter-patter of rain hitting the poncho. Other strange noises breaking the silence of the night came from the woods, which conjured up moments of fear to play tricks on your mind. Combine this with the stunts your eyes are playing on you. Seeing everything imaginable moving through the night. Of course, the trick here is to filter out what's real and what's not.

Wasn't long before the brain slipped into the why was I here stage, which at the time seemed a valued question; what was I doing here in the pitch darkness of the night, laying in a wet hole in the ground watching some drug dealers at work?

Couldn't be for empathy for the millions of people using drugs as that is something that eludes me. My therapist once told me, 'I'm just a cold-hearted bastard', not wholly accurate. Granted, I don't give a crap about other peoples' problems. So what if they die, I don't know them so who gives a shit about them. What I do care about are my family and a few close friends.

Maybe it's because I hate things, anything or anyone who are not following the rules. Let's face it, drug dealing is not, for sure, abiding by the guidelines in anyone's book. Now it might be because I have always struggled to get anywhere in life and find it hard to ask for help. I want to assist people without them asking for assistance, similar to the woman yesterday.

Could it merely be because I've done this so many times before, it is like a job to me? When it came to the money side of things, recently one thing was for sure, I definitely needed that, with the travel business not doing that well. OK, decided I'm here for the dosh.

A light that came on to the rear of the house snapped my mind back into focus. A check of the time, it was 04:23, being extinguished about ten minutes later with no movements spotted; made a note on my notepad.

Looked down at Mickey, it would soon be first light; a time all military personnel serving or otherwise cherished, as it brings about the sense they lived through another night with no issues. Even if you're deprived of sleep, those first rays reinvigorate you as they welcome you to a new day.

Day Two of Observation Post

The first lights of the day started to penetrate through the canopy, then the first crackle of the radio on a new day broke the morning silence of a new day.

"GD, OK."

"TS, OK."

Pressed the transmit button, "S3, OK," great to hear the boys had made it through the night.

Reached into the Bergen and pulled out a small flask, poured out half a cup of coffee. Always amazed how this tiny object could keep liquids warm for such a long time. Especially as it was given to me on an integral cruise of Norwegian Bliss. Replaced the flask before reaching in again, this time for one of the cookies Abbie provided. One of the things the Army had drummed into you as a recruit was only taken one item out at a time. Then replace it before taking out another as you never knew when you would be attacked and have to grab your kit and bug out.

One thing that always brought a smile to my face, when I thought about this, was the fact if you all ran away together, it's called a tactical withdrawal, but if you ran away on your own, it's called desertion.

Held the cup in one hand, sipping on the coffee, picked up the binoculars and scanned the whole property. From what I could perceive, our lazy drug dealers were still getting their beauty sleep, apart from the two on guard near the water tanks.

08:27 - Several people emerged into the front yard, stood in a group and started smoking; checked my notes to confirm, this was about the same time as yesterday. Maybe a pattern is forming, such as this is about the time our drug dealers rise from their slumber.

09:00 - A group of four men and two women came from the warehouse and climbed aboard the lorry and headed towards the gate. Couple of interesting points here, as I hadn't seen anyone enter this morning. They must have slept there last night, something that would be very handy when it comes to the final mission. The second point, at 09:00 six people leave the compound, reducing the number of people still on the property to only fourteen.

09:56 - Appears another pattern is forming here, same as yesterday, three men left the house and entered the vineyard.

This information was helping into the start of a plan of attack; of course, need more info from the other two before jumping to any conclusions.

Down on the property were the usual activities you would expect from any operation for the next two hours, with people coming and going from the warehouse, people going backwards and forwards from the vineyard.

In fact, the only movement that was out of the ordinary, and something we hadn't seen yesterday was at 10:36 people were seen leading five large looking German Shepherd and Rottweiler dogs from the gatehouse to the field.

12:00 - The cheating bastard Sam arrived and entered the house, leaving after six minutes and made his way into the warehouse. Guess he'd come to fix something; this was confirmed twenty minutes later when the sound of some type of machinery was heard coming from inside.

Became apparent we are going to need an idea of the layout of that place, maybe Abbie can help with this.

13:00 - The lorry returned from town, presumed this was where it had been as it was now unloading crates from the back. On a closer examination with my binos, confirmed it was food or at least that's what the boxes led us to believe.

Sunset would be in about thirty minutes. Needed to collect my claymore before it got too dark and I had to make my way to the RV following the same procedure, as yesterday when placing it into position. Made my way over the ridge to the stump, crawling on my belly. After disarming the device, paused for a moment, using the opportunity to check out the warehouse from a different angle. Glad I did as I noticed a rear door I hadn't seen before.

Back in the OP, ensured everything was packed away apart from the radio, still needed that to send the last check message, plus everyone's signal to bug out.

Dead on 19:17, sent my message, "S3, OK."

"TS, OK," and, "GD, OK,"; guess the boys were ready to call it an end to the observation phase.

Final check everything was away, left the location and proceeded to where I placed my rear protection, carefully removing this and packed it in the Bergen. Now a simple process of making my way down to the track where I was dropped off to wait.

By the time I arrived at the edge of the tree line, it was dark so ensured I stayed inside of tree line until I heard the sound of the Land Rover coming down the trail as the lights would be off.

The area was quiet, so should not be any chance I would miss Simon as he approached. Had just taken out my torch with the red lens when in the distance, the noise of the vehicle's engine broke the morning silence.

As it got closer, I gave two flashes, the car pulled to a stop close to where I was crouched. George was already on board when I scrambled onboard, "Morning all, hope you've both had an uneventful OP."

George's Observation Post

Calculated that, at the speed of the vehicle once they had crossed the road, I would have five seconds before reaching the location where I needed to be. Approaching the crossing, Simon slowed down to a near crawl, observed for any signs of movement before accelerating away; if he had floored it, the increased noise could have attracted attention.

"Get ready to jump, mate." Five, four, three, two, one; I leapt from the vehicle, landing on the fringe of the tree line. No need for a compass bearing, all he had to do was keep the road to my right. Making sure I stayed a minimum of fifty metres away, made my way to where I would be carrying out the OP, according to the map. A stream ran twisting and turning past the front gate about seventy metres away, with any luck, a suitable place could be found on the far bank.

Managed to make a good pace, so soon arrived at a position about a hundred metres short of the location and went to ground. As I did so, a car drove along the road away from the target. Scanning in front, could see that the stream started to bend to the right then left again once it reappeared from under the tarmac. This is where I would place the OP.

After a quick assessment of the area, made my way as quickly and quietly as possible, stopping again at the edge of the stream. On closer inspection, the bank dropped down five feet with the water running along the middle, about three feet wide before raising back up again. To the left on the opposite bank, a part which had fallen away, perfect.

First task: needed to put out rear protection tripwire, more than likely the threat was more likely to come from the road, so that would be the best place to locate it.

Spotted several possible routes our friends would take, being none too professional, surely they would take the easy way, this was where the alarm would be set.

Made my way past the location for about twenty metres before scrambling down, jumping the river and landing on the other side. Still below the height of the opposite bank, made my way to the location of my OP. Shit, as I landed on the opposite bank my right foot slipped into the water. With any luck, I would manage to remove my boot before water had time to penetrate the leather. The last thing I needed was to spend 48 hours with cold, wet feet.

Wasn't long before I reached the point where I would be carrying out the observation from, kept as close to the ground as possible and crawled into position. Thankfully there was sufficient undergrowth available to conceal the location from view. Turned around, placing my head where my feet should be confirmed that the place could not be seen from the road.

Placed the Bergen to my right, took out my binoculars, notebook & pencil and poncho, which would provide some protection if it rained. Could not see any prominent location for the claymore, so going to have to do without it for now.

The time had now reached 06:17, time for the first check-in.

"S3, OK."

Picked up the radio and pressed transmit button; waited for a split-second then spoke clearly, "GD, OK."

After what seemed like a long pause, which felt like it lasted forever, but in reality, was only about twenty seconds before, "TS, OK."

Looked back towards the gate, in full view were two men dressed in jeans, a black jacket, and if I had to estimate their height, it would be around 5' 7". Both armed with AK47s, which slung over their shoulders. One man was holding the lead of a Rottweiler which sat by his side.

Just to the left of the gatehouse, spotted the kennels Sam had told us about, they consisted of four separate areas constructed of galvanised welded mesh wire fence about six feet high; inside each was a small doghouse.

Bearing in mind our drug dealer friends had moved in on someone else's property, they had done an excellent job on constructing them, or was there something Henry was not telling us.

08:30 -- Looking through the gate, a man and a woman came from the house, stood smoking for about ten minutes, noted this down on my pad as every detail counts on this type of mission.

09:15 -- The sound of a vehicle coming down the road from behind me grew closer. As the car stopped, managed to work out that this was Sam along with a young lady I didn't recognise sat in the passenger seat. The woman waved at the two guards who then opened the gate to them in, Sam drove up to the house, climbed out and went inside.

09:17 – Finished writing down some notes when it was time for the next check-in with the other two.

11:05 — The young lady, around 5' 10" tall with a slim model type figure, with long blonde hair which reached halfway down her back, dressed in a light blue dress, and Sam left the house and walked towards the gatehouse, stopping to speak to the two guards on the gate before entering.

If I didn't know better, would say they had known each other for a long time. Understood this from the woman. From the impression Sam had given us up to now, he didn't know these people.

Didn't bother me doing an OP during the day as always plenty going on, it's the nights I hate as usually not much happening, so time just drags on at a slow pace. The point of the radio checks was it continually refocused your mind, talking of which it was time for the next one.

11:17 — Simon initiated the first call this time, TS, OK."

Picked up the radio, "GD, OK."

This was followed up a couple of seconds later by, "S3, OK."

11:55 - Re-emerging from the gatehouse, Sam and the woman walked back to their Jeep. Once Sam had finished shaking hands with a stylishly dressed man around 5' 9", who was standing near the front door to the house both Sam and the women climbed into the jeep. It was Hadley, I recognised him from the photos I had seen earlier, always best to be able to identify your enemy.

Was starting to feel peckish so pulled out the napkin-wrapped food parcel Abbie had kindly made for us all, inside were some sandwiches, fruit and a few biscuits. Took one of the sarnies. Was just about to start eating when the sound of a single shot caught my attention, sounded like it came from behind the house. Couldn't actually witness what it was, probably one of the idiots firing off recklessly into the air to the amusement of his mates, made a note of the time, 14:00

14:10 — Hadley emerged from the front door, along with three others and climbed into a Land Rover and drove to the gatehouse, stopping for a short time to talk to the guards who had opened the gate.

15:00 — People left the house and walked over to the gatehouse leaving, after 15 minutes with two dogs, one Rottweiler and a German Shepherd. Then proceeded to walk to the right of the house where I lost them; with any luck, Steve will pick them up from his location.

A few moments later, two women came from the warehouse with two other hounds and swapped places with the two men on the gate, guess this was their idea of a shift change.

Must be the sound of running water, but now had to attend to the call of nature; one advantage of having a stream behind me so no need for bottles or pissing myself. Got back into the OP in time to watch people milling around in the doorway to the warehouse.

18:25 — Henry's Land Rover returned and drove up to the house, was that fucking Sam getting out of the car along with the person he had left with earlier.? Two small children also exited the vehicle. Maybe the woman and the little ones are Hadley's family. Scratch that if they are, why's Sam now got his arm around her? Plus, I hoped the kids were not here when the preverbal shit starts flying in a couple of days. The last thing I want to do is top two small children.

Not long now until sunset, so time to make sure everything that shouldn't be out was back where it should be. Placed everything in a position where I could intuitively reach without fumbling. The light was starting to fade, so put my hand inside the Bergen and took out the small thermos flask I always carried. Poured myself a warm cup of tea. By the time I'd drunk it, the time was approaching the last radio check of the day at 19:17, after which we will all settle into our night routines.

"S3, OK."

This followed by, "TS, OK."

Transmitted my call sign, "GD, OK."

The last rays of light were disappearing over the horizon, took my poncho out and draped it over my back. At least it would provide some shelter tonight if the weather gods weren't on our side.

20:30 — A small group of six people emerged from the house, led by Sam pointing towards the skyline, they then proceed to split into two smaller groups. A short moment in time passed, when they started to shine powerful torches into the tree line, one in the direction of Steve and the other in the path of where Simon would be.

This can't be a coincidence, what the fuck is Sam playing at? Hope he hasn't compromised the whole mission. Mind you, if he has, this might be one of the last things he ever does.

Now that it was dark, they had turned on the lights, one bright light covered the front gate, no lights were covering the back where the kennels were located, which left them still in darkness. Ensured I made a note of this as I may need this info during the mission if I have to take out the dogs.

Must have been about 02:00 when it started to rain; at first a gentle trickle before opening up into a full-blown tropical rainstorm. Thank God I put the poncho over myself, hate the rain, but nothing I can do about it so might as well have listened to the sound of it dripping through the trees and landing in the stream.

You would be amazed at the number of strange sounds and sights your mind puts in places that don't exist. For my part, I started to get flashbacks from my time in the military.

The rain started to pour heavier, making me think why I was here getting soaked laying on the ground with only a poncho providing any type of protection while watching some idiots stood on a gate; thought I left this life behind.

This could be something to do with the fact I hate the idea of someone taking advantage of other people, not individuals as really don't care about them, thanks to the PTSD. Suppose this type of work is perfect for to my anger issues, you know the one where someone hits you with a stick, so you take a metal bar to them.

Of course, the most essential thing in my life, that of my family and looking after them, you need money, something my current official job provides but not in a sufficient amount to support them to a standard I believe is required.

Think it's the same for the other two and dosh is the primary reason I was laying here getting piss wet through.

04:23 — Was brought back to the here and now as a light

came on, just inside of the doorway, managed to distinguish the shape of a lone figure having a sneaky cigarette.

Day Two of the Observation Post.

Soon be first light, mine and many other veterans favourite time of the day as we had made it through the night without a scratch. Can't be our drug-dealing friends best time of day as no sign of them running about the place, apart from two who were walking the dogs back and forward near the gate.

Looked at Mickey the time was now 06:17, time to check-in for the first time today. Reaching for the radio gave the transmitter button a push, "GD, OK," followed by, "TS, OK," then a couple of moments later with,

"S3, OK," what's the matter, Steve, you half asleep?

Poured another cup of lukewarm tea, taking several sips and enjoyed some biscuits, a nice way to start the day in my book. Once finished, again ensured everything was put away, a habit I haven't been able to shake since my Army days.

08:27 — Almost the same time as yesterday, three people emerged from the house and into the front yard, stood in a group and started smoking. A routine could be forming here, this may be an indication of when they finish their beauty sleep; made a note on my pad.

09:00 — A small party of people, consisting of four men and two women came from the direction of the warehouse, climbed into the lorry and drove towards the gatehouse.

The guards must have been inside, as the driver honked his horn to attract their attention. Followed by what sounded like a lot of abuse as the guard opened the gate to let them leave.

From what's been said beforehand, this must be the food run.

10:36 — Our friends must be fed and watered and was now the turn of the pooches. A party of three people were leading five large looking German Shepherd and Rottweiler dogs in the direction of the vineyard. Fascinating, as this only left one dog at the gatehouse. Returning about an hour later, this would give us a one-hour window where I would only have to deal with one pooch during the attack.

11:50 — Sam arrived at the gate and spent ten minutes talking and laughing with guards before driving towards the warehouse, possibly he was here to fix some type of machinery; confirmed a short time later when the sound of an engine firing up came from inside.

12:55 — The noise of the lorry returning came from the direction of the road. As it passed the gatehouse, could distinguish several boxes which contained food and multiple crates of drinks, this could be why the lazy bastards hate getting up in the morning, they are all hungover.

Looked like the whole place was quiet for the moment; taking advantage of this, slipped out of the OP into the stream.

Made my way along to the left a short distance, until I reached a better position to get a closer view of the kennels. From here, managed to confirm there was only one way into the enclosures, and that was from inside the gatehouse; this left one massive blind spot which we may perhaps be able to use to our benefit.

With sunset being in about twenty-five minutes, ensured everything was packed away, ready to bug out straight after the 19:17 check-in.

Dead on 19:17, my radio crackled into life, "S3, OK," penetrated the airwaves followed by, "TS, OK."

Instantly after sending my call sign, "GD, OK," I slipped back down the slope and headed back to where I had laid my tripwire. Removed the last end, when a vehicle stopped fifty metres away. Immediately hit the ground. Watched as a woman shone a torch into the trees like she was searching for someone. Crap, hope I'd not been seen. Hope that Sam had not informed his buddies that someone may be in the area. Of course, he wouldn't know where anyone would be, we had ensured nobody had overheard any of our conversations.

Waited a couple of minutes before continuing to pack away the tripwire. Now a matter of making my way to the collection point and on time, as Simon would drive straight past.

Was dark when I finally arrived at the pickup point, took up a position as near to the track as possible, still ensuring I remained in cover, took out my torch with the red lens and waited until the sound of the vehicle was close by.

Been in my current location for five to six minutes when the rumble of an engine approached. Delayed as long as possible, before signalling Simon with the prearranged two flashes of the torch. "Welcome aboard," came the voice from the front as we drove to collect Steve.

Simon's Observation Post

The two numpties dropped off, the first port of call, or in this case the bay, best find my way off the tarmac and find a way through the trees, which won't slow us down too much as we may be coming this way at high speed. Another fifty metres down the road a trail, which looked like it headed towards the inlet; right let's find out where this trail leads us to.

By the look of things would guess this route hasn't been used in a while, useful on the one hand but on the other why hasn't it? Could be a dead-end, or perhaps a massive obstacle making unpassable, just the type of challenge I like.

This was going to take some skilful driving, as the trail twisted and turned with far too many potholes, now I know why not many people come this way. In front, a near-vertical drop, which shouldn't be an issue; however, it could be a problem getting up the other side. Only one way to find out, time to put the transfer box into low range by pulling back on the red lever and engaging four-wheel drive. First gear selected, gently does it, bloody hell this was steep as the vehicle edged over the ridge.

Easy part completed, now for getting back out of this ditch, there wasn't enough room here to take a run-up. So kept the old girl in first and kept her rolling. Very close to the top and the wheels started to spin, come on girl, you can make it, only another eight feet. If talking to a vehicle would improve its performance, I should have said more at this point, she began to slip backwards.

Bottom of the ditch looked wide enough; with a couple of movements managed to turn the Land Rover around, better drive along the base of the trench for a while to find another way out.

Travelled about one hundred and forty metres, when on my right spotted what looked like a landslide. Perfect, could use this to climb out. There was someone looking down on me today, as the vehicle crested the ridge. That's handy, the inlet was about two hundred metres in the distance.

The trees were blocking my view, so would have a closer look on foot. Grabbed the rifle and made my way to the creek, ensuring I stayed in the tree line. Scanned the vicinity looking for a suitable landing point for us to wait for Derek and his boat.

Took a rough sketch of the surroundings, would need this for the planning stage. Must have got carried away, as I looked down at my watch the time was 06:16, one minute before the first radio-check.

Fuck! I had left the radio in the vehicle, only one thing for it. I sprinted as fast as my legs would carry me through the trees back to Land Rover. By the time I located it, I was twenty seconds late. Picked up the transmitter and pressed transmit button, "TS, OK."

Missed the other two and procedure prevented my asking for another, so would have to wait for the next one at 09:17 to find out if the others are in place.

Needed to find my way back on the trail. Going the same way I came was not an option, would never get back up that hill, would have to find a different way from here. Took a general bearing of where I wanted to go. Then I would have to rely on the great sense of direction built up over the years commanding a chieftain tank.

Thirty minutes or so of weaving in and out of the trees, I found myself near the track. Stopped short, climbed out and made the rest of the way on foot for a quick recce of where the trail I was now following met with the tarmac. Marked down some notable features either side, may be required to find the turning again which could be after dark.

Calculated the bridge must be about two hundred metres to my right and I still needed to check-out underneath for Steve; not sure what he's planned but knowing him, it will more than likely involve a boom of some sort.

Would be conspicuous if I drove through the wood to get to the bridge, might as well continue going down the track. Arrived five minutes later, reverse parked the Land Rover, concealing it in the trees and made my way underneath. Noticed the tide was now in, so made a quick estimate of the height from the water level to the lowest part, giving an inch or two made it about seven feet. Time was moving on far too fast, so decided the best way was to take photos with my phone rather than make notes.

Better get back to the primary mission of setting up an observation post overlooking Henry's place. Travelled along the track for about one click until it started heading off in the direction of the sea. On the apex of a bend, could see another smaller one which ran almost entirely the way I needed to be. Drove past the turning for about fifty metres then turned off into the undergrowth, stopping after several metres and went back to remove any signs that this is where I left the track.

Joined the new trail a little way up from the junction, now it was time to find my new home, until tomorrow night that is.

Rather than make lots of noise with the Land Rover, parked it for a while and continued on foot, until I found the ideal location which provided not only cover for me but the vehicle as well.

This was going to take time, needed to drive at a steady pace to reduce the constant humming of the engine to a bare minimum if I didn't want to be spotted. Found the ideal position on the forward edge of the tree line looking down onto the target.

Located on the top of the hill, gave me the advantage of being able to survey both sides of the house plus the whole of the vineyard; the only area I couldn't cover from here was the gatehouse, but George would have that covered.

Now the first priority, camouflage the Land Rover. Folded down the windscreen to prevent any glare as the sun or light reflected off it. Reached in the rear and grabbed the old hessian sacks, placed them over the front and back, preventing any possible reflections.

Next task, to collect some local vegetation to help blend the vehicle into its surroundings. My watch was telling me there was only another eighteen minutes to the 09:17, not going to be late for that one as well, I'd cam up after the radio check.

09:17 Time for the first to check-in. "TS, OK," this was followed by, "S3, OK," then soon after by, "GD, OK."

Radio check over, back to setting up the OP, reversed the vehicle in case I needed to complete a fast getaway. Now required vegetation leaned up against the front that wouldn't impede me when leaving.

Completed the same for the sides, the roof covering would be a tad different. Placed the four 3-foot posts I custom-made in Sam's garage into slots on the rear compartment. Stretched out the tarpaulin, securing each corner to post; I had purposely kept them short to maintain a minimal profile. Plus, if the heavens opened up, there was no way I was going to get piss wet through, unlike the other two.

The OP was ready to go. Taking advantage in the lull in activity, made a brew via the boiling vessel set up in the back, perks of being the transport guy.

10:45 — A small group of three men left the house and enter the warehouse, only to emerge around thirty minutes later carrying several sacks between them and headed towards the vineyard. Upon reaching the middle, they started to carry out some type of work under the vines. Guess it had something to do with the drugs they were growing, made a note of this on my pad.

11:05 — Through the binos spotted Sam and the woman 6' tall with a skinny figure, with long blonde hair dressed in a light blue dress leaving the house via the front door together and walked in the direction of the gatehouse.

11:17 — Time for next radio-check, pressed the transmit button, waited for a second remembering my radio training, "TS, OK."

"GD, OK."

"S3, OK." That's all three checked in and more importantly still alive.

12:00 — Not sure what Sam and the women had been up to when they disappeared, spotted them again making their way back to Sam's Jeep where they stopped to shake hands with a man about 5' 11" who was standing near the front door.

Needed to make a closer observation of our stranger, so picked up the binoculars. A person I recognised from the photographs at Abbie's place, took a few seconds to register it was Hadley, the so-called leader of this outfit.

Felt hungry now, so pulled out the wrapped bundle Abbie had made for us all. Inside were some cookies, sandwiches and several items of fruit. Took out an apple, should keep me going for a few hours.

Forward recce was one of my prominent roles in the Army, so didn't mind carrying out OPs unlike the Grunts, (Ground, Reconnaissance, Untrainable) AKA Steve and George. Dissimilar to them, I always had a nice warm vehicle to sit, none of that laying in the cold, wet mud for me. Well, enough gloating for now, what was happening down on the property?

14:00 — A lot of shouting attracted me to the back of the house, an unknown woman and Hadley were facing a man kneeling on the floor. Behind him, another man dressed in beige shorts and a white Polo shirt was holding a pistol to the back of the man's head. Wonder what that poor fucker had done.

Even more shouting and pointing at the man on his knees, couldn't understand what he was saying. Moments later I heard the distinctive sound of a 9 mm shot filling the air and the man fell face down on the lawn blood staining the green of the grass. Saw Hadley take something from the man's pocket, and along with the others went back indoors.

14:10 — The three men and Hadley climbed into a Land Rover and headed for the gatehouse.

14:26 — From my vantage point I managed to see a tad into the warehouse if they left the door open, which they'd now done. Inside I could just about see a vehicle and a massive pile of sacks, two men were throwing them up to a third on the back.

18:25 — Henry's Land Rover returned and drove up to the house. Had to look twice as Sam got out with the woman I saw him with earlier, along with two children I would estimate to be between 4 & 9.

Wonder who the kids belong to? Think I knew the answer as they ran over to her. What I wasn't prepared for was what I watched next, as Sam put his arm around her.

What is the prick up to? Nothing annoys me more than a person cheating on his partner, the man needs a slap.

19:17 - Grabbed my radio ready for the check-in, Steve's voice came over the air first with, "S3, OK," followed up with my call sign, "TS, OK," Finally George checked-in "GD, OK."

Must have been a long day, needed to go back to the little boy's room. Another advantage of being the transport guy, reached over and grabbed the empty black container and problem sorted.

The day was starting to close, as darkness crept in as last light was fast approaching, time to begin to think about the night routine; which if I'm honest with myself would not be a lot different from the day, the hardest part when nothing is happening is staying awake.

20:30 — Group of six people emerged from the house, one of which was Sam, splitting into two groups. One of them, led by Sam was using a bright light, they started to scan the tree line. One in my direction, the other in the area where Steve would be. What is that bastard doing, I hope he hadn't told Hadley what was happening? Mind you if he had, he doesn't know any of the details, we made sure nobody was in earshot when we discussed our plans.

01:50 — Black clouds had been forming over the last couple of hours, they had decided now would be a good time to empty their contents. My tarpaulin was doing its job apart from the middle, which was starting to fill up. Dam it, would need to go and get a stick to hold up the centre.

Spent some time using my hand to push the water out, but this was making a loud splashing sound. Far better to ensure the water roll-off the tarp. Wasn't long before the gentle rain turned into a full-blown tropical rainstorm, and I was now wet.

Sat here for the last hour in the silence listening to the massive drops of rain hitting the canvas. Pondering life and why I was now seated in a Land Rover on top of the hill in a foreign country; and why I had taken Henry's call, after the scenes I had witnessed in Iraq of innocent people caught up in war. Vowed to myself if possible, I might be able to help someone I would, nobody should be treated like that again.

For being up here on my own, I preferred to be on my own where I don't have to be around anyone. Yes, Steve and

George were about, but the difference with them is trust has been built up over the short time we knew each other. When it came to hurting other people, this was not my thing; saying that I had a job to do and I would rather it was them getting hurt than me.

Thinking about it, we were all here because we needed the money. I'd known in my case it was the real reason I was here, as things were not going too well since leaving in the military.

04:23 — Brought back to the here and now as a glow came from one of the windows of the house.

Made it through another night with the rays of first light breaking over the horizon; really love this time of day, even got up early to watch the sunrise most days. Hope the others made it as well, would have to wait to find out, it was time for the first check-in of the day, 06:17.

The first checked-in came over the air, the first was George, "GD, OK."

Followed up with, "TS, OK," Steve was the last to call this morning with, "S3, OK."

Day Two of Observation Post

08:27 — That was two days in a row three people emerged into the front yard, standing in a group and smoking, maybe some sort of pattern was starting to form or this was when the lazy bastards get out of bed.

08:50 – The warehouse doors opened, and the lorry pulled out, stopping near the house. This vehicle was followed by four men and two women who climbed on board, then drove off towards the gate.

10:36 — Saw some people leading five large looking German Shepherd and Rottweiler dogs from the gatehouse to the field. Guess it was their walkies time. Remember Sam saying there was six of them in total, that means only one dog was left near the gate. George would have spotted this as well, but I'll still make a note of it.

Time for another brew and one of Abbie's sandwiches, managed to save half from the previous day. While I ate, checked the vineyard; more people than yesterday were busy working, whatever they were doing under the vines. Did notice that more sacks were leaving the field today, maybe they've got a drug run coming up.

11:50 — Sam arrived and drove into the warehouse, stopped at the far corner, took out a small metal chest and a handful of tools and started to work on generator type machinery twenty minutes later, when the sound of an engine was heard firing up inside.

13:00 — Managed to spot the lorry returning, the people in the back were seated on wooden crates. Looking through the binoculars, could distinguish what looked like food boxes and even more creates of drinks. Must be the reason they hate getting up in the morning, they're all hungover.

Noted down all the activities that occurred this afternoon, wasn't anything out of the ordinary considering they were a bunch of drug dealers. Not long now before last light, so started to take down the tarpaulin and ensure all my kits were fully packed. Wouldn't begin to remove the cam until after the last-light check-in at 19:17, which should be around about now.

19:17 — A voice came over the radio, it was Steve, "S3, OK."

Beat George to it and transmitted, "TS, OK."

A few seconds later, "GD, OK," was heard.

This was the sign for George and Steve to make their ways to the pickup points. Would leave in fifteen minutes, once I'd removed the foliage and checked the location for anything that could have fallen on the floor that may be traced back to us. Confirmed the area was clear, then inched forward slowly knocking the branches that were leaning on the vehicle to the ground.

The route to the pickup points would be much simpler than the way here but still had to be completed with caution. This is when a lot of people fuck up and end up being killed. Drove to the edge of the trail but still in the tree line, pulled over, turned off the motor and listened. Couldn't hear anything so proceeded back on the route and on to the track using the same way I had come in.

Once again, once I had left the woods, stopped to conceal my tracks. Didn't want any nosey bastard finding them, that may well lead back to where the OP was if they put all the pieces together.

Made sure I noticed the markers I had taken note of when I came from the inlet, to ensure they were fresh in my mind. Nearing the point where George had leapt out and spotted two flashes of a red torch, this must be the first pickup. Slowed the vehicle down to a crawl as I passed, then I sensed the suspension sink a little as George climbed on board.

"Morning mate, hope you slept well?"

"Fine thanks, and yourself?"

Goes without saying this was just banter, as we were all professional and sleep would be the last thing on our minds.

"Right let's go get the ugly one."

Same as yesterday morning, drove past the road to Henry's place as quickly and unobtrusively as possible, slowing down as I approached the location where I had dropped Steve; wasn't long when I spotted the two red flashes of his torch. Again, slowed the vehicle down to a crawl, Steve jumped on board.

"Morning all, hope you've both had an uneventful OP?"

"Couldn't tell you, mate, was asleep most of the night."

"Take us back to Abbie's then, Simon, George stinks."

"Did you get a chance to look under the bridge?"

"Sure did, boss, you want me to stop now?"

"Chuck over my Bergen, George, need to do something underneath."

Simon reversed the vehicle into the trees. Taking a small pack with me, I jumped down, ran across the road and disappeared.

"Wonder what that mad man is up to?"

"Not sure, but you can guarantee it is going to be a nasty surprise for someone."

A short time later, I reappeared minus the bag, "Take us home, mate."

Pre-Mission

"STOP, we have a problem. Take a look at the vehicle tracks. They go right up to the house, as we are all aware Abbie doesn't allow this. I, for one, am not taking the fucking chance, get us out of here, Simon.

"Park over behind that bush, let's make a plan of how we're going to tackle this. Suggest we approach from the rear of the house by using the tree line as cover. Then we can climb over the fence behind where we've been kipping, that should keep us out of view. Remember the fence is electrified, so don't want anyone shouting out if their meat and two vegs are fried. Once we're over, we are confronted with two entry points, one on each side of the house; I'll take the front while you two take the rear.

"At this point, we still don't know the reason for the tracks leading to the house, and perhaps all could be innocent. And Abbie might be inside giving them a right earful for getting dust in her home, so do not go in all weapons blazing. Once we've entered and found this not to be the case, we can then take the necessary action. Anyone we find that shouldn't be there we need to be able to talk, got that, George? We all know what you're like when you're angry. Grab your kit, boys, let's go."

The trees and undergrowth gave us enough cover as we made our way to the back of the house. Stood off from the house to observe for any noise or movement, once we were satisfied it was safe, and nobody could be seen in the vicinity, I went over the electric fence first. Took up a firing position on the peripheral of the building, looking towards the rear door. Once Simon and George were over, they took up similar stances.

"Give me two minutes to make my way around to the front then we all enter concurrently, safety catches off, boys let's go."

On the facade of the house was a window into the living room, I needed to confirm nobody was inside.

Only had one chance at this, a two-second glance via the bottom corner confirmed at least one person I didn't recognise sat on the sofa. Could conceivably be more, as it wasn't normal in my experience for one individual to be left after an extraction in case someone came back; in fact, their mission was hostile, and we still hadn't a clue what the issue was.

Thirty seconds remaining before the planned entry, standing to the right of the door I gave it a knock; you never know if some smart twat is going to put a couple of rounds through the door.

Counted down, instantly on reaching zero, entering the house simultaneously with the other two, who entered via the rear door. Headed straight for the kitchen, Simon and George would enter the living room first, so would let them deal with the person I saw through the window.

My rifle was in the ready position as I entered. What a mess, signs of a struggle were everywhere. The table was face down on the floor, complete with an assortment of cooking ingredients. Looked like Abbie must have been making something when she was attacked. Of course, it could have not been Sam as we knew what he'd been up back at Henry's place.

About to leave to join the others when I caught a glimpse of a man in the corner of the room raising an AK47, he hesitated for a split-second, I didn't. Turned around and without thinking double-tapped two rounds, both hitting him in the centre of his face. As though in slow motion, a massive part of the back of his head exploded against the wall. The lifeless body slumped to the floor, to my right. From the other room, I could overhear the commotion in the other room, swung around again and ran to help.

By the time I arrived, the man was pinned to the ground as George landed a hard kick to his face with his right foot. At times like this, your adrenaline would be pumping around your veins on overtime, but we needed to bring ourselves down to ascertain the situation and fast.

"Tie him to that chair. Don't gag him, we need him to talk. You will find another one dead one in the kitchen, Simon. Can you do a sweep of the house in case any more of the fuckers are lurking about, could do without any nasty surprises."

"Didn't find anybody else about, Steve, so what are we going to do with this arsehole?"

"First, we need some information, then depending on what he tells us will depend on whether we kill him or not," making sure he understood every word I was saying.

"So, what's your name? No need to ask who you work for, as we can guess you're working for Hadley." The silence said it all.

"Loosen his tongue a little, George."

With full force, George slammed his fist hard into the side of our friend's head. "Want to talk now, arsehole?"

Ten minutes later and getting nowhere. "Time to up my ante."

Collected some safety fuse and a detonator which I had left under my bed, so goes to show these people are not professionals, the first thing I would do is check the place over for weapons etc.

"As you're uncooperative to my simple questions, you leave me only one option."

Reached down, wrapped the fuse around his legs ending with the detonator resting delicately on his manhood.

"Right, my friend, that is a safety cord which is coiled around your legs, it has a burn rate of sixty seconds per thirty centimetres.

"From what I calculate, that is about one-half metres giving you hardly five minutes from the time I light the fuse to saying goodbye to the bottom half of your body, so I suggest you answer my questions.

"For the last time, what has happened to Abbie, and why are you here?"

"You're bluffing."

"Why would you want to take that chance?"

Reached down again and ignited the fuse, "Start talking."

The man started to talk, there was a tremble in his voice, "Hadley had us come over here and snatch Abbie. She has been taken to Henry's house, we're left here in case you came back."

"How much information do you know about us and our activities since we have been on the island?"

"Sam is a close friend of Hadley's, he told us you were up to something, but he wasn't sure what. I've told you what you wanted, now pull that fucking fuse out."

"Don't think so."

At that moment, the detonator exploded blowing the bottom half of his body across the room, spattering body parts and blood everywhere, the cheeky fucker even got some on me. Within seconds of him starting to scream, Simon put a 9 mm bullet into the back of his head.

Was something about Sam I didn't like soon after meeting him, now we have the proof.

"Any of you spot Sam with Hadley at the house?" enquired Simon.

"Yeah, and the bastard was shining a torch in my direction with a group of men."

"Saw him arrive in a car with a young lady and far too familiar with the people on the main gate for my liking."

"One man who shouldn't be walking in a week, if I have anything to do with it."

"There are seven days left to complete this mission, I suggest we make it sooner than later, but first we need to get some sleep, let's head back to the Land Rover."

Back at the vehicle, the first task was to move the Land Rover undercover while we got our heads down. A quick search not too far from the house located a spot that provided sufficient cover. Simon still had the hessian sacks he had used in his observation post, placed them over the Land Rover and with the aid of the local foliage, camouflaged the area.

"I'll take the first watch, you and Simon decide between yourself who will be going next. Shall we say two-hour stags?" Wasn't going mad taking the first one, at least I would be able to catch a straight four hours to sleep. It is the poor sod on the middle stag I felt sorry for as his nap will be broken. This turned out to be George as he'd drawn the short straw.

This gave me time to start mulling over some type of plan for the actual operation to retake property from Hadley and his gang of drug dealers. What was disturbing me was how much information on our mission they were aware of, thanks to Sam. Realistically this couldn't be much, as he only knew parts of what was going on from Henry. Plus we had made sure we did not speak about the mission where anyone may accidentally overhear us.

Still, I had to take this into consideration when planning. Might be more safety precautions being made by our friends with extra weapons near the gatehouse. Could only really start to create a strategy once the boys and myself had time to reveal what we've all seen during our individual OPs.

Thank God the two hours went fast, as I was now finding it difficult to keep my eyes open, it been a long hard couple of days. Found George laying by the vehicle, gave him a nudge and stepped back; seen him lash out before from being woken from a deep sleep.

"Your turn to stag on, mate."

"No problem, just getting up."

For want of a better place, laid down in the same place George had been moments before.

Several hours passed and Simon had taken over as sentry. Looking down at his watch, time to wake the others out of the land of nod, gave them both a gentle tap with his boot.

"OK, you two sleeping beauties, Mickey says it's time to get up."

"Got any water left in your boiling vessel on the vehicle, do with a brew?"

"Thought you may say that, so switched it on a few moments ago, be ready soon."

"Cheers, mate."

"Don't know about you two but starting to feel hungry, suggest we make a move into town to grab some food before comparing our observation post notes."

Before going into Jal, found a secure place and buried our notebooks in three different locations near to where we were now; the theory was if some idiot finds one set of documents they would be denied access to all three.

"Just need to make a quick change out of these muddy garments," we had all stashed extra clothes in our Bergens along with scent-free wet wipes, you can never be too prepared.

Similar to what we'd done on the two previous occasions, we parked on the outskirts and walked in. The place seemed empty for an afternoon, wonder why, let's hope the influence of Hadley does reach as far as Jal. Saying that, Paul, who runs the police is connected to him.

Bearing in mind that we had been lying in a ditch for two days, well at least two of us had we still looked dirty even after the wipe down with the wet wipes and stunk a bit, even with the change of attire. The plan was to grab a quick meal at Katie's café before obtaining supplies from the supermarket.

Joshua Boulevard was as empty as the rest of the place nearly halfway down the street, when a small party of people looked in our direction then ran off around the corner towards the port. Both Simon and George were doing the same as me and double-checking their pistols were still tucked away in their jackets.

"Definitely something out of the ordinary was happening here in town today, even for a place like this."

"Agree, let's make our way into the café asap."

"Stop right there! You dirty gits can sit at the back of the room, you're not getting dirt on my clean tablecloths, where the hell have you been?"

"Been camping for a couple of days, and Simon's cooking is not up to your excellent standard." Katie gave us a knowing grin as to say 'I sold you weapons, I know where you're more likely to have been'.

"What can I fetch you, gentlemen?"

"Three house specials please, and why is the place so quiet?"

"Sure, and don't panic, it's nothing about any activities you may or may not be up to. There's a charity event going on at the port to raise money for the poorer people on the island."

"What a relief."

Wasn't long before Katie returned with three colossal plates piled high with the house special. "Take it, you look like you might be starving, enjoy."

Must all have been hungry; the three plates were finished in short order along with several mugs of coffee and tea.

"Bloody hell, Simon, the first time I have ever known you finish a whole meal before."

Time was now ticking past, and we still had to talk over our findings and make plans.

Now that Hadley would possibly be expecting something before the end of next week, we needed to bring forward the project if we had any chance of still maintaining the element of surprise.

"Cheers, Katie, the food was excellent."

"See you later, boys, stay safe."

Next stop was the local supermarket to pick up some supplies for the next couple of days. Didn't need too much, as the attack would go in within the next forty-eight hours at the latest.

Most of the foodstuff were items we could either boil in Simon's cooking vessel or things we may perhaps throw together, something we used to call an 'Army Chuck In'. Favourite of many a squaddie as they travelled in the back of an AFV 432.

Couldn't chance going straight back to Abbie's place, as when the two men we had killed earlier didn't show up around at the vineyard, someone would come looking.

Back at the location we had been before, we each retrieved our notes from where we had hidden them. Before getting down to business, a final sweep of the area confirmed nobody was in the vicinity that might overhear what we were about to discuss. The easiest way for us all to find out what the others saw from their perspective was each to take it in turns to read out their notes on the OP. I went first, followed by George and then Simon.

A few things that stood out from all the reports.

First, that Sam couldn't be trusted, something we already knew from the house combined with his behaviour back at Henry's place.

Second, there seemed to be a resemblance of a routine with the signs of life being around 08:30 when people first appeared from the house. This happened on both days, confirmed by us all.

Third, there was always two armed guards near the water tanks.

Fourth, the dogs were taken walkies at around 10:30 every morning, leaving only one dog at the gatehouse.

Fifth, we knew that people slept in the house and the warehouse.

Sixth, they are well-armed.

Finally, Hadley was using the woman and the children as protection, fully aware most people have an issue with shooting kids, they are probably unwitting participants in this.

As for the layout, George confirmed the area around the back of the kennels was dark. Plus, the dogs and handlers could only reach the rear via the front door, this may perhaps be one of the ways in. Then we have the back door of the warehouse, another possible way if the door opened from the outside. A potential way in would be to approach through the vineyard. This would involve skirting the coastline, from a point off from Henry's place to somewhere on the peripheral of the property.

This had merit, as we were aware that there would only be two armed guards in the area until 10:30, the dogs and their handlers would be out around the same time in a place where they can be dispatched quickly. Gone was the plan of putting the pooches to sleep, was planning on using Sam for this part, but now we can forget that idea.

"Steve, I'm about to make an Army Chuck In, and brewing up."

"Sounds good to me, mate."

Simon opened a couple of tins of stewing steak, carrots, peas, spam, and beans and placed them all into the same pot.

"Should be ready in about half-hour."

"Have to run the Land Rover for a few minutes to recharge the batteries, if nobody as any objections?"

"Do what you have to, I'll do a sweep of the area to ensure there are no nosey bastards around." Found nothing, so joined the boys who were now seated near the rear of the vehicle enjoying a few beers.

"Throw us one over, George."

"Excellent nosh."

"You know me, can chuck in with the best of them."

"Before we drink far too much, I would like to run some possible scenarios past you both."

"You are the planner among us, Steve, whatever you have come up with."

"Yes, but a good planner always listens to their troops. Here is a rough plan of actions."

"Simon and I will approach from the vineyard, after making our way along the coast from here. This is after confirmation tomorrow, as we recce the route to find out if it was practical to go that way. You will be in the same position you were for your OP, George. From which when you hear us taking out the men and hounds, you will dispatch the people at the gatehouse and the last dog.

"Once you've done that, find a place where your shooting skills will be of assistance. Simon will be entering the warehouse via the rear door, we can find out if it opens while on our recce. How you accomplish this, I will leave to you.

"Once I've dealt with any remaining people in the vineyard, I will be heading towards the house, where you two will join me to take out more bad guys. Can go over the find details tomorrow, ready for the mission the following day."

"Any questions?"

"Like you said, need to complete the recce first before we can go into it more."

"May need to be able to get into the area of the kennels before you start shooting, as there is a small fence to deal with."

"Tell you what, George, there are some wire cutters in Sam's garage, let's make a night raid."

Was now starting to get dark, "You stay here, and I'll go and get them for you, just need my bag of tricks."

Was just enough light to see what I was doing, but enough that other people couldn't see me. Taking the same route we had taken earlier today, made my way past the house, which was quiet and still in darkness; with a bit of luck, the idiots wouldn't come back to check on their mates. To be safe, better peek inside, the house was still in the same state as we had left it, with parts of our friend even now staining the walls.

Was wrong about them coming back, as the man in the kitchen was no longer there, plus the half-man had gone as well, wonder why they hadn't come searching for us. While I was here might as well help myself to Sam's beers, he isn't going to be needing them.

Once inside, I identified the tools on the bench, spotted the wire cutters attached to the back wall along with a crowbar. Replaced items in my bag with them and proceeded to the sliding door of the garage and half-opened it--time to leave a pleasant surprise for anyone returning.

Strapped a detonator to one of the cans of fuel Sam had stored here, running a wire from it along the front of the door towards the small wall to the left, making sure it would be seen. Attached to this was another wire, leading to a second device situated in a bush close to the wall.

This one contained an electrical circuit, which was set up with a break being maintained by a piece of timber held in place by a clothes peg. If the line I left on view on purpose was pulled, this would pull out a bit of wood on the other, causing a complete circuit and boom.

The trick here is most smart arses would notice the prepared bomb, as I'd ensured it would be hard to miss. Thinking they were outsmarting me, attach a line to mine, placing themselves around the corner and behind the wall before pulling the cord. Sorry folks, you just put yourself next to the explosion, idiots.

"There you go, George. One pair of wire cutters, plus a beer I relieved Sam of his stockpile."

The rest of the night was spent enjoying a few drinks and telling old war stories, might as well relax now as there is nothing we can do until tomorrow.

Henry's Place

Hadley sat back in the leather-bound chair, looking warmly at the photo of his wife and children situated on the desk in front of him. Reminded him of the days as a young boy growing up in Tortola near Cane Garden Bay, then working in the bars and restaurants along the beach. Watched as his parents struggled, as the tourists came and went, splashing their cash as if there was no tomorrow. This was when he made a promise to himself that when he had children, they would not go short of anything as his family had.

The shortage of work and minimal pay was the reason he had gotten into crime to start with. At first, starting with petty stuff; from overcharging customers and pocketing the difference, to stealing bags left unattended under the rows of yellow parasols on the beach. Once he got an appetite of a better life, nothing could stop him as he rose through the ranks, until he now found himself running the operation on St Halb.

There was knock at the door. "Come in."

A couple of men and Sam entered the room, taking a seat on the two sofas across from where Hadley now sat.

"Tell me, gentlemen, when will the next shipment be ready for export?"

"If all goes well, in the next few days, we're starting to cut and bag the crop today."

"Thank you, please leave us now, I wish to talk to Sam

alone." With this, the two men who'd come in with Sam got up and left.

"So, what's the latest from your three friends."

"Nothing since I last saw them back at my place; these three are professionals, so we need to start taking extra precautions around here."

"Any idea when they might try something?"

"From what Henry said to me regarding a function to be held here next week, I would say any time between now and next Friday, at a rough guess possibly next Wednesday or Thursday."

"Need to do me a favour and go back to your place and find out if our friends have been about."

"Sure, I will go in a minute."

Once Sam had left the room, Hadley picked up the phone located on his desk and spoke for around twenty minutes to someone in London about the next shipment of marijuana.

After leaving the office, Sam walked past a reception room where two people were slumped on two soft chairs, their eyes fixed to a programme on the television. From the looks of them, a gunshot wouldn't get them moving. On the way past the kitchen, he looked inside for no reason, but that of habit; two women dressed in chef's whites could be seen preparing meals. On the right just passed the kitchen, he located a small wooden door which led to the cellar.

Stone steps made their way down to several rooms, most were full of wine bottles fermenting, each room protected by a secure iron gate, apart from one which had been broken into the lock laying on the floor. Towards the rear was a door, behind it the tunnel to the warehouse; giving it a firm tug confirmed it wasn't locked.

Next to this, another solid door secured by a thick plank resting on two metal hooks, one each side of the door. Didn't need to look inside, Sam knew who lay behind this door. It was Abbie, he did not want to face her, so he started to leave quietly as possible when his leg hit the table in the centre of the room.

"I know you're out there, and you better fucking let me out."

Followed by multiply hard hits on the inside, as Abbie tried in vain to smash down the door. He walked away without saying a word, making his way to the second floor and into one of the bedrooms, exiting a few minutes later with a 9 mm Browning like the one he had used in the British Army.

Passed several people standing near the door smoking, made his way to the warehouse to collect two men who would accompany him back to his house looking for any signs that Simon, George and I had been back to the house.

Calling over two people who were busy doing nothing in the store, they all jumped in a Jeep and drove towards the gatehouse. The gate was being protected by two men; one of them held the lead of a German Shepherd, which started to growl at Sam as he passed.

Inside the gatehouse, three people were seated behind an old wooden desk situated a little back from a counter which faced the door, drinking bottles of some type of alcohol. In contrast, four others disappeared out the back to return with the remaining German Shepherds and Rottweilers. After travelling a short distance, one of them turned around and shouted out, "What's the time?"

"10:35," came the reply.

"Thanks, see you in an hour."

They headed to the vineyard to give the dogs time to run around out of the kennels, once they reached the corner of the field near the two water tanks, they let them off their leashes. This was a routine they completed every day; let the pooches off, walk around the perimeter for one hour before placing the leash back on and returning them to the gatehouse.

Hadley walked at a slow pace over to the warehouse to check on the progress of the packing. The store was almost entirely full of oak wine barrels that were being stored to mature, stacked in neat rows on shelving which reached the top of the building. Towards the back wall was a semi-automatic bottling plant which ran off a separate generator located on the left near the door.

Centre on the floor in front of filled barrels, marijuana was piled high, which had been freshly cultivated from the vineyard that day. A group of people were taking the leaves of the plants and repacking them into sacks to be wrapped.

Another trio of people were then wrapping them in thick white plastic before stuffing them into oak barrels, ready to be loaded on to the lorry and shipped off as wine from the St Halb Vineyard.

"So how many do we have prepared?" asked Hadley.

"Around thirty."

"Excellent, will be able to fulfil the complete marijuana plant consignment in the next couple of days?"

"No problem, boss."

Looked at his watch, then returned back to the house. It was lunchtime, he was feeling hungry on entering the dining room. His second in command, Claire, a well-built woman, six-foot of solid muscle and ex-forces was already sat at the table, along with Carol and her two children. Just because he was away from his usual home, didn't mean he couldn't be civilised. Besides, Henry had excellent taste in dining furniture and silver cutlery, shame to let them go to waste.

A young woman in her early twenties, dressed in a chef's whites poured wine for everyone, including the kids. One time, Carol allowed them to drink a glass of wine with their meals as it was custom on the island. A delicious lunch was served with polite conversation. Not once was there any mention of the activities taking place at the property. It was taken as read everybody knew what was going on.

"My apologies, you will have to excuse Claire and me, we have work to discuss."

Back in the office, Hadley sat behind his desk, paused for a moment or two before saying, "You managed to get Abbie to tell you anything about the men Henry sent, plus where they collect weapons on this island?"

"Not yet, but she will after a little persuasion of the physical type."

"Leave that to you, but the shipment goes out in around three days from now, we're going to need info by then if we are going to protect our assets."

Meanwhile, Sam and the other two had arrived back at his house. He chuckled to himself when he noticed vehicle tracks leading up to the house, knowing that Abbie would go mental when she saw someone had driven up to her home, but that wouldn't be an issue anymore.

Part of the deal he made with Hadley was for her to disappear, enabling him to create a new life with Carol and the two children, the youngest of which was his.

He had met her over four and a half years ago when they came to the island, in the bar on Joshua Boulevard.

To start with nothing serious, he was seeing her when Abbie was working at Henry's place or when he told Abbie that he was at work. Knowing that she would not agree to divorce, when Hadley offered him a way out of the marriage, he decided instantly.

"You go around the back and come through the back entrance, I'll go through the front; be careful, we don't know if anyone else is home. On the off chance, if someone is here, I will play innocent and ask if they have seen Abbie as I've been looking everywhere for her."

A search of the house found no people dead or alive, apart from the bits of body and blood sprayed all over the walls of the living room. One of the men was throwing up at the sight of all the carnage.

"Stop throwing up in my house, take it outside. While you're at it, check the garage for signs of anyone."

"OK," came through a muffled hand, as they tried to hold back the sick that was now engulfing both his mouth and hand. The boys had been back and guessed that Abbie would be missing, and that on the wall must be one of Hadley's men. As expected, they had picked up all the stuff when they disappeared for a few days, might as well go and check the two idiots outside.

"Stay there, Sam, we have discovered a suspect package next to the sliding door, John has found a wire leading from it."

"Where the fuck is he?"

"He's tied some string to the wire and gone behind that wall to pull the line, wants to find out if the package is anything of concern."

Sam was about to shout "STOP, don't yank on that cord" when the deafening sound of a massive explosion, which could probably be heard by Simon and George, along with flames which reached at least five feet high into the sky came from where John used to be.

"Don't touch anything else, come back with me now."

Meanwhile back at Henry's place Claire and two women made their way to the cellar for a conversation with Abbie.

"This is what's going to happen," looking at the other two, "you lift off the wooden restraint once the door is open, we all take hold of her; remember she will put up a fight."

A split-second after the door opened, they all raced in and grabbed Abbie; a well-placed kick to the back of the knees forcing her to the floor.

Claire moved to within inches of Abbie's face, "Right, you bitch I need some information, I don't believe in the easy or hard way, so this is going to be the latter."

A powerful punch landed on the side of Abbie's face knocking her sideways, the only thing preventing her hitting the ground was the two people holding her by her arms.

Through gritted teeth, "I don't know what you want from me. Even if I did, I wouldn't fucking tell you, wait to my husband finds out about this, he's going to kill you."

Claire laughed loudly, "You idiot, who do think told us where you would be, Sam is upstairs with Hadley."

Several harder punches were landed, one to the face and the other in the stomach. Abbie gave out a loud agonising scream, she had never felt this amount of pain, or been treated in this way.

"Where is Steve, Simon and George?"

"The last thing I heard was they were planning to stamp all over your fat ugly face. Let me go and I'll give you a preview, bitch."

"Throw her back in there, we will try again later, I've other stuff to complete." The door slammed shut and locked again.

Once again, Abbie was left alone in the cold, dark room of the cellar, crouching down in the corner cupping her hand around her now swollen face. Tears started to roll down her face as she grasped to work out how she had found herself locked away like an animal. Why Sam, the man she had been married to for many years would do this to her. 'Why does everything I touch go wrong?'

Mission Minus 24 hrs

As always, George was the first one up and sat on the rear of the Land Rover while drinking a hot cup of tea.

"Morning, the water has boiled if you want your usual gallon of coffee in the morning."

"Cheers, mate, you been up long?"

"About thirty minutes or so, Simon's gone to the woods for a dump."

"Far too much info this time in the morning."

Grabbed myself some boiling water from the vessel, poured it into my metal mug along with a splash of milk from the armoured cow and made a brew, and went to join George.

"Shift up," I took a seat on the back of the tailboard.

"There is a lot to do today, so when his lordship comes back, George, I'll 'get some scran going'.

Breakfast was not going to be anything fancy, just sausage, bacon and eggs all fried together in the same pan on the embers of a fire someone had already started.

"You will make a good housewife one day, Steve. Sorry house person, wouldn't want to upset some fucker."

"Thanks, George, but you know what you can do."

"Yep, grab some plates."

Come and get it then, remember I cooked so one of you two can clean up the mess."

"That went down well, Steve, how did you know my favourite was burnt sausages and smashed fried eggs? How was yours, Simon.?"

"Food is food, mate. Better we start cleaning up, George before grumpy over there starts on one."

Once breakfast was out of the way the plan of action this morning; ensure that all kit was packed, A first parade check on the vehicle. Then make a strategy of how we were going to recce our way to the back of the vineyard. Once back from that, we had to go over tomorrow in minute detail. Especially if we were going to get this pulled off with all three of us getting the mission done without a scratch.

"Bring over the map, let's check today's route."

Placing it on the tailboard, Simon orientated it to the land. From our position, we were about one kilometre from the coast, which could be reached by the track that wound its way through thick forest until it came to the coastline. From that point, it would be a straightforward matter of following the shoreline until we reached the boathouse that protruded out into the sea from Henry's property. This would be the first real obstacle on the route, due to not knowing if any guards or anybody else had located themselves here.

On the plus side, this would provide us with the perfect opportunity to peek inside to find out if there was, in fact, a boat housed here and what condition it was in. May need it as a backup strategy for leaving, even if it's only away for us to reach the inlet where Derek would be waiting for us if everything goes to plan.

"Got any ideas, anyone, of how we do today's recce?"

followed by a couple of minutes of silence, as all three of us mulled it over in our minds.

"Let us take the Land Rover to the coast, conceal it someplace while all three of us make our way along the shoreline."

"Sounds like an idea, gents. Simon, if you sort out the vehicle while we disassemble the camp."

As always, it wasn't just a job of putting out the fire. The whole area needed to be checked for any accidental dropping of paper or food. This still made me think back to my time a young solider and still learning. Caught trying to bury my rubbish rather than lug it about for several days. The section commander at the time, instead of ripping me a new arsehole, took time to explain that so much can be learned from what people couldn't be bothered to carry back with them like numbers and morale etc.

Due to the terrain, this was going to be slower than anticipated, as Simon skilfully manoeuvred along the track. Which didn't leave much room to drive with the thick undergrowth, coming so close to the trail you were able to reach out and touch it. Rounded a tight bend and started to head down a steep incline, to be faced with a small stream imitatively in our path.

"Didn't spot that on the map, you think you can drive across?"

"That depends."

"On what?"

"Are you getting off your fat arse and going to investigate

how deep the water is and whether the ground underwater is hard enough. Would do it myself, but I'm driving, and Steve is navigating."

"No problem. Unlike you two pussies, I'm not afraid of a little water."

George broke off a branch from a nearby tree, to use to keep his balance and test the hardness of the ground, tentatively inching his way in the cold running water, which now came just above his knees, making his way to the other side of the stream tapping with the stick as he went.

"All good to go, mate, I'll wait for you on this side of the river."

Selecting four-wheel drive, drove the Land Rover at a speed which was neither too slow, which might result in vehicle becoming stuck as it sank into the riverbed, nor too fast it would cause the water to enter too high in the engine compartment, resulting in an electrical short circuit.

"Think you've maybe done that before, Simon."

"Once or twice. Somewhat different in a tank as you wouldn't even stop, the only person who would find themselves getting a complete soaking would be the driver, if the idiot kept the hatch open. Perks of being the commander."

The track continued to wind its way through the trees for about another six hundred metres before it finally came to the shoreline. Took no time at all to find a suitable location to conceal the Land Rover among the undergrowth. Grabbed our kit and made our way to the edge of the tree line overlooking the shore.

The warm, clear waters of the Caribbean Sea were lapping at the shore about a hundred and fifty metres away from where we stood. A distinctive row of seaweed stretched along the sandy beach around sixty metres from the breaking waves, a sure indication that the tide was out. From our perspective, there were ninety metres from the seaweed and the tree line. If we were spotted by anyone at sea and came towards us, they would need to cross ninety metres of open/killing ground.

The easiest way would be to walk along the beach to the boathouse and beyond. We couldn't afford to leave a nice set of footprints in the sand that even a person with half a brain cell would be able to follow. No, we would have to use the tree line. This would make the going a little slower but provide some cover from view.

A quick check of the time, 09:00, which meant if we want a closer observation of the dogs and their handlers, we had around one and a half hours to reach a spot we might be able to observe them from.

"You two ready? Good. Let us go." I led off in our usual formation with me leading, Simon following me and George taking up the rear.

At first, staying inside the tree line the going was easy, made reasonably good time covering the first kilometre in around thirty minutes, at this rate should arrive at the boathouse in plenty of time for a quick investigation.

Located where the stream crossed earlier emptied into the sea, which now presented us with a little open ground of our own. On its own this shouldn't be an issue, but about two hundred metres out at sea was a small boat, softly bobbing up and down in the ocean. Through the binoculars, the shape of two figures fishing could be clearly seen, one of which was facing the shore.

Making my way carefully so not risk being seen or heard to the edge, I crouched down behind a bulky green bush, placed my hand on top of my head; seen by Simon and George, they were on my position within seconds.

"If you go across first, George, followed by Simon. Once you are both over I will cross and proceed to pass you, take up your normal positions," liked to mix our routine in crossing obstacles to confuse anyone who was watching us.

While one observed the direction we had come, the other kept an eye on the two fishermen still bobbing up and down on the crystal blue waters of the sea. Soon my turn to cross, a quick check behind me, the coast was clear so entered the stream. The water at this point may have only come up just above your shins, but you always got that sinking sensation as the water started to enter via the tops of your boots. You knew that for the near future you would have cold, wet feet.

As I passed George, a voice went, "Now you know how I feel."

Crossing the stream had cost us a little time, so now needed to open the pace to reach the objective in time. The time now, 09:50, which gave us fifteen minutes to check inside where the boat was kept without being seen. Fortunately, going on the second part was as easy as the first, reaching the area in no time.

The boathouse was in the natural break in the forest at the end of a fifty-metre-long wooden pier standing almost one metre high. The structure was constructed out of shiplap timber. At a guess would say it was about ten metres long by six metres wide and stood on concrete pillars buried into the sand, giving it a height of around three metres and painted bright red.

From its position, a boat would be able to launch at any time. Didn't need to rely on the tide being right level. Needed to take a look inside to what type of craft was being stored, if any.

Between us and the pier was seventy metres of open ground that we would need to clear. Additionally, at the end of the pier an area of around one hundred square metres had been prepared and well-maintained, from the look of the short length of the grass. A compete contrast to the rough vegetation of the forest. At the far end, you could distinguish where the path from the house broke through.

No words were required here as we'd done this type of thing hundreds of times. George adopted a prone firing position close to a bush at the edge of the clearing, aiming the rifle at the break in the trees at the far end of the grassed lawn while I covered the boathouse.

After taking a deep breath, Simon sprinted across the seventy metres before finding cover under the pier, in a place, where covering fire can be given if required. Next up was me, a final check to ensure the coast was clear before making a dash towards the safety of the boathouse. Must have been about halfway across when I stumbled and fell face down in the soft, wet sand.

Shit! I laid motionless, listening and watching for any movement and feeling like a real prat. From where I was, the stupid grin on Simon's face was visible, I'm not going to live this one down. Picked myself up and continued to run the rest of the distance to underneath the boathouse, from here I would cover down the beach as George raced across to join us.

The floor above me was made of wooden planks with a small gap between each one, possibly to allow water to drip down from the boat when it had returned from the sea or after washing off the seawater.

What was strange, still couldn't spot any sort of ramp to launch the vessel, maybe this will become clear once inside. No sounds were coming from within plus no sight of anyone through the cracks between the planks, time to investigate.

The plan was simple, George would stay outside to provide cover if anybody showed up while Simon and myself would take a peek at the interior. Looks like we had only one way in and that was via the small door from the pier. This would make us exposed from people coming from the direction of the house, so as little time on entry would be paramount.

Giving the thumbs-up signal to Simon, we jumped up and took positions either side of the door. Grabbing the door handle, I gradually pressed it down and pushed the door; I guess we weren't expected, that's why they hadn't locked the door. Waited twenty seconds once the door was open before we both rushed inside.

Situated in the centre of the floor and taking up the majority of the available space was a grey ridged inflatable complete with two Honda Orca 15 hp outboard motors. That should do us if we need it. Was now clear why I couldn't spot a ramp for launching the boat. At the far end was a hydraulic ramp which guessing would be lowered once the two large barn doors were opened.

An assortment of spare boat parts lay on a makeshift bench. Several jerry cans were lined up in a row along one side, under lifejackets that were hanging down from hooks on the wall. On the opposite side was a set of stairs leading up to some type of loft. About to start going up when Simon grabbed my arm while raising one finger to his mouth. Both stood motionless, daring even not to breathe for a few seconds when the sound of someone moving on a higher floor could be heard.

Whispering into his ear, "When I say, we rush upstairs. I'll lead, try to detain who is up there without firing a shot." Simon gave me the thumbs up to indicate he understood.

The loft was a small space with hardly any headroom; ropes and old anchors lay across the floor. In the far corner behind an old metal locker, we managed to perceive the shape of a person doing his best to blend into the background. Both dashed to grab him, the man mustn't be expecting anyone as he was unarmed. Wasn't long before I held him a headlock.

The man thrashed about trying to claw at my face. Only one thing for it, as I hurled him to the floor. Bringing down the full force of my body, I soon had him pinned down on the ground, while Simon prevented his legs, kicking frantically as he tried to free himself.

We were now faced with a dilemma, we couldn't tie him up because when someone came looking for him, and they would, Hadley and the rest will know someone is up to no good. And I'm positive he's no fool and will soon realise it was us, Sam would have bound to have said something.

Couldn't risk the noise of a bullet or even the large blood splatter if we slit his throat, was only one thing for it. Placed my arm around the front of his neck in a similar fashion I'd used on the man on St Bethanie and strangled him. Wasn't long before his lifeless body lay on the floor.

Couldn't leave his body here to be discovered, we had to dispose of it where it couldn't be found.

"Pass me the rope, and a few of them anchors, Simon."

Once we had sufficiently attached several heavyweights to the lifeless body with the ropes, we carried him downstairs, there was only one thing for it. Would need to throw his body into the water channel used when they launched the boat, with any luck the water level will stay high as he sinks to the bottom.

"Better hurry up if we are going to get to target on time."

Once outside, gave George a tap on the shoulder, "What happened inside?"

"Will tell you later, mate."

Still had five hundred metres to go until we reached a position where the activities in the vineyard, including the daily walk for the hounds might be watched, if there was indeed such a place. The primary objective was still to check if a viable location to launch could be found, plus a route into the warehouse via the rear door. The time now was 10:25, no way we would arrive in time to monitor the direction the dog handlers took to and from the vineyard.

Arrived at the point where the forest ended, and the sandy beach and growing fields merged. A hedgerow had been planted along the perimeter, probably providing shelter for the marijuana plants from the slight breeze blowing in from the ocean. Sand had blown up across the shore and was piled up against the bottom of the hedge, forming a natural sandbank. Will be able to use this to reach the other side of the vineyard towards the second of the two water tanks which provided a constant water supply.

No point in staying there as the position was below the lay of the land and gave no line of sight, so called the boys over to talk about our next move. "Any ideas?"

"Need to go and investigate if it's possible to enter the warehouse via that back door you mentioned. If you transverse to the water tank, George can stay here ready to cover our withdrawal as he will not be coming this way when it's time to take out the bad guys."

"Sound like you have a plan, so I will go along with that proposal."

"Good to me too."

"OK, we meet back here in exactly one hour from now."

Observed as Simon headed for the warehouse and George was in position before crouching as low as possible behind the bank but still, in a way, I would be able to cover the ground quickly without being seen. With any luck, the people working will be too absorbed in what they were doing to even bother looking towards the ocean.

Reached the corner in no time, now just a short distance until I arrived at the water tanks, unlike the other tank on the far side I didn't spot any guards here. The reservoir stood on iron girders which stretched across a walled structure, inside the base was a water pump which was running with a nearly silent murmur. Perfect, this should cover any noise I made as I scrambled up the ladder on the outside of the tank.

Lady luck was with me today. The top consisted of a two-foot metal lip which ran the whole circumference, in the centre was a loading hatch. By design, this must have been repurposed from a completely different use. Why would a water tank need a protective lid, maybe they used it for storing wine, hence the rim; not wanting to waste any spillage? Not complaining as it was now giving me excellent protection.

From my advantage point, I could identify the dogs running freely among the rows of vines while their handlers walked in a group around the perimeter, stopping only occasionally to speak to the people working on the plants. Took out my notebook and sketched a plan from this view. Made sure I noted down landmarks with approximate distances from both the water tank and the place where George was now concealed.

If the guards stuck to their routine of staying together, there shouldn't be an issue taking them all down from here. Then it would be a case of sprinting as fast as my legs would carry me over what I'm estimating would be two hundred metres to the grounds of the house.

Having covered the short distance, Simon found himself on the back edge of a small metal building. Between it and the warehouse was a thirty-metre exposed dash. Peeking around the corner as he crouched close to the floor, nobody was in sight, so propelled himself across.

A scan of the area confirmed that they had not placed CCTV cameras at the back of the store. Which is surprising as Henry had said some wines are priceless. Right better check the door, which was six metres away along the back wall of the warehouse. Hoped it wasn't locked, a simple twist of the door handle established it wasn't.

Now for the tricky bit. Needed to find out if it would open and hope and pray no lazy bastard who should be working is looking straight at the door and spot any movement. Not even a little amount. Typical, nobody had been doing maintenance around here as the door squeaked and groaned as it opened, just enough to confirm it wasn't locked.

Closing the door as carefully as he had when opening it, confirmed it was shut properly. Let's hope no one now locked the bloody thing. The thought crossed Simon's mind to leave the door ajar to be safe but then the vision of the wind blowing the door shut swept, so that idea was shelved.

Ten minutes left to arrive back at the RV.

Back in the tree line George looked down at his watch, the other two had better start making a move. They had only twenty minutes to the pre-arranged time. As he did, a man started to walk directly toward his location. The rifle was pulled firmly into the shoulder, his eye looking through the optical sight he was ready to fire.

The approaching man stopped three metres short, turned to face a nearby bush, then the recognisable sound of flowing water; he was having a piss, oblivious to the fact three metres away from him a gun was pointing right at his head.

There was a rustling of leaves and broken twigs coming from the forest. These were no ordinary noises, but that of a person deliberately moving with caution to his left, again he was ready to fire when he saw it was Simon. Looking to his right, he managed to see Steve approaching along the hedgerow towards the RV.

"Is everyone OK? If so, let's make a move back to the Land Rover."

Taking the same route back as the way we came, we paused for a few minutes near the boathouse to ensure no unwanted people were looking for their mate. Good job we did, two men emerged from inside and proceeded to walk along the pier before jumping down and looking underneath, calling out, "Paco".

This must be the man we dispatched earlier.

About to make plans on dealing with the situation when the two men walked off in the direction of the house. Left it for a few more minutes to ensure nobody else was in the area before crossing.

The Land Rover was only a couple of hundred metres away, we had no intentions of making a stupid rookie mistake by walking straight over to where we had concealed it.

This would be a three-point pincer movement; we would all approach from different angles, stopping short and standing off and observing. I would be the bait as Simon and

George covered me from safe distance, rifles at the ready.

Took my time and slowly moved into the location, prepared for any nasty surprises. On reaching the vehicle checked around for any signs of tampering, which might indicate it had been found and could be some type of trap waiting. Gave the all-clear signal to the others who then, ensuring they still followed the same procedure, joined me at the Land Rover.

"That went well, boys, how about we set up camp here for the night. I'll put out a few booby traps out just in case, if one of you two fancy putting a brew on?"

Grabbed two of the home-made claymores and some wire and headed off to the track that brought us here early this morning. Found the perfect place towards the bottom of a tree and placed the device, ensuring the wire ran the full length across about a metre from the floor. This route, I would be expecting vehicles rather than people. Walking back in the direction of the beach, I laid the second claymore. By the time I got back, Simon already had made the brew and was lighting a small fire. I take it, we were all hungry.

There were still several hours before nightfall so limited chance of it attracting attention. But to be safe, he was building a fire inside a hole he'd dug in the ground.

"From tomorrow, boys, we will either be running, talking or shooting, so there'll be no time for eating. So might as well use up what's left of the rations, I'll bung them all in the same pot."

"Yummy, my favourite Army-Chuck-In."

The fire had burnt down to glowing embers before Simon put the pan on. "That should take about thirty minutes or so."

"Once we've eaten, we need to start making plans for the assault tomorrow."

"No problem, as you like your coffee here is another one for you, just make sure you don't trip on the way over!"

"Knew the moment my face got implanted into the sand that you two bastards would never let me hear the last of it." Simon and George started to laugh with stupid grins. Always good to relieve tension after a hard day's mission, so joined in laughing at my own expense.

"Scran's ready, boys, come and get it. There you go, one huge dollop of chuck-in."

"Got a wine list, waiter?"

"Now let me see, we have a vintage bottle of sparkling or still corporation pop, or maybe sir would like a glass of kiss my arse, a rare vintage."

"Let me think, I'll stick with the sparkling, no make that still water with ground coffee beans."

Once the scran was completed, everything was put away and the fire dowsed; we were ready to move at a moment's notice.

The Plan

"OK, gents, down to business; time to start making plans for the final attack. Cast your eyes over here to the model of the target I've made on the floor, let us go over the plan one step at a time. As we discussed this will be a two-prong attack, I will split these down in a moment.

"Objective – To remove as many people from the location as possible, either willingly or by deadly force. Rescue Abbie if she is here, lastly collect the envelope from Henry's safe. Once all this has taken place and the mission completed, head back to London via St Bethanie.

"Drop off – First light tomorrow morning is around 05:30. Will need to be in our relevant starting position before then. You will be dropped off first, George, at the same place as at the start of the OP phase," drawing a line on the ground with a stick from our present location to the drop off point.

"Simon and I will return back here, concealing the Land Rover before heading up the coast again following the route we took today; bearing in mind the time it took us and the driving time for dropping off, George, this will commence at 03:00.

"George – Once dropped off, proceed to a location where you can conceal yourself close to the wire fence, ready to make an entry once you hear the attack underway. The signal will be when I fire at the first person. Once in, you will need to gain access and deal with any of the occupants.

"Once you've done this, dispatch the people at the gate and

the dog. Then take up a sniper's position on the roof of the gatehouse where you will have three objectives. First, as people flee out of the warehouse, make sure they can't take part in any more activities. Second, when you see Simon run to the back of the house, shoot anyone who runs out the front door. Any questions so far?"

"Not at the moment," came the reply from George.

"What about you, Simon?"

"I've got a question, or more of a point. George, make sure when I come running out of the store, don't take fucking aim."

"Third, when you have made the call and satisfied nobody else could run out from the house that you need to shoot, join us inside the house, making sure you enter from the rear, would hate to put a bullet in you.

"The route to vineyard - When we arrive back here after dropping off George, after concealing the vehicle, we will make our way briskly along the shoreline close the tree line, no need to hide our movement. Earlier it took us about fifty minutes to get to the boathouse, and that was in daylight, tomorrow will be making our way in the darkness. Staying on the sand, we should be able to cover the ground flat-out. On arrival, we will only pause fleetingly to ensure nobody is about.

"On reaching the corner of the field, I will continue to my location while Simon positions himself around the back of the warehouse. Any questions on anything up to now?"

"Not from me."

"Nor me."

"Ok, gents, let us move on to the assault part of the mission."

"The attack will be initiated by me once I have all three dog handlers and their pooches in the field and in my sights. Once I confirm this, I will take down all three and anyone else I see. This is your signal to make your entry into the gatehouse, and the warehouse from the rear.

"Warehouse – Simon, you will enter from here," again pointing to the model on the floor. "Once inside, any people you find in there will need to be dispatched with extreme prejudice. Don't worry about people running out, George will sort the problem out. Once you have made sure there is nobody who could impede the mission, ensure no vehicles you find are operational apart from one.

"Entry to house – When there is no further threat from the people in the growing fields, I will sprint as fast as my short legs will take me across the marijuana field to the back of the house, disposing of anyone who gets in the way. On arrival, I will wait to be joined by Simon. On gaining entry via the patio doors, we will start to clear the rooms on the ground floor, only making our way to the cellar after being joined by George. Upstairs to be made safe once we are satisfied with the basement, and lower levels checked and cleared of any bad guys.

"Rescue of Abbie – Once we have located her, we need to remove her to a place out of harm's way. This could well be the cellar until we are ready to leave. Talking of Abbie, if we manage to catch hold of Sam, he must be kept alive and handed over to the police on St Bethanie. This man needs to suffer for a long time, not given the satisfaction of a rapid death from a bullet to the head.

"Retrieval of the envelope - According to Henry, the package is in the safe situated in his study, Simon, you have the combination?"

"Yes, here on my mobile."

"Write the number down, the last thing we need would be a loss of your phone or you, and give each of us a copy."

"Roger."

"After locating the study and removed any obstacles, I will open the safe while Simon reads out the combination, and George covers the door.

"Withdrawal – As soon as we have Abbie, the envelope and possibly Sam, we will make a tactical retreat. On leaving the house, there should be one of the vehicles out the front. If not, we take one of the cars from the warehouse, Simon, make sure you leave one working. This can be made inoperable as we go. Soon as we are clear of the property, we will drive the route Simon recced to the inlet where hopefully Derek is waiting.

"Continuity Plans – If anything so should go wrong, we will take the following actions. The most critical; if anyone becomes injured and unable to continue before the attack, they are to make their way to the Land Rover. If the assault is underway, RV at the gatehouse. God forbid I'm killed before the initial raid, Simon, take my place on the water tank.

"Once we arrive at the inlet and if Derek is not there with the boat, after waiting no more than thirty minutes, we will make our way to the port ready for the flight already planned back to St Bethanie.

"By any chance, if we find Hadley still in the house and hasn't escaped, not sure. We will deal with this situation as it arises, I'm expecting him to make a run for it the moment any shooting starts.

"Is everything clear in your minds, gents? If not, ask now as everything tomorrow needs to go like clockwork if we are all going to get out of this alive."

"Regarding the Land Rover, are you going to rig this to explode, Steve, would be handy to know if we need to use the vehicle and you're not about?"

"Hadn't thought about it, Simon, but now you mention it, this is what I'll do."

"I will half fill both rear lights with petrol, after breaking the glass of the bulb ensuring the element is not damaged. Under the brake lights, will run a plastic tube making sure it is not visible, this will be full of fuel leading to one of the jerry cans. Now once someone drives off and presses the brakes, boom."

"One question leading on from Simon's, how do we disarm this if you're not around, Steve?"

"Will leave two wires hanging under the dash, if you know where you are looking that is, just separate the cables to break the circuit. If you two have no more questions, I would suggest you check your equipment. George, nearly forgot, if you take the LMG, will give support in your sniper position."

Every person now ran through every tiny detail until the plan ran step by step in their minds as they prepared their kit in silence.

"Make it around six hours to go time, I make that two each for stag duty. George, you take the first stag, and I'll take the last one."

Seemed like the four hours had flown by so rapidly without me getting any real sleep. Not that it was easy on the night before any battle do any sleeping; your mind was always mulling things over. Ammo checked and placed in jacket pockets and fastened to ensure nothing would fall out. So nothing to do but listen to the quietness and silent night, watching the shadows of the night flicker in the moonlight.

Time for thinking was now over, "Time to get up, boys, it's go time."

The Mission

George's Mission

Jumping down from the vehicle, George collected his equipment and started to head for his start position, but not before looking over his shoulder. "Meet you two on the other side."

Following basically the same route taken to the OP as last time, soon arrived at the stream close to the old observation post. With a giant leap, landed on the far bank and crawled into a location where it was possible to keep an eye on any movements at the front gate.

Can't stay here, need to move closer to the fence ready to cut through once Steve started shooting. Spent a few minutes observing the borderline, two available hold-up positions; one behind the gatehouse, the other being past the kennels. Which one would depend on which way the wind was blowing? Must be in luck, it was coming from the right, across people standing around near the gate. Needed to make sure the location was downwind, so those dogs don't pick up the scent.

Not much going on, so might as well make my way to the start location to the left of the kennels, about a hundred metres from my current position. Had plenty of time so no need to rush, would take this silently and cautiously. Slid back down into the stream and headed downstream, before climbing back up towards the edge of the bank opposite the place I needed to be. From what I could detect, the best course of action would be breaking this down into sections, making my way from three different locations.

Keeping myself close to the ground, crawled a little distance at a time trying not to make any sudden noise that might attract attention. Made it to the first spot, which provided concealment via a clump of small green bushes. Stopped motionless, watching, and listening for any movement from the direction of the gate. Only when satisfied, continued with caution on to the next batch of cover.

Repeating this twice more before stopping short of a patch of foliage along the fence, this would the waiting position for the go. Being downwind of the dogs, didn't mean they would not be able to detect the slightest noise, so would have to be more careful. Inching forward one inch at a time, clearing any twigs that might snap as you crawled over them.

Eventually reached the point from where I would commence my part of the operation; from here it was possible to make out several of the hounds; half in, half out of individual kennels, from lack of movement, assumed they were asleep. Took out the wire cutters and placed them on the ground ready, while observing the area around waiting for the off.

The hardest part of this stage was controlling your emotions, such as self-doubt; debating with yourself if you are capable of completing the mission or not.

Then there was fear, if anyone ever tells you they never feel scared they're lying, even Steve with his absence of any emotion gets scared before an operation, a little fear is what helps to keep you alive.

Steve's Mission

Meanwhile Simon and I had arrived back where we had parked earlier this morning.

"Simon, if you start on concealment, I will prepare the brake lights and the booby-trap."

First, I needed to separate the two wires under the dashboard as safety, fill the lenses with petrol and insert the bulb minus the glass back into its housing. The pre-filled plastic tube would run close to the lights then into the cap of the jerry can ensuring we got a big bang.

"Grab your equipment from the vehicle, Simon, then I'll reconnect the wires."

"You ready, mate, time to make a move."

"When you are, Steve."

Not long before we had reached the shoreline, a slight breeze came in from the sea and the moonlight flickered off a calm ocean. Turned left and headed up the beach at a brisk pace, with Simon following a short distance behind. Was making good time but couldn't afford to slacken the pace if we were to get on target on time.

The boathouse was now only eighty metres to our front when I spotted a man in the light of the moon. He left via the door and was walking down the wooden pier towards the grassed area. I imminently headed for the cover of the tree line ten metres to my left. Once Simon had closed in on my location, now a little distance short of the opening in the trees, snap plan was made as we had to get past him without being seen.

"OK, from what we see he is patrolling up and down the pier at a slow pace. Once the man starts to walk back in the direction of the building, I will sprint across and take up a position under the pier. On the next cycle, you make a run for it and join me, we will do the same on the other side, ready?"

Waited until he had turned around and taken several steps of his return trip, sprung up and sprinted as fast my legs would carry me across the open ground and slid under the pier as he turned again and started his walk back.

Once again, Simon held back before making his dash across to join me. Our friend must be either trying to keep himself from falling asleep inside, or he was for some reason doing his job as instructed, which was out of the norm from what we've seen so far. Turned around again, started to walk back to the boathouse.

Was about to make for the protection of the tree line when Simon grabbed me; our friend had, without warning stopped. A few heart-stopping moments later, he continued along the pier; at the precise second he did, I launched myself towards cover, reaching it within seconds. Similar to before, Simon waited then legged it across to join me.

A quick check of the time told me we had only thirty minutes to first light when we had to be in position, with at least another 12 minutes to cover along the coastline. Leading off at a faster pace than before, due to the hold-up we headed for the corner of the vineyard where we would split up.

It was still dark when we reached the edge of the woods, but the first rays of light starting to breakthrough, did not have time to hang around.

"I will meet you at the house later, Steve," making his way back inside the woods in the direction of the warehouse.

Following a similar route as the other day, Simon quickly and noiselessly made his way, looking for any signs that someone had spotted his tracks from last time, covertly proceeding to the first of the outbuildings.

Simon's Mission

Standing next to the door for the next few hours might be too risky if anyone used it for any reason. Needed to find a secure location where it would be possible to watch any coming and goings, which still provides cover, but also close enough to be able to reach the exit when required within a short moment.

A scan of the area provided the perfect spot back among the green undergrowth of the forest, set around about forty metres from the entrance, which gave an ideal view. Would make final decision once in position. Moving back away from the building into the woods, travelling a hundred metres before turning right, the plan was to approach from the rear as this offered the most protection and out of the line of sight.

An abundance of natural cover made it easy-going. Finally reaching a spot within thirty-five metres or so from the warehouse door. Simon took up a prone position, amidst the fallen leaves and crawling into position and waited. Nothing to do now but to wait for the fun to start.

Steve's Mission

After leaving Simon, I was now making my way to the start position using the available protection of the hedgerow and build-up of sand. Made my way to the far edge, pausing to listen for any movement among the vines. In the distance, the unmistakable shape of two people standing near the water tank, too dark to notice any individual features; apart from the distinctive glow of a cigarette moving up and down, with the light becoming brighter as the person took a drag. Kind of them to let me know where to aim, somewhere between the top and bottom.

My hold-up position on the water tank was a hundred and twenty metres away, along the rear edge of the vineyard which ran close to the shoreline. Making use of the darkness, approached from the beach immediately behind the tank. Stopped at the bottom, using the cover of the small brick wall of the surround and slung my rifle across my back.

One of the few times I would allow myself to do this, as it was usually ready in case something happens. Still, I needed to stop any chance of the metallic parts banging against the metal of the tank.

Taking a pause between each step, started my ascent up the ladder until a point just below the rim; this was the tricky part. Had no choice, I would need to skyline myself while clambering into the space between the tank and the rim. Once on top of the tank, took up position behind the perimeter in a position where I could see through one of the tiny splits dotted around the edge.

Wouldn't be able to fire from here, to do that I would have to take up a different stance where I would be exposed, but I would have the element of surprise on my side.

All there was to do now was to wait. The last few weeks preparation and planning comes down to what happens next.

Laying here motionless in the morning light had my mind wandering into the moral dilemmas on taking a life, or if I would make it to the end of this day. No time for thinking now, the three guards were approaching.

The heart started to pump faster as adrenaline flowed throughout my body. We'd reached the point of no return. OK, one deep breath, with one fluid movement adopted a kneeling position. Found the first target in my sights — the procedure now running through my mind. Breathe in, breathe out, hold your breath, remember to squeeze the trigger, don't pull.

My finger took up the first pressure, followed by the second. The mechanism recoiled as the first round left the rifle. Almost like in slow motion, the bullet struck home. The back of the man's head exploded, with blood and brain matter dispersing in all directions.

The others started to scream and shout, in a daze of the moment; confused, their reactions slow, not knowing what happened. No time to waste. Found the next target and fired, like the first went down with a silent thud as the round found its target. Took aim at the third man, now composed and running towards me at high speed. Too late, my third bullet hit him in the chest, forcing the target to fall backwards, still screaming in pain as he clutched at his wound, trying in vain to stop the bleeding.

Soon as the third round left the barrel, turned and ran to the ladder; descending as fast as possible, my feet hardly touching the rungs. Can't afford to let this man live. Within seconds, I was standing over him, the eyes of a dead man now glaring into mine. He mumbled something incoherent as I rested the barrel on his forehead and squeezed the trigger.

The sound of barking filled the air, looked up in time to watch five dogs heading my way. This was not the time to panic; taking aim the first went down, closely followed by the remaining four.

While waiting, had spotted two men working in the field. They had now gone to ground, had to find them and fast. Sprinted to the location, where I had seen them before. There was no sign of them, where are the fuckers? About to leave when a noise to my right attracted my attention. Buried under a heap of marijuana plants, the shape of two bodies could be seen hiding. Emptied four rounds from the magazine into the pile. No more visible movement came from the undergrowth.

Turned in the direction of the house and started to sprint across towards the other water tank. Still two more guards to deal with. They would be confused, as three attacks were currently happening in separate areas of the property. Looking up, saw one man standing on the tank aiming a weapon in my direction. I leapt to the floor and crawled a few feet to my left as a round struck the deck where I had dived to the ground moments earlier.

Cheeky fucker! Raising my rifle into a firing position, placed the pointer of the optical sight on the centre of his face and fired. The body staggered before dropping off the tank and hitting the brick wall surround with a thud.

No sign of the second person, probably headed off to help elsewhere, so made my way to the rear of the house to wait for Simon.

Simon's Mission

On hearing the first shot, Simon sprung to his feet and rushed towards the door. Placed his hand on the door handle and raised the rifle to a firing position, taking up the first pressure.

Right, time to compose yourself, then with one smooth movement flung the door open, rushing inside. Imminently in front stood a man and woman packing sacks. Before they had a chance to turn and investigate the sound, he let several rounds fly into them. Both bodies fell forward and now lay motionless, face down in the plants they were planning destroying people's lives with, a fitting end.

A lot of shouting and the noise of running people came from his left. Turned towards the threat and took up a position behind the vehicle. Took aim and waited. Seconds later, three people came sprinting from in between the barrels of wine, firing in his direction. Time to stay calm and pick up the first target, as a hail of bullets came his way, some missing by only inches, others ricocheting off the metal to his front.

Nanoseconds after the arrow of the sight landed on target the first fell, blood soaking the concrete floor. No more than five seconds had passed when the rest lay beside the first; they had lived by the gun, and now they died by the gun.

No time to waste here, the remainder of the warehouse needed to be checked, don't want any nasty surprises. Systematically clearing each row in turn, was about make a turn to go down the third aisle when a shot rang past his ears. A woman was spotted as she took cover behind the row of barrels.

Got you! A plan was quickly formulated, couldn't allow this turkey shoot to carry on, had places to be. Took up a prone position and took aim down under the bottom row of wine barrels.

This bitch needed to be brought down. A rookie mistake, the bottom of her feet were exposed. This was going to be a difficult shot as it wasn't possible to rest his elbows on the floor as you would in a normal prone firing position. Took one deep breath, exhaled and squeezed the trigger. Two rounds in quick succession shattered both her ankles and the body crumpled to the floor.

The woman's screams could be heard as he sprinted as fast as his legs would carry him with adrenaline pumping throughout his body. Now stood over her when another person appeared in the doorway about six metres away and to the left. After finishing the woman off with a bullet to the head, launched at the entrance, catching the man with the butt of the rifle below the chin. As he reeled backwards, three rounds were emptied into the man's chest.

Not sure on how many rounds I'd fired so better change magazine to be safe, just in case. No time to waste, I needed to make two of the three vehicles parked at the other end inoperable. Placing a single bullet into two tyres of each of them should put them out of action. The next task was to join up with Steve at the back of the house.

Racing towards the open door of the warehouse, found a person raising his weapon into a firing position when suddenly the side of his head exploded, throwing a mixture of blood, brain and skull over the wall. Looking in the direction of the gate, I mouthed the words, 'Bloody good shot,

George'.

George's Mission

On hearing the first shot, George sprung to his feet and hurled himself against the wire fence, cutting a hole just big enough for him the fit through. A check to the right confirmed the person from the gate had vanished, along with his mutt. Next stage to enter the gatehouse via the dog kennels.

What he had not seen from his OP was a door to the rear on the far edge of the building, this would be his way in. Grabbed the door handle, pushing it down to ease the door. Shit, it was locked, would have to go the same way as the dogs went.

Cutting another hole, entered the first compound, the small entrance to the front was open. Through the opening, it was possible to see two guards taking cover behind a huge oak wooden counter which ran most of the way across the room. Observed for a few seconds to ensure nobody else was present before sliding the LMG gingerly in first.

It was a tight squeeze but I managed to get through. Crap! As I stood up, my arm knocked a chair which made a loud scraping noise along the floor. Both men swung around and were now facing in my direction, ready to fire. With the LMG at the hip, let rip a short burst cutting them down before they had time to move.

That was easier than expected, but I'm not complaining. Now needed to get to the roof. Moving to unlock the door at the rear of the room, I was grabbed by someone, their arm tightly secure around my neck, the pursuing struggle knocked the machine gun to the deck.

Grabbing at his arm, tried to remove it from around my neck without any luck. Turned and ran backwards, slamming the person's back into the edge of the solid desk. This loosened their grip sufficiently enough to enable me to retrieve my knife from its housing. Without thinking, I rammed the blade deep into their side, turning it to inflict as much pain as possible; he cried out as I dug the knife deeper. Used this opportunity to get myself free. No time to pick up the weapon, the blade would have to do.

With one swift movement, I drew the sharp blade across his throat. There seemed to be a fraction delay in time when nothing happened. Then slowly droplets of blood started flowing from the cut gradually at first then with ever-increasing pressure. While they clasped at their neck, I picked up the LMG and fired a shot into his head from close range, splattering it against the back wall.

Now needed to make my way to the roof by clambering over the wire mesh at the back, collecting one of the weapons from the bodies dispatched earlier, this would be handy as a spare. Leaving the gatehouse, slung the LMG across my back, throwing the spare one on top of the mesh and started to climb.

The building's roof was higher than I could reach; would have to run across and take a leaping jump for it, hoping I could take hold of the edge to heave myself up.

Failed on the first attempt, the second was successful with my hands making contact with the metal edging which ran the perimeter. Using all my strength, which was still weakened by the encounter downstairs, managed to pull myself onto the roof. The small apex ran from the rear towards the gate. Perfect, this would give me a fantastic sniper position over the house and ground, but leave me open at the back.

Unfolded the legs of the LMG and rested them slightly down from the apex, leaving the barrel as the only part showing over the ridge. Settled down to watch for anyone exiting the house or enter the warehouse while Simon was clearing the inside.

Not been there long when I spotted a man approaching the front of the warehouse. Watched as he lifted his weapon to fire, took up the first pressure on the trigger aimed at the right side of his head. Controlled my breathing and took the final pressure. A split-second passed until the round struck the person's head. He fell where he stood. A few moments later, Simon appeared looking in my direction; don't worry, mate, I've got you covered.

<u>All Missions</u>

On reaching the rear of the house I could hear the reassuring sounds of Simon and George fulfilling their parts of the mission; found the nearest cover and inserted a new magazine with a confirmation tug, to ensure it was sitting correctly in its housing when Simon arrived at the back of the house.

"Glad you could make it, you ready?"

Taking up a position against a concrete wall either side of a glass-fronted door, which led into the dining room. I started to count down on my fingers, ensuring they were visible as I counted down from three. We would go on zero.

Three, two, one, zero, go. With one complete movement, grasped the handle, swung the door open, and both of us ran inside, with me taking the lead. A fast sweep of the room confirmed the room was devoid of anyone. Sounds of shouting and running people came from the rest of the house.

Done this on many occasions and today would be no different. Once inside I covered the area forward, and to the right, while Simon covered the other half.

Facing me when I entered the corridor was a man armed with an AK47 which he brought up ready to fire; let him have two rounds in the chest, knocking him backwards, screaming in pain. Still, not before the bastard had managed to get one off himself which struck me with a glancing blow to my left arm.

No time to think about the excruciating pain now pulsing through my arm, anyway the adrenaline should keep it in check; for now, we have more pressing matters to attend to. Behind me, the sound of gunfire attracted my attention, turned around to assist, finding several bodies already dispatched.

Tapped Simon on the shoulder and pointed towards the corridor. Moving with caution and hugging the walls, we inched forward, rifles ready for instant action. Rounding the corner and now facing the front door, caught sight of someone fleeing out the house, a moment later the distinctive sound of the crack and thump from the LMG was heard.

Cleared each room as we went, finally we were confronted with the open door of the kitchen. Using the same procedure, entered to discover two women dressed in chef whites, their hands held high above their heads, shouting 'don't shoot'. Simon kept his rifle aimed at them; they were now both visibly shaking with fear. Made sure Simon was covering me before searching for anyone else who might be taking advantage of the moment.

Looked like our chefs were not part of this drug gang, but innocent locals caught up in this mess. Involved or not, can't have them running around the house, if for nothing else than their own safety. Plus, didn't fancy receiving another hole in any part of my body. Along the wall, past a preparation table stood an American type fridge freezer.

An idea sprung to mind. Removed its contents and shelving from the fridge, 'bring them over here', forcing the women inside. Inserted a few kitchen utensils between the two handles of the fridge, which gave just enough room for them to open for air to breathe. Found the mains cable and unplugged it from the socket, don't want them to freeze to death, I'm not a complete bastard.

The sound of a door being opened towards the rear of the house had us taking up a firing stance. Seconds later, a voice cried out, "Steve, Simon, it's George, don't fire."

"Stay there, we will come back for you." Not stupid enough to shout out 'we are in the kitchen', in case someone else overheard it.

We had two more locations in the house still needing to be cleared, the study and the cellar. Couldn't risk being trapped in the basement, so we would make our way to the study first. The door was open when we arrived. Sprinted across the opening to take a stance on the other side.

A single shot came from the back of the room. Not sure exactly where from, we would need to draw the shooter's fire again. Only one way to do this was to rush the room, with everyone firing at possible locations of the shooter.

Go on two, deep breath, all three accelerated through the door, firing several bursts at every possible place our shooter could be hiding. The area now looked a mess, with sections of the whitewashed walls full of holes, the expensive-looking sofa lay in tatters. Priceless bottles of wine now dripped down from the glass-fronted drinks cabinet. Now silent, we must have hit our target. Not letting complacency set in, moved with caution, checking every location we had shot at for any signs of life.

"Think we got them, gents." As I spoke a muscle-bound woman around six feet tall darted from behind the solid oak desk and launched herself in my direction.

Haven't got time for this shit, raised my weapon and placed a bullet between her beautiful blue eyes. The body dropped in slow motion, bouncing as it hit the wooden floor, blood now matting the long blonde hair which lay about her.

Located the safe embedded in the wall behind the desk, about a foot wide by about two feet tall with an electronic keypad mounted on the of the left edge.

"Read out the combination, Simon."

Reaching into his pocket, he pulled out a piece of paper, "OK, the number is 2-4-5-0-7-1-8-3."

The safe opened, inside was as Henry had said, a large brown envelope with a blue stripe running down the middle, along with several posh-looking bottles of wine. Might as well have them, placed everything into the Bergen.

The stairs leading to the second floor were located near the front of the house, consisting of two sets of stairs, one on each side of the grand entrance hall decorated with fine art leading to a separate landing; which in turn led to a different set of stairs which continued up to the first floor.

The plan was simple. Would make my way up one side while Simon took the other. George would remain in the hallway as a backup in case any idiot tried to surprise us, then make his way up once we had reached the top. The second floor spanned out in two different directions; time was escaping us fast. Needed to secure this level and quickly.

"You two take that corridor, I'll take this one."

Had nearly finished checking the rooms on this half of the building. When leaving the last bedroom, a single shot came from down the corridor. Turned instantly and raced towards the sound of the gunshot. Both George and Simon were standing inside next to quilt-covered double bed overlooked by a patio door which led to a small balcony.

Crouched down in a tight huddle was a woman and two small children. Half in and half out of the patio doors, laying on his back with blood staining the lush white carpet was a dead man. This must have been the shot I had heard.

Of course, we all recognised her from the OPs. This was the woman we had seen with Sam, "She says her name is Carol," said George as he continued to check the room.

"Relax, Carol, nothing is going to happen to you and your kids as long as you do what we say," she nodded gently in acknowledgement that she understood what I was saying.

Stay in here, do not come out again for the rest of the day, if you do, you could be killed. Say yes if you fully understand."

Carol responded in a faint scared, trembling voice. "Yes, I understand."

"When we leave, make sure the door is locked and don't answer the door to anyone until tomorrow.

"Boys, grab that body and throw it over the balcony. These kids have seen enough horror to last a lifetime, without having to look at the bloke's ugly face all day." Closing the door behind us as we left, waited until the sound of the key turning on the other side confirmed the door was locked.

"Follow me, boys, we need to check the cellar; with any luck, this will be where Abbie is, if she is here at all," working on the assumption we hadn't found her yet.

The door to the basement was somewhere near the kitchen, if I remembered correctly from our briefing on the place.

Passing the kitchen once more, spotted the doors of the fridge freezer repeatedly being shoved violently from the inside; if I didn't know better, our chefs were trying to escape. Just for the fun of it, George fired two well-aimed shots which pierced the wall directly above the fridge, the doors stopped moving. "Should keep them still for a while longer."

Located the door a little further along on. The steep stone steps led down into a large room which, even though the lights were on, it was still dimly lit. Several smaller rooms led off the main chamber, each protected by metal gates, apart from one. Off to the right was a wooden door locked with the aid of a giant wooden plank. Made our way around the room, checking every nook and cranny for any signs of the low life.

Faint sounds of a woman sobbing came from behind the timber door, this could be Abbie. Not taking any chances, George positioned himself with a direct line of sight inside once the door was opened, ready with a killing shot if required. Simon and I once again took positions either side of the door. Confirmed we were all set, grabbed the plank and removed it from the two hooks it rested on. Final check to see if George had a good aim, with one swift movement flung the door open.

In the back corner a woman sat on the floor, knees drawn up to the chest, held in place by two arms wrapped around them, rocking backwards and forwards, her head resting on them as she sobbed quietly. As if in slow motion she lifted her head, looked at me with swollen eyes.

"Abbie, it's OK, we're here now to take you home." She gave a small hint of a smile. "Stay here until we search the rest of the place, we will be back for you, we promise."

"That must be the tunnel to the warehouse, see if the door is locked, Simon."

"Yep, it's open, and look what I found inside," as he dragged Sam screaming in pain and clutching at his head; letting go of his hair to throw him into the centre of the room. Sam was now kneeling down on the floor in the middle of the cellar and being flanked by two pissed off men, each with a rifle pointed at his head.

"Before you start giving us any bullshit, you know we were watching this place. Tell us what you've been up to before one of the boys' fingers twitch on the trigger. Begin with you and

Carol, yes, we saw you and have now spoken with her, so no little porkies. Then follow up with you and Hadley and the connection with Henry, you have five minutes." Took out my 9 mm and placed it just out of his reach, but close enough to tempt him to go for it. Wanted an excuse to waste this arsehole.

"Met Carol not long after coming to the island and been having an affair since, the youngest child is mine. I was planning on telling Abbie, just have not got around to it yet," turning to look at where she had been kept.

"Don't fucking look over there, arsehole look at me," watched as his eyes spotted the pistol on the side, part of me was saying 'go on reach for it, you little fucker'.

"If you've not managed to work it out, here is a news flash, Henry and Hadley run the drug business together. Henry wants Hadley disposed of as he is starting to get sloppy and mess up, parts of the shipments to St Bethanie started to disappear. That's where you three come into it, to remove him and the people loyal to Hadley."

"Keep talking, dickhead, where do you fit into this?"

"What do you think happened to the parts that went missing?"

"Enlighten me."

"I would take the surplus over to our contact on St Bethanie who, shall we say distributed the merchandise."

"You are doing fine, there is a good chance I might not kill you yet, name of the contact?"

"Edward, he runs the black market trade, among other

things on the island."

"Final question before we gag you, what's the deal with you, Hadley and Abbie? She looks rather beat up. Be careful with your answer because if that was you, see the two rifle butts close to your head, they will come down with such force they will break every bone in your skull."

"Knew she would never leave me with anything. If she was dead, I could collect the two million dollars life insurance I took out on her."

Knowing he might not get out of this alive, Sam glanced over to where the 9 mm was placed. Noticing this I also looked, fuck it's gone. With that, a crack came from over my shoulder as a 9 mm bullet exited a smoking barrel followed by the thud as the round found the shooter's target; the centre of Sam's face. George and Simon leapt away as blood and brain squirted from the back of his head.

Turning around rapidly to discover who had fired the shot, stood behind me holding the gun in both hands and shaking wildly with tears running down her face was Abbie. Can't say I blame her, the bastard deserved it, besides, saved us dragging his sorry arse over to St Bethanie.

Walked over to Abbie, still trembling, prised from the 9 mm from the vice-like grip she now had on it. "It's OK, we'll take it from here. Need to move now, Abbie, make sure you stay behind Simon, George will be bringing up the rear. Ready?" she nodded.

"Let us get the fuck out of here, boys."

The tunnel came out near the back of the warehouse behind the row of wine barrels. On entering, there were two dead people, one with her ankles blown out. With as much speed as possible, made our way to where the vehicles were parked.

"Which one, mate," Simon pointed to a jeep in the far corner.

Once we had all scrambled aboard, with George in the back with Abbie, Simon turned the key to kick the vehicle into life. Nothing, the battery was flat.

"Don't say a fucking word, George."

"Sam always kept several batteries on charge, there over by the generator."

"Thanks, you're a lifesaver."

Climbing down, George took up a position by the door looking out towards the house. The battery was replaced in short order.

"Let's try again, shall we?" This time she fired-up the first time. "Thank fuck for that."

The front gate was shut and locked when we approached, "The switch is in the gatehouse, Steve, near the window." Stepping over several dead bodies, located the release mechanism, watched as they started to open before returning to the jeep.

Nearly back in the vehicle when a massive Rottweiler appeared from nowhere and took a bounding leap towards me, knocking me flat to the floor. Managed to throw it to one side as George reached over a put a bullet through its skull.

"Were you not you suppose to make sure there were none of these mutts still about, George?"

"Was wondering where it went."

Racing through the gate at high speed, we headed for the tiny inlet where Derek should be waiting to take us back to St Bethanie. Making significant progress along the tarmac road, I reached into my pack and took out the brown envelope removed earlier from the safe.

"Now, let's see what crucial information is in here." Carefully peeling back the lip, tried not to tear any part.

If the info was nothing of importance, I'd reseal it later. Inside was a pile of A4 sheets of papers, each page containing contact details of some description. One, in particular, drew my attention as it was an address in Southampton.

"Looks like Sam might have been telling the truth, gents, Henry was part of some drug underworld, the envelope's full of names and addresses of undesirable distributors, take a gander for yourselves."

At this point, the vehicle exited the road joining a dirt track, winding its way through the dense undergrowth. No point asking where we were going as Simon had the route under control. He would have already checked out the course. Within minutes, we came to a stop near to the inlet, but not too near, we would need to check the vicinity in case it had become compromised.

Jumped down and grabbed my rifle, "Abbie, wait here, we won't be long."

Spanning out and each taking a different route, headed forward using all the available cover towards the pickup point, stopping eighty metres or so short and observed.

No sign of any movement apart from Derek moored under the overhang of an enormous tree, whose branches arched over the water providing excellent protection from view. Placed my hand on top of my head to signal the others to close in on my location. Ensured that everyone had seen the boat, we headed back to the Jeep to collect our equipment and, of course Abbie.

"Best you come with us to St Bethanie for at least a week until everything settles down here, you can always come back later."

On reaching the boat, there was no sight of Derek, where the fuck was he? Turns out we weren't the only ones standing off, he had done the same and was watching us from about fifty metres away hidden among the green and brown bushes which frequented the area.

"Hi, gents and lady, glad you could make it without nearly being shot," pointing at my left arm. "Who is the young lady?"

"Not as much as we are to see you, and this is Abbie, she'll be coming with us."

"No problem, let's get moving out of here before any of your friends show up."

Once all on board, the vessel fired into life and headed out towards to open ocean and safety. Had settled down when Simon gave me a kick, "Is that Hadley over there?" On the bridge was a group of around five heavily armed people, taking centre stage was indeed Hadley.

"I wondered where that sniffling little wimp had got to. Well, he isn't getting away this time." Reached down to pick up the rifle when a gunshot was heard from behind me.

Turned round to see George still in the firing position.

"What! You're a crap shot, if you had missed we would have never heard the last of it."

"True."

Hadley's body had fallen into the ocean and now drifting out with the tide, along with the others Simon had kindly killed for us. Taking us back to St Bethanie, Derek opened up the formidable engine as we skimmed the water heading out to sea.

Journey Home

"The weather is on our side so should be back to St Bethanie in no time. Thought you might be hungry after a hard day's work, so the wife knocked you up some sandwiches etc. You already know where the stuff is for a brew."

"Thanks, Derek, you're a lifesaver, anyone else fancy a drink?"

"Sounds like a plan to me, Steve, you volunteering?"

"No problem, George, I will be your bitch for the trip."

Abbie was inside the cabin sat in one corner, staring out the window in her own little world.

"You OK?" Abbie gave a small nod as an acknowledgement she was OK. "All will be fine, everything will turn out for the better, best you stay away from St Halb for a few weeks to be safe."

"What about Sam, I killed him? Surely the police will come looking for me, I don't want to go to prison."

"That is not how the boys and I understand what happened, positive he was caught up in the crossfire by our drug-dealing friends. Last time we spoke, you were back at your place cleaning up the mess from a burglary."

"Thank you so much, just not sure where to go from here."

"That's an easy one, give us a hand with the brews before the gents in the back start moaning." Raising out of her seat, Abbie walked over and grabbed the tray, loaded it with an assortment of sandwiches and followed me to the stern.

"There you go, you lazy gits, what more does a person want, but a brew and a sarnie after a long day at the office."

Must have been about an hour before we sighted St Bethanie emerging over the horizon. The plan after reaching the port was to make our way directly to the airport and take the next available flight back to the UK. Already had return tickets, but due to our plans being altered, we would need to leave one day early. Would need to use our charms and blag our way on to an earlier flight. Let us hope Edward and his gang were nowhere to be seen and not discovered the young man buried in the woods.

"Any comeback from the explosion on the dock when we left, Derek?"

"Funny you should say that, the police arrested four men from the island, part of the underbelly I told you about; they swear blind they were not involved in any explosion anywhere on the island. Of course, the constabulary did not believe them, wonder who could have planted such a device!" turned around and smiled at the three of us. "Who indeed."

"Any chance of you giving us a lift to the airport, our usual driver might be unavailable?"

"Fine by me, will need to pop home first to collect the car and make sure the wife is OK. What are you doing about the young lady, if you need somewhere for her to stay she is more than welcome to stay with us for a while."

"Cheers, I will ask Abbie what she wants to do."

"We may have a greeting party, Simon, grab the binos and see who is eager to find out if we arrived OK."

"Your friend the taxi driver, Edward is the man at the end of the pier, another three men stood behind him, another one is over on the other dock. Can't tell if there were any more at the moment, but more will be around I guess."

"Appears we are going in hot, check your weapons." George took up a sniper position in the cabin and through the window with the LMG.

"Don't shoot unless you need to, or you hear me shout fire."

"Go inside and stay there until I give you the all-clear, Abbie."

We gracefully touched the marina a few minutes later. More men were stood on the opposite pier, looking in our direction and fully armed. Edward and his goons were making their way along the dock to meet us. Waited until he was close and threw him the painter line to tie up the boat. This was a two-fold reason; first, to ensure he did not have a weapon in his hand; the other, we needed to secure the vessel, might as well put him to use as he is stood there doing nothing.

"Hi, Edward, lovely to see you. We don't need a taxi today, Derek here is providing us a lift back to the hotel."

"Stop fucking about, you know why I'm here, you have anything to do with the death of my nephew I sent to follow you a week or so ago? More importantly, words got back to me; you are responsible for the interruption of my supply chain from St Halb."

Need to keep him talking while Simon slipped tenderly without a sound over the side and into the water. Worked with him a long time now so could second guess he was going to sneak past them and surface behind and slightly to one side of them.

"Not us, mate, been doing some R&R and a little sea fishing with Derek here." Out of the corner of my eye spotted the men on the other dock raising their weapons ready to fire. No need to worry about these people, they were being covered by Derek who now had one of the rifles trained on them from a firing position.

"Enough of the games, Steve, you and your friends will be coming with us."

"One moment, let me ask them, gents, anyone want to go with Edward? Sorry, they said no." At the end of the pier, observed as Simon climbed out of the water, taking up a position behind the last boat. His rifle was in the aim ready for me to give the command. Final check to ensure everyone was in place, my task was to jump out of the fucking way as I was unarmed.

"Fire," the sound of instantaneous gunfire reverberated from three directions around the dock, matched only by the curding screams of men taking their last mortal breath. Took the 9 mm Browning and headed to where Edward was now laying on the floor. Thick red blood dripping through the gaps in the planks, his eyes gazed upwards towards the heavens.

As I approached, he tried to say something, as he was in the last throes of life. Couldn't afford to leave anyone alive that could come after us later. Aimed the 9 mm at his head and fired. At least I had given him a quick death and not left him to suffer, or thrown him in the water to drown, this was out of courtesy as I liked the man.

Over on the other pier, three single shots could be heard as Simon ensured the others would be joining Edward. After collecting all the bodies, placed them in small dinghy. Made several small holes in the hull and pushed it out to sea. The tide was leaving the harbour, helped by the wind gently blowing from the shore. The boat should sink some way offshore, with any luck we shall be well away from this area. The only concern was for Derek and Abbie.

Think we better make a move before some nosey bastard arrives poking around asking questions on the gunfire. "You can come out now, Abbie, we need to make our way to Derek's place."

Tucked my 9 mm into the rear of my trousers and the rifle in a green refuge bag along with the rest of the weapons. The plan was to keep them with us until we arrived at the airport then hand them over to Derek to hold, in case we ever came back this way.

Could not see anyone in the vicinity apart from some people in the distance, they would without a doubt have overheard the firing, but they were too far away to be able to recognise any of us, so not an issue for now.

Arrived at the Zum-Kuhstall about eighteen minutes later, proceeding inside and taking a seat at one of the tables.

"Give us ten, and I will be with you, help yourself to a beer if you want one."

"Cheers, bottle or draft, gents?"

"While Derek is away, this is the plan from here to landing back in Heathrow. No point in playing silly buggers anymore. The rifles will be transported in the car with us in case any of Edward's gang is still looking for a fight.

"We will pull the vehicle up short of the airport, where we will stash the weapons in a hide for Derek to collect up later. The last thing we needed is some fresh-faced police person to choose today to prove himself and inspect the vehicle.

"Once inside the departures lounge, pick on the nearest airline staff member sat behind the check-in desk and showing signs of being bored and having a bad day, so doesn't give a shit. Then with charm and finesse try to blag an early trip home, so you two ugly bastards bring a smile."

Turning back to face Abbie, "Before we leave to head back to the UK, not sure if you have made any plans yet of what you are going to next, but Derek offered for you to stay with them until things quiet down."

"That would be wonderful, Steve; one slight problem, all my money is at my place on St Halb, so can't pay him."

"Doesn't want any, but here is a little something to tide you over. Just in case I forget here is a gift for the future, a bottle of Domaine de la Romanée-Conti Grand Cru. An overpriced wine I personally rescued from Henry's safe, must go for anywhere between $19,700 to $551,314 according to the search I did on my mobile. The greedy git Henry had four of them; no don't feel guilty taking them, more likely than not paid for with drug money."

"Wow not sure what to say, Steve."

"Thanks not required, you can buy us all a drink later. Do not panic, boys, have our retirement fund safely packed securely away."

Derek went upstairs, returning a few moments later with a woman in her early fifties and about 5 foot 5 inches with long brown hair.

"Let me introduce Claire."

"Delighted to meet you. That's Simon and George, and the young lady is Abbie, and I'm Steve."

"Come with me, Abbie, let the men carry on with whatever they were doing."

Handed over one of the bottles of wines to Derek, "This is for you, mate, and thanks for all you've done. I wouldn't put it behind the bar if I was you, far too expensive for the locals."

The first part of the trip to the airport went without any hassle, weapons stashed for easy pickup later once things calmed down a bit. The same can't be said when entering the ring road. Local police must know about the shooting at the docks and are carrying a checkpoint, looking for someone to blame. Airing on the side of caution we still had with us the three 9 mms. Reminds me of the time in Northern Ireland when I stumbled across the ambush.

Slipped my Browning under my arse away from prying eyes, hope they do not ask us to get out of the vehicle. No need to turn around, the others would be doing the same.

Took my passport out of my pocket, placing it on my knees ready. Shit, the occupants of two cars, further along, had disembarked, were now standing with both hands placed on their heads. One copper was gesturing with his gun for the men to stand away from the vehicle.

OK, deep breath, gents we are in; flashbacks came flooding back and sweat started to run slowly down my spine. Once the car came to a complete stop, grasped the handle of the 9 mm with my right hand, the open passport with the other as Derek lowered the windows.

"Afternoon, Officer, something happened on the island we've not heard about or is this normal practice?" True professionals might have picked up the slight uneasy edge to my voice.

"Where you off to, gentlemen?"

"Home, we have spent a couple of weeks exploring your beautiful island."

"Passports."

The officer gave our documents a quick check over, he must have been satisfied as he waved us on without another word.

"That was fucking close, gents."

Departures were a few minutes away from where Derek dropped us off. Inside was buzzing with the movement of people as they hurried through check-in and customs.

The British Airways desks were located at the far end of the hall, past the multiple coffee outlets selling overpriced drinks to weary travellers. A collection of gift shops were busy trying to prise the last of the peoples' holiday money before they boarded their flights to all corners of the world.

A small group of people were inching their way through the maze of sheep pens to speak to someone and collect boarding passes. Stood off to observe for a while before picking up on a young man sat behind the business class desk, who didn't look like he was having a good day; he would be the target. With all the added security going on, we could not afford to spend another night here so important we go today.

"Hi, sir, looks like we are not the only ones having a bad day."

"Just one of them days I suppose, but I am fine but thanks for enquiring, how can I help?"

"Need to rearrange our flights from tomorrow to tonight, an emergency back in the UK, any chance you could change the flight?"

"Let me take a look at your tickets." After a few minutes of tapping away on his keyboard and looking at the monitor,

"Have both bad and good news, gents, business and economy class are entirely booked for tonight; however, I have room in first."

"OK, thanks for trying." We had the money to afford first class, but I was still trying to grab a free upgrade.

"There is some good news for you as well, gents. Here are three upgraded seats to first class, courtesy of British Airways, always pays to be polite, enjoy your flight."

"The plane doesn't leave for four hours, boys, if you're anything like me could do with a decent meal, anyone for a mixed grill once we exit through customs?"

Slipping past customs this end was a breeze as they are only interested in what you might be carrying on to the aircraft, not who you are or where you may be heading. The intense part is once you arrive and need to pass through both immigration and passport control.

We all held electronic passports so would enter via the automatic gates, with a bit of luck nothing about our exploits had reached the UK so it should be plain sailing straight through, we would all be able to relax from then on. Then there was the small matter of collecting the remainder of our fee from Henry.

The departure was comparable to what you would find at most international airports, once your gate number was displayed, made your way to the gate to be confronted with another check of passport and boarding pass before ushered to another waiting area. A mixture of holidaymakers and businesspeople now filled the space, all trying to be the first one on the aircraft and the all-important battle of the overhead lockers. Majority of people are not aware that the plane doesn't have enough storage if everyone boarded with a carry-on bag.

First class travel on a flight was a unique experience for most people, from the over intensive crew to the lavish meals served whenever you wanted far away from the feeding frenzy in cattle class at the rear of the aeroplane. Besides us three there were only two other people on the opposite side, so plenty of room.

Managed to stay awake for the safety brief, unlike Simon, who was horizontal on the lay-flat bed. Looked over to George, who was making the most of the opportunity with a table laid out similar to what you would find in any five-star restaurant complete with several glasses of champagne. Think I will have some of that and called over Lorna, the same stewardess I had on the way over.

Things seemed to be running too smoothly, as we had no delays at either immigration or passport control and soon found ourselves with luggage in the arrivals hall.

"Make contact with Henry, Simon and arrange a meeting, might as well complete the mission today as we are in London."

"Sure." After five unsuccessful attempts, "He is not answering, will try again in a few minutes."

"Do you know where his office is?"

"Yeah, it is not far from where we met him in the pub a few weeks back."

"In that case let's make our way there while you keep trying, he owes us £250,000."

"If we catch the Heathrow Express to Paddington, we can take a cab from there to the coffee shop where George and I met up with you in the boozer."

A short fifteen minutes train ride followed a twenty-minute taxi journey due to the traffic in London always being terrible, no matter what they do to try to improve the flow of vehicles. The shop was virtually empty, so took up the seats we had occupied previously near the window overlooking the public house across the street. Only been there for a short time when Simon's phone rang.

"Was that Henry?"

"Yes, he says he will meet us across the road an approximately half an hour from now."

"Hope he brings the rest of our money, or the bastard can go back and fetch it."

Looked down at my watch. "The arsehole is late, what's keeping him?" at that moment George gave me a nudge.

"Appears like he's turned up with the goon he was with last time."

Watched as he took up a seat inside the pub; for some reason he sat on his own, so where was the bloke he went in with? Waited another couple of minutes before crossing over the road and entering. The hired help was spotted on the other side of the room, facing Henry.

"George, go and keep him company while we have a chat with our friend, in case he tries anything stupid."

Took up a position either side of Henry, so he couldn't get out from behind the table.

"Hello, gents, nice to meet you all again."

"Shall we cut out all the bullshit, we know the real reason you sent us there, which was nothing with the removing any local thugs. Spoke to a few people while we were there and seems like you ran this little enterprise with Hadley and you wanted him eliminated, correct?"

"So what are you three going to do about it?"

"Nothing, Henry, we completed your mission, and they are now all gone, pay us what you owe us, and we will be on our way."

"Do not have the money on my person, I need to go back to my office and take it from the safe, will take time."

"Don't play games with us, Henry, you have exactly one hour to collect the money and be back here."

Been in this game far too long to actually still be sat here waiting for him and any other thugs he decides to come back with, along with a few nasty surprises. Once he had left, we would follow him at a discrete distance to the office. Then at some point invite Henry down some dark alley, depending on his actions he may not come back out.

For our own security, George stayed behind for a few minutes after we departed to follow Henry in case someone else had the notion of repaying the gesture. Turned left when leaving the boozer and walked down a local high street with shops, cafés, and banks of multiple descriptions lining the edge of the newly pedestrianised area.

Running down the middle, people were seated on benches chatting with friends or watching the performance of street buskers of varying levels of skills. Others were loaded down with heavy bags, went about their daily business of shopping. Businesspeople with drinks in one hand and mobiles held to their heads hurried about the place.

Made my way down one side, with Simon taking the other side of the street; both keeping a close eye on him, now one hundred metres in front of me and ambling along as he talked on the telephone, momentarily stopping on numerous occasions to check around to see if anyone was following. Every time he did, I would instinctively turn to pretend to be window shopping, preferably with some unexpected shopper between him and me.

Something I had learned the hard way was to try to stop in front of the same type of shop each time. Far better than looking at an electrical store one minute followed by a sports shop the next. Would be surprised how much a beating focuses the mind.

Situated on the end of the high street was a glass-fronted tall office building. Counting the windows, must have been about twenty storeys. Placing the phone back into his jacket pocket, Henry entered via the front revolving doors. Ideally situated opposite the main exit were several metal benches, but this would be taking too much of a risk. For any reason Henry looked out of the window, we might be spotted. Instead, located myself a bit further down the street among other happy shoppers. Sat on a bench, pretending to read a leaflet I just collected from one of those annoying people trying to part you with your hard-earned cash, but with a full view of the exit.

From the seats behind, "He is in the building, shall I check the rear in case the building has another exit point?"

"Good idea, Simon, I'll give you a missed call if he comes this way and vice versa if he comes your way." At that moment George took up position next to me.

"Doesn't look like he had anyone follow us, the hired help went off in the opposite direction."

"Give him no more than thirty minutes to come out, or we will have to go in and find the bastard."

Time was nearly up when Henry emerged from the office, heading down the high street, in the opposite direction from the agreed meeting point; what's he up to? Gave a missed call to Simon who came legging it around the corner, knocking Henry to the floor, stunning him for a few seconds.

Once he realised it was us, picked himself up and sprinted down one of the side streets; the first mistake as this was an alley with no way out apart from the way he came, which was now blocked.

"Grab him, boys, let's see what the dickhead has to say." Taking one arm each and slamming him hard against the brick wall, I planted my fist into the side of his head, so he knew the time for being polite was now over.

"Not thinking of bailing on us, were you?"

"No, I was on my way to the bank, honest."

"Now we have a problem, Henry, I fucking don't believe you," as I slammed my fist as hard as I could into his gut, forcing his to flinch in excruciating pain.

"Money."

"It is in my bag, let me go, and I will remove the envelopes containing the money for you."

Another blow landed in the centre of his face, resulting in streams of blood running down his face. "That's for fucking lying."

Reached down and grabbed the small brown leather bag he had been carrying, which was laying on the floor by his feet. Inside was a stack of fifty-pound notes. "Keep hold of the arsehole tightly, boys, while I check the money."

"All there, what shall we do with this idiot?"

"Think we should let the arsehole live, for now, he may come in useful in the future."

"Must be your lucky day, Henry you stay alive. But remember we will be watching you, and the slightest issue and you will be a dead man walking." Gave him one more good smack to ensure he got the message.

Once George and Simon realised their firm grip on him, he slumped down to the floor and curled up clutching at his stomach with both hands, sobbing uncontrollably as agonising pain flowed throughout his body.

Turned and went to walk out of the alley and back down the high street, when for some unknown reason I turned back for one last glance at the figure curled up on the floor. We had made a rookie mistake and not checked for any weapons. Henry was staggering to his feet with a 9 mm in his right hand.

Unconsciously I ran towards the danger, closely followed by the other two as the characteristic sound of a crack as the bullet left the barrel echoing as if flew past. Striking him hard with the full force of my body, knocked him to the ground. A split-second later, Simon had wrestled the pistol from his hand and now had the dangerous end resting squarely on the side of the man's head. Only managed to get the word 'what' out, when the trigger was pulled.

Not stupid enough to leave the weapon anywhere for the police to discover, I would dispose out at sea in a few days. Leaving the alley, we made our way through the crowed high street to Paddington station and boarded the first available train out of London in the direction of Kent, where we would double back on ourselves and head for home.

The carriage was empty apart from a few people seated towards the far end. Made the decision not to stop at the ticket office, as the majority of these now have cameras watching the person selling you a ticket, partly for their safety and part making sure they do not rip off the company.

Would purchase ours from the guard as they came through, with the excuse the train was about to leave, the truth was didn't fancy being caught on camera.

Waited for several minutes after we pulled away from the platform to ensure nobody would pass us looking for a seat, before discussing the next move.

"Make sure once you arrive home you burn what you're wearing, have a cold shower before soaping yourself down with pumice soap, this should remove any leftover gun residue from Henry's pistol. Would suggest once the train arrives at our stop, we go our separate ways and meet up again at Simon's place in four days from now."

"Sounds good to me, what about the dosh?"

"Give it all to Simon, we can divide everything equally then."

About an hour later, the carriage pulled into the final stop. Disembarking into a crowded platform, pushed and shoved our way to the exit, said our farewells and I headed home. Feeling exhausted after the last few weeks, either that or downright lazy, decided to take a taxi home rather than walk the hour or so back.

Now was not the time to relax yet, knew about too many

missions that failed on the final hurdle. After placing my Bergen near the door took an amble around the area, checking for any new signs of activity. A last check of the hair I had placed between the door and frame, the seal had been broken, someone had been inside.

Picked up the small metal bar I always kept hidden in the bushes for just such an emergency. Inserted the key and quietly pulled the door open, with my right hand holding the bar, ready to meet any assailants who might still be inside.

Moved from each room, in turn, couldn't find anyone, and nothing looked disturbed from the way I had left it. Was about to go back outside to grab my bag when I noticed the note on the side. The park's maintenance team had been inside to check the gas supply.

Couldn't be arsed to do any washing, that could wait until tomorrow. Time for a brew and a check on the news to see if anyone one had found our friend, Henry, plus more important do they have any suspects. They say no news is good news.

Was about to make another coffee when the bloody phone started to make like a canary and sing its fucking head off in the kitchen. Now who the hell can that be, I've only just reached home. Better answer it; hopefully, it will be the arseholes from the council, so I can tell them where they can do one; it wasn't.

"Steve, it's Simon, a friend of mine got a job we might be interested in."

Glossary

Dubby Dust	Washing Powder
Mickey	Cheap Wristwatch
Egg Banjo	Egg Sandwich
PAYG	Pay As You Go
Chimp	Mind / Anger Management programme used in the treatment of PTSD
Call Sign TS	Tanky Simon
Call Sign GD	George Dog
Call Sign S3	Steve 3 (RGJ)
Escaped Librarian	A term used in the treatment of PTSD
Donkey Walloper	Tank Driver
Click	Kilometre
OP	Observation Post
Polo Donkey	Horse/Donkey

RV	Rendezvous – Meeting Point
Bergen	Backpack
Stag	Sentry Duty

ABOUT THE AUTHOR

In 2017 after many years of suffering, I was diagnosed with PTSD from three life-threatening events during my service. Part of my recovery at Combat Stress someone suggested I should begin writing. During my last two week stay at Combat Stress in Apil 2019, I started to write. Have now published my first ever book on poetry called Poetry from the PTSD Mind which takes you on a journey from the bad times to the good. I have also written two other books called 'The Lighter Side of Cruising parts one and two.

For details of our other books, or to submit your
own manuscript please visit
www.green-cat.co

Printed in Great Britain
by Amazon

86496617R00173